The Fate of Us

I0599045

♫ THE BROKEN LYRICS DUET ♫
BOOK TWO

TORI FOX

1

NOAH

The hardest part about chasing after someone who runs for a living when shit goes bad is that they're good at not wanting to be found. Or maybe I am just bad at finding them. Hell, it took over a year to find my wife when she ran from me.

I tried to get ahold of Anna for three hours. Her sister and her parents did too. I drove to the daisy field, which wasn't far away, hoping I would find her there but no luck. We all figured she somehow got a vehicle because there is nowhere else she could have gone in this town.

I feel bad for ruining her sister's engagement party, but Jessica took the high road. Well *a* road and blamed Becca.

I can't believe Anna's best friend was the one that her fiancé cheated on her with. Anna talked to Becca almost once a week and made no hints about it. Anna relied on that friendship with Becca. It gave her the support she needed when she felt that she was doing everything wrong with her life.

Becca had even sent Anna pictures of her kids, though she always hid their face enough you couldn't see any resemblance to Kyle in her oldest. I know Anna is hurting badly. She was finally accepting the loss and moving on. But this must have thrown her back seven years.

"If you grip that beer any harder, you might break it."

I look at my hand and see how white my knuckles are. It's not until then that I notice the ache in my hand.

"She will call. Eventually."

I look at Jessica and sigh. She has been optimistic the last few hours. And as I sit at her parents' kitchen table, I can't figure out why. It took her almost two years to get in contact with Anna after Kyle died. And after that, Anna talked to her a handful of times a year. They don't have an easy relationship. Not like they used to when Anna was younger, or so Anna told me. Although, last night when we came here for dinner, it was like no time had passed between them.

"God, you know how to brood. Maybe that is why Anna is in love with you. She always likes the brooding type. Of course she could pull it off quite well too."

I try to contain my anger. I know it's just that I am worried about her but Jessica's overoptimistic attitude isn't helping. "She isn't in love with me."

Jessica snorts, and it pains me to hear it. Anna has the same mannerism. "Okay, you tell yourself that. But the way she looks at you, the way she talks about you. I am ninety-nine percent sure that is love."

I shake my head and take a sip of my beer that's gone warm.

A cold beer is placed in front of me by Jessica's fiancé. He places a hand on her shoulder. "Jess, why don't you just lay off it for a bit. Let him try to think."

"Whatever," Jessica huffs as she gets up and leaves the kitchen.

Connor sits in Jessica's seat and takes a long sip of his

beer. "I think she is projecting. Trying to remain positive. She doesn't want to lose her sister again."

"I know."

"You don't want to lose her either."

I look at him and see something in his eyes that relaxes me. I grab the new beer he brought and chug half of it.

"I think Jessica is right though. She will be back. Or answer her phone. Finding out about the thing that ruined your life in such an abrupt way can be devastating."

"She was finally getting over it. Learning to move on," I tell him. Finally finding the words to speak after sitting for hours in silence.

"I didn't know Anna. I wasn't around when Kyle died. Hell, no one even knew about the affair—"

I cut him off. "No one did. She didn't want to give him a bad rap after he passed."

"She sounds like an amazing person. To keep that secret hidden. And with everything Jess has told me, damn, she went through the wringer."

I nod. "How long has Jess known?" I can tell Jessica knew about the affair, didn't believe Becca's story of a one-night stand.

"Ever since Becca had the baby. Jess was friends with Becca and she knew Kyle really well. She grew up with him too. She was scared to tell Anna. Didn't know how she would react. Jess finally told me after a few months of us dating. She had kept it secret for almost five years. I always wondered why she was so cold to Becca when we saw her at the country club or when her parents would invite Becca over. I don't know how Becca convinced this whole town about her baby being the result of a trip to Anna's college but it worked. Maybe because she married her husband soon after no one saw her as a bad person for having a child out of wedlock."

I drink the rest of my beer. "It's fucked up, man."

"This whole thing is," he agrees with me.

I grab us two more beers. I don't give a shit how much I drink tonight. I just want Anna to call me back.

A knock on the door causes us both to jump. But I know it's not her.

We hear Jessica answer it before she starts yelling.

"Fuck," Connor and I say in unison.

We both bolt for the door as Jessica pushes Becca hard against the chest causing her to stumble down the front stoop.

"I told you to leave her alone. I've been telling you for years. Yet, you had to talk to her constantly, feed her lies, drive her away from her family. You are a bitch and you need to get out of this damn town. Everyone knows what you did. You know how quick news travels here. And there isn't one goddamned person who wants to see your face again."

"It wasn't like that. We—"

"Stop with your bullshit excuses!"

Connor grabs Jess before she can throw another punch at Becca. But she pulls away, her anger fierce.

I step between her and Becca, Jess' body presses against my chest, peering around my shoulder. "You should have told her."

"Why didn't you?" Becca hisses.

The one statement causes a sadness to fall over Jess' face as she takes a step back.

"That's right. You didn't want to be the bad sister, the bad friend. Let her know the secrets you've known for years. Isn't that right?"

Jess stumbles back into Conner's arms.

"He told me," Becca sneers. "He told me everything. How you caught him years ago with another woman. How you tried to tell Anna but she wouldn't believe you. How he made a move on you."

Jess shakes her head. "That's not true."

"Which part, Jessica? It's all secrets and lies. Things you should have told your own blood. But Kyle told me everything. How that one night Anna was too busy to go to that party because she was writing music. But you were there, and Kyle said he always thought you were the pretty one. He told me how he dragged you into that room. How his fingers slid up your thigh under that pink dress you had on. How he fucked you with his fingers before you passed out on the bed."

A shiver runs down Jess' arms. "I was drunk."

"You wanted it."

"I didn't—I didn't know it was him. I was so drunk. I could barely stand."

"All lies. You can pretend you didn't know it was Kyle. But you and I both know you knew the truth. You are just as guilty as I am."

Tears pour down Jessica's face. "I didn't know. I didn't know." She falls to the ground and Connor wraps his arms around her before picking her up.

"I think you need to leave, Becca," Connor says before he carries a bawling Jess into the house.

I turn to Becca, shocked over her words. "Leave," I command.

Becca crosses her arms over her chest. "Anna deserves to know the truth. And now you will be one more person she loves that will keep it from her. Such a pity."

"Get out!" I shout, trying my best to maintain my composure as I tower over her.

She takes a step back before turning around and walking to her car. Before she gets in she says, "I would have told her, you know. Eventually. When I was sure she could handle it."

"Then why did you show up today?"

She shrugs. "I don't really know."

I watch her as she backs out of the driveway and drives down the street. My hands clenched in fists. I need an outlet for all this anger. To break away the pain I know Anna is feeling and the revelations that will hurt her more. I just need her. And I know she needs me too.

2

NOAH

I POUR A CUP OF COFFEE FOR JESS THE NEXT MORNING. Her eyes are red rimmed and raw, no doubt from a night of crying. Connor and her parents had to leave for work, so it's only the two of us in the house. She hasn't said a word since she came down the stairs twenty minutes ago. And I don't know how to start the conversation.

I set the cup down in front of her and take a seat across the table. She takes a sip of the coffee before speaking. "Thank you."

I nod at her and go back to looking out the window, trying to piece together all my memories of Anna. Looking for any clues in anything she could have said to me. I'm startled when Jess speaks.

"I didn't know. I swear to it. I don't want you to think that I am as bad as her."

I look over at her, confused.

"That story Becca told. I swear on my life, I had no idea it was Kyle that night."

I nod, not really knowing how else to answer. Do I think it's shitty that Jess messed around with Kyle? Fuck yes. But from the look on her face, I can tell she didn't even know it was him until last night.

"God, I was so drunk that night. I don't even know how it happened. I only had one drink when I got there, but it was strong." She sniffles as she circles her finger over the wood of the kitchen table. "I started dancing with my girls and then got super dizzy. Someone wrapped their fingers around my waist and I just followed them... fuck, I am such an idiot."

My body stiffens as I hear Jess retell the story. A story I've heard one too many times as a cop in a college town. One I've heard from my sister. "Jess."

She looks up at me as tears leak down her cheek.

I stand up, grabbing a tissue from the box on the counter, and squat in front of her. "Jess," I whisper as I hand her a tissue. "I think you were drugged that night."

Her quiet tears become more audible as I speak. "I've seen it happen a lot. And everything you just said sounds like every other case I've had." I grab her hands. "It wasn't your fault. If Kyle did that to you, he is worse than I thought he could be. If Kyle did that, Anna will forgive you."

"Are you sure?" she squeaks out.

"Anna has the biggest heart in the world. She would never blame this on you." I sigh before I continue. "And who knows if it was him. Becca hasn't proven herself trustworthy to me at all. She could be lying."

"B-b-but I was wearing a pink dress the night it happened."

"And Becca was at the party. She could have easily known what happened to you and made that whole thing about Kyle up. From everything I know about her, she seems like she has been jealous of Anna her whole life. And she will do what she can to tear her world apart."

8

"How can you be so sure?"

"I'm a cop. I've seen it happen more times than I can count."

Jess squeezes my hands back before letting go. "Thank you. I needed that. That night has been burned in my brain since it happened."

"You were assaulted, Jess."

She shakes her head. "I knew what I was doing. Kinda."

"It's assault if you've been drugged."

She nods. "I guess I never thought of it that way. I never reported it."

"Most don't," I say quietly as my thoughts race back to my sister.

"God, this is all so fucked up. Kyle never deserved my sister. He was a piece of trash."

I look at her confused. Everything I know about Kyle I heard from Anna so I don't know the other side, don't know how others viewed him. But Anna made it sound like he was the boy next door, the hometown hero.

"He never loved her like he said he did. He had this whole town and everyone that knew them playing the fool. The summer after they started dating, I walked in on him fucking some girl we went to high school with. When I brought it up to him, he played the whole thing off like it wasn't his fault. He was such a fucking dick. Said he needed better pussy sometimes. Wanted to wrap his hands around a girl, not lose his grip in her fat."

I shudder at her words. Christ, this guy was a dick. If only Anna knew before he destroyed her life. "Why didn't you tell her?"

She snorts. "Because that girl was head over heels. I tried to tell her but she just wouldn't listen." She takes a sip of her coffee as she tries to find her next words. "I don't even know why he proposed. Maybe things changed over time. I stopped talking to him after I confronted him. Only words I exchanged were cordial ones at family gatherings. I should have pushed it on Anna again. But she was so in love. And I thought he might have changed. Realized he truly loved her and not what he could get on the side. I was wrong.

"And Becca played that damn one-night stand lie so well." Jess looks up at me as she talks. "That's what she told everyone when she got pregnant. Even Anna thought it was true. Anna was there holding Becca's hand when Becca had to tell her parents. Breaking the news she had sex out of wedlock. Anna even let Becca crash at her and Kyle's place when Becca's parents kicked her out."

Fuck, this shit gets more fucked by the minute.

"I can't even imagine how much those two fucked behind Anna's back while she wasn't home. I bet you anything that is why Kyle quit playing music with her. It was around the same damn time Becca moved in. Eventually Becca's parents agreed to let her move back home. It was a few weeks before Anna and Kyle were supposed to get married. And then we all know what happened.

"I feel so bad for my sister. That this was all happening under her nose. I waited for years for her to tell me but she never did. I thought maybe she never knew. But after seeing her face when she saw Becca's kid, I knew she knew an affair had happened." She rubs her hands over her face and takes a deep breath. "I wish I had been honest with her sooner."

"I think you both could have been." I think back to Rosie and how I wish she had told me or Carson or Everett about what she was going through. Opened up to us for support rather than tumble down a dark path. "But you two are still here, you two can still make amends over the secrets you kept."

"I hope so."

I give Jess' hand one last squeeze before rising from my chair. "I'm going to make some phone calls. See if I missed anyone that might know where she is."

3

NOAH

I take a seat at a local bar in town just in time for happy hour. The first one goes down easier than I expected. I don't even think as I order my second, foregoing my rule of one beer in public. I press my face into my palms and groan. I feel like I have gone through every resource to try and find Anna.

Seraphina hadn't heard from her but checked on all the places she thought she might go. Luckily all her stuff including her car was at her house, so she didn't up and run.

Mason said she hasn't been by the studio.

I was even able to get ahold of her friend Liam from The Beer Garden and he hadn't heard from her either.

The police here in Hartswell can't help because they don't think she is a missing person. Which I have to agree with.

But I just want some clue, some kind of answer that can lead me on the path to her. I don't want to outstay my welcome here but I worry if I go back home to Asheville, I'll miss her along the way.

I just don't know what to do. I'm torn inside, not over just Anna but my past. I don't know what to think. The effort I have spent looking for her is more effort than I feel like I put in looking for my ex-wife. I don't know what that says about me. Are my feelings stronger for Anna than Claire? We haven't been together that long. Should I be feeling this way? Is it too soon?

Fuck, these thoughts are going to make me need whiskey. And I don't think that's a good choice right now.

I take another sip of my beer but before I can let the thoughts fog my brain again, I hear the scrape of a stool next to me. I sneak a glance to my side and see a young man. The bar is nearly empty, he could have chosen a different seat.

He orders a beer from the bartender and takes a sip before he turns my direction. "Noah, right?"

I turn to face him, not sure how he knows who I am. He must be in his late twenties. He's wearing an EMT shirt. When I meet his copper eyes, I know he must be related to Kyle.

He reaches his hand out to me. "I'm Jed, Kyle's brother."

I shake his hand but don't say anything.

He runs his hand through his hair before taking a sip of his beer. "I... ugh... I ran into Anna yesterday."

I tighten my fist. He is the first person to admit he has seen her and failed to let her family know after hundreds of phone calls to neighbors and friends.

He must see me begin to fume because he holds a hand up in front of me. "Look, I know you're pissed. I know her family is looking for her but I promised her I wouldn't say anything. Which isn't like me. I'm not my brother. I'm a good guy. And I upheld my promise to her."

He has my attention now.

"Anna told me to give her twenty-four hours. So I did."

"What did she say?" I blurt out.

He bites his lip before talking. "She needed time after

what I told her and she needed to be alone. She told me to find you. She knew you would be looking for her."

"What the hell did you say to her?" I grit out.

"I'm a paramedic. It's what I've wanted to do my entire life. Save people. It was my first week on the job, finally certified, excited and anxious all at once."

I don't have time for this. "Get to the point."

He looks at me with a raised brow and I know he isn't one to take orders. "There was a bad storm at the end of my first week. Rain turned to ice. The roads were slick, icy. It was foggy as hell, all a fucking mess. I worked twenty-four hours straight as it was accident after accident. My boss finally told our team to call it quits for the night. To head back to the station. We were on our way when we saw a car flipped on the side of the road. It looked bad. It was near a creek and the guardrail along the bridge on the opposite side of the road was mangled and smashed. We pulled over to check on the occupants of the vehicle. As we got closer, I could finally make out the model of the car through the fog, saw the plates. I fell to the ground. I knew it was Kyle's car. I could also tell by the scene of the accident, there was a low chance he survived. The driver's side was smashed in, glass and blood everywhere. He hit a rock on the side of the road that caused his car to flip.

"I almost quit my job after that. My dream shredded by the loss of my brother. But then the cops that were at the scene gave me a letter they found in the car. None of us got closure with what happened with Kyle. I mean, who does in an accident. No one ever gets to say goodbye. But Kyle had something to say to Anna, he just never told her."

I grit my teeth. "He was cheating on her."

Jed nods his head. "He was. She told me yesterday she knew about that. But I gave her the letter anyway. She needed to see it. Needed to read those words."

I know Jed isn't going to tell me what the letter said, even though he clearly read it. I just hope they weren't words to break Anna even more. "She say where she was going?"

He shakes his head. "Nah but I did let her borrow my car. And she only said 'Give me twenty-four hours. Then find Noah Taylor, he'll be with my family. Tell him I needed a sanctuary.'"

I grip the back of my neck at those words. Thinking, searching my mind for any hint she might have given me in our hours of conversation.

I knock my beer over when the memory hits and jolt from my seat. "Thank you Jed. I—ugh—I need to go." I throw a twenty on the bar and turn to head out but Jed's voice stops me.

"Treat her right, man. My brother didn't deserve her. I hope that you do."

I nod at him as I rush out the door. I hope I deserve her too. Yet for some reason I feel that I don't.

I jump into my SUV and throw it in drive as I fumble with my phone to dial Hunter.

"What's up, Noah?" he answers, sounding winded.

"You busy?"

"I just got done with a run before heading into the hospital. What's wrong?"

"Can you give me the number of your friend that's a detective?"

He chuckles into the phone. "Dude, how many times have I told you? You are going to do fine on that damn test."

"It's not about that. It's—ugh, work related."

"You sure you're okay, man? You sound flustered."

I take a deep breath before answering. "Yeah, I just need some information for a case."

"Isn't that what detectives do?"

"Can you just stop with the questions, please? I am looking for someone."

"Okay geez, man. I'll text you his number." He pauses before asking me another damn question. "You sure you're alright?"

"Yeah." I clear my throat. "I'm fine."

"Okay well, let me know if you need anything."

I hang up the phone before I answer him. I make a quick stop at the hotel we were staying at, grab our bags, and check out. I hit the gas once I hit the interstate. I look at the GPS that tells me it's about a four-and-a-half-hour drive to the islands south of Charleston. That gives me just enough time to try and remember which island she hinted at that damn cottage being.

I leave a message for my brother's friend, hoping he can help me out. He works for Beaufort County PD and I can only hope that he might recognize my description or he has records that can help me.

I race against the sun hoping I can make it before dark so I can find her tonight but as I get closer to the coast, the horizon darkens.

I pull into a gas station just outside Hilton Head Island when my phone rings. I pray it might be Anna but an unknown number pops up on my screen. "Hello?"

"Hi, is this Noah Taylor?"

"Speaking."

"Hi this is Detective Tyler Marks. Hunter Taylor is your brother, right? I got your message, but he also told me you might be calling."

"Yes, Detective."

"Please call me Tyler. I don't need formalities with you. Besides, if I remember correctly, you are a police officer up in Asheville."

"I am."

"What can I do for you? Need help with a case?"

I rub the back of my neck before I answer. This is against all protocol. I know as a cop we aren't supposed to use the police systems for personal use but many of us do. "I was actually looking for a missing person."

I hear him rustle papers in the background. "Is there an APB out on the subject?"

"Ugh—no. This is personal."

"You know I can't—"

"Look, I am not asking you to do anything crazy. I just want to know if you can run some plates. See if a car has been pulled over or at least passed through a toll."

I hear Tyler sigh on the other end of the phone. "Is that it?"

"Yeah. I hate asking this, especially because you don't know me. But it's my girl and she got some bad news and ran off. Her family is looking everywhere for her."

"Why would she be out here?"

"She told me once about a cottage she used to go to. She never told me where it was specifically, just that it was outside Hilton Head. I am just praying that it's in your jurisdiction and maybe you have some evidence that she was around."

"I hear ya, man. And I get that you're a cop. So you know that this might sound suspicious? I'm not saying you are abusive, but you know what I am saying?"

"I know. But I swear I am telling the truth. You can call my brother."

"Oh I will." He clears his throat. "Let me look into a few things. Make some calls. If you can text me the license plate of her vehicle, I can start looking."

"Thanks, man. I appreciate it."

"Sure thing," he says before he hangs up.

I send him a text of the make, model, and plate of Jed's

vehicle, explaining the situation. I text my brother and tell him not to be a dick, to tell his friend this has to do with Anna.

My brother met her once and fell in love with her. So I know he will do what he can to help me out.

I pull into a hotel for the night. It's too dark out for me to try and find a lime green cottage with pink shutters. Not to mention there is a lot of coastline to cover.

I wake up to my phone ringing just after midnight. My neck cracks as I sit up from the awkward position I fell asleep in sitting on the balcony of my room. I see it's Detective Marks and quickly answer the phone.

"I didn't get any hits on the plates," he says.

"Fuck."

"I'm sorry, man. I talked to Hunter. He told me you filled him in on everything with your girlfriend. I'm sorry and I know you hate to hear this, but I am sure she will go home eventually."

I groan as I stand up and head inside. "I know. Thanks for checking, man. If you ever need a favor up in Asheville, you know how to reach me."

"Will do. So what's your plan now? I am assuming you're here."

"Yeah. I am going to drive the coastline tomorrow. See if I find the cottage she told me about." I bite my lip as I recall our conversation for the hundredth time. "If it is around here, it shouldn't be too hard to find a lime green cottage."

"Lime green, you say?"

I nod even though he can't see me. "She told me she used to go to this tiny cottage on the coastline to relax and rejuvenate her mind. Hell, it could be in Georgia for all I know. Or torn down. I just need to find her. I need to make sure she is okay."

I hear him whispering in the background before he gets

back on the phone. "My wife is a real estate agent. She might know of the place."

"Really?" I ask.

"Yeah. Do you have any more of a description?"

I tell him about the pink shutters and any detail I can remember Anna telling me.

"I'll call you in the morning. She might know of the place."

"Thank you."

"But I am still being cautious on this whole situation. Mind if I follow you just for her wellbeing?"

I chuckle into the phone. "I wouldn't be a good cop if I told you I mind."

4

ANNA

I sip my coffee on the porch of my great-aunt's cottage as I watch the waves roll in. I haven't been here in over seven years and I forgot how peaceful it was. The taste of salt in the air, the steady beat of the ocean waves, the smell of sunshine keeping me warm even when it's barely fifty degrees.

I came here in anger. To yell at the void. Find some way to roll the wrath off my body when I found out Becca's secret. But the letter Jed gave me made me let it all go. It gave me the peace I didn't know I was looking for. That letter felt like the most honest thing Kyle had told me in years. I didn't know I needed it so badly to move on. To realize the last seven years of mourning was all a waste. I finally saw the real Kyle, the one he kept under lock and key, the hidden secrets behind my back. The person I never would have loved if I knew the truth.

I grab the letter out of the pocket of the oversized cardigan I have on. My aunt knitted me one every summer I came here and I always thought they were hideous. But as the years passed, I found comfort in her knitting, comfort in her words, the knowledge she passed down to me every year

I came here to visit. I wish she was here now. Still alive to give me the advice I never knew I needed.

And I don't need it about Kyle. I need it about Noah. My feelings for him are all-consuming and reckless and maybe coming too quickly. Falling for him was like being struck by lightning. So sudden and intense it leaves me breathless.

I never thought I needed someone like him. I never thought I could move on from my past. And now I am scared I am making the wrong decision. Is being with him the right one? Now that I have finally come to terms with Kyle's mistakes and indiscretions, should I be looking for more happiness in myself? Or do I already have it and being with Noah is letting me truly be free of the past?

I glance down at the letter I've read a hundred times since I got here two days ago. I take a deep breath, clutching the rings around my neck, before I read it again.

Anna May,

I don't know how many times I told you I was sorry tonight but I want you to know I really am. Fuck, I fucked all this up. Our life, our future. But mostly you. You trusted me with every ounce of your soul and I tossed that trust in the trash. All the times I came up with excuses, I should have told you the truth. I should have told you I wasn't worthy of you.

You, Anna, you are the perfect being. You are beautiful and talented. You have a presence to you I have never found in anyone else. When we first started playing music, I knew what we had was special. I knew you were special. It's when I first started to fall for you. The fifteen years of friendship we had before that never opened my eyes to the tenacious, incredible woman you are. I always told you I wished I real-ized it sooner. You always told me we would have dated in third grade and broke up by fourth. Maybe you were right.

I never should have done what I did to you. And every plate you threw at me tonight I deserved. I am selfish and unworthy. I broke the one thing I promised to you and that was forever. I don't think you'll ever believe how much I was looking forward to marrying you. I still want to. God, I love you so much. I know it's hard to believe me when I told you earlier I cheated on you but it's the truth. I thought once we were married I would put the past behind me. Focus on you. That is what I wrote in my vows, at least.

But maybe that's a lie too. Maybe I won't stay faithful to you but I will try so hard. I didn't tell you about all the girls. I felt like an asshole telling you earlier. But if I have any chance to still walk down that aisle with you next week, I want you to know the entire truth.

I got a little bit of the taste of the rock star life when we started playing bigger and bigger shows. You were busy packing up the van with the rest of the guys. I was talking to fans. You always said I was better at it than you were. The first time I cheated was with one of those fans. She gave me a blow job in the bathroom. Later that night I fucked you, still on a high from that blow job and you had no idea what I did. It gave me a high. Made me addicted to the thrill of cheating. It's not an excuse. I know that now. And I don't want to tell you there were lots of girls but there were. Each one of them a one-time deal. You were the one I wanted to come home to every night.

It wasn't until the last girl I thought maybe we weren't meant for each other. Because she wasn't a one-time thing. She was what I could get when you were too busy. I never meant to fall for her. I never meant to get her pregnant. And I know if you still marry me next week, that is one thing you need to know. I was too chickenshit to tell you face to face. But I can't deny the fact, I can't pretend it's not mine. I also need you to know who it is. She can be manipulative. Hell, I *think she manipulated me into this entire relationship. You need to know that I will choose you, baby. I will always choose you. I love you more than I can say. You know how much I love you.*

Becca has never meant to me what you mean to me. Even when I thought she did. I was wrong. I know that now more than ever. I went to her house tonight to break it off. Because seeing that look on your face when I left broke me in a way I didn't know I needed. I needed to feel what it was like to lose you, to know I needed you. Because I do need you, baby. I need you so bad. We aren't us if we aren't together. Isn't that what you always say?

I know you don't want to see me tonight. That's why I am leaving this in the house for you. I'll be at a hotel. But I hope you find this before you go to sleep. Hope you realize it's you and me, baby, if you can forgive me for all my indiscretions.

I love you. I need you. I want you to be my wife.

You and me forever.

Kyle

I throw my head back and laugh, my voice carrying into the wind, mixing with the sound of the waves. It's almost magical, bringing a melody to my head.

I laugh until I start to cry as I crumple the letter back up and shove it in my pocket. I don't know what I ever saw in Kyle. I guess I was just naïve and in love. But I know better now. I know I won't ever let a man have that kind of power over me again. Seven years wasted, thinking I could have forgiven him.

What a dick.

He is the worst person I have ever let into my heart.

Into my life.

And if I had known Becca was the one he was cheating on me with, I would have let her have him.

I wipe the last tears I will ever let myself have over him.

Being back in this place has given me the clarity I need. Maybe I should move here. Continue to live this peace I have found in such a short time. But leaving Noah makes my heart heave. Just thinking about not seeing him again leaves me nauseous. But I don't want to admit the feelings I have for him yet.

I should text him.

I should call him.

I know he is going crazy over the fact I left without as much as a note. Hell, his ex-wife gave him more. But deep in my heart I know he knows I'll be back. He knows better than I do when I need space.

By now, Jed has talked to him. And I hope he can forgive me for leaving with such haste.

I stand and stretch as I head inside to grab more coffee. I cross through the tiny living room into the outdated kitchen and pour a cup from my aunt's percolator. I smile thinking of how many times I bought her a real coffee pot and each time she would return it. She loved making her coffee the old-fashioned way. And I don't blame her now, the taste is better, or maybe it's just the memories.

I hear a car door slam and glance out the window to see a black SUV barely visible through the tall beach grass. I blink a few times, swearing I am hallucinating when I see the top of Noah's head.

There is no way he could have found me. Is there? Did I even tell him about this place?

I search my memories as I recall the conversation we had about sanctuaries. But I know I never told him exactly where it was.

My mind must be playing tricks on me.

Maybe I do need him more than I think I do.

I grab my coffee cup and head back to the porch,

choosing to sit on the rail instead of the old rocker I pulled out of the storage shed next to the cottage.

I sip my coffee as I glance back and forth from the water to the path that leads to the road. My mind and my heart battling. My heart wanting the glimpse of a man I saw to be the man I am falling for. While my mind is telling me I am a crazy person and hallucinating.

I look back out to the ocean and take a deep breath as my hands go back to the necklace around my neck. Today is the day I am letting go of every piece of my past.

The sound of footsteps on the worn-out boardwalk my great-uncle built pulls my eyes back toward the road.

My heart clenches when I see a man wearing a Beaufort County PD shirt. Not the police officer I want to see. I bite my lip in worry. Who would be looking for me here? My parents didn't even know that Great-Aunt Sheila left this place to me, they weren't close to her at all. Even my sister doesn't know and she spent almost as much time with me here as a kid.

A soft breeze floats through the porch as a shiver rolls down my spine. I pull my cardigan over my bare shoulder and stand, scared of whatever news might be coming to me.

But then I see what I thought I was for sure dreaming about.

Behind the officer is a tall, husky man with light brown hair and blindingly blue eyes. And those eyes are focused right on me.

My stomach flips and my heart seizes.

I drop my coffee cup on the deck, not caring about the shattered ceramic as I skip down the few steps to the boardwalk.

I ignore the police officer as he tries to ask me a question and throw myself into Noah's arms. He lifts me up as I wrap my legs around his waist, burying my head in his neck. Tears flood my eyes as I grip him as hard as I can.

I didn't know I needed this.

Needed him.

"I never should have run like that," I murmur into his neck.

"Shh... you did what you needed," he says as one of his large hands strokes my back, the other holding tight to the wild curls in my hair.

"I'm sorry... I'm so—"

He cuts me off before I can apologize, pulling my face to meet his, his forehead resting against mine. "You needed space. You needed—"

"I needed you. I didn't know. I didn't know," I whisper just as his lips find mine.

That fire and crackle that's always been between us increases tenfold with this kiss. Two days apart and it's like my heart forgot how to beat without him around.

My hands find their way into his hair, pulling him as close to me as I can get him. His hand slides down to cup my ass as his other holds me possessively in the back of my hair. One swipe of his tongue against my lips and I come undone, moaning into him, clawing at his back. I can feel his hard erection against my center and I want nothing more than to drag him into the cottage and show him how much I truly need him.

But the clearing of a throat behind us causes us both to stop. I slowly slide down Noah's body, a blush flooding my cheeks, forgetting there was a police officer with him.

Noah speaks, a raspiness to his voice as he slides me in front of him, my back to his chest, hiding the erection I now feel pressed into my back. "Sorry Tyler, I forgot—"

The man, Tyler, holds his hand up to stop Noah from speaking. "Don't worry. I know how the feeling is. I just wanted to stop you before I arrested you both for public indecency."

Noah chuckles at that. "Don't think that would look too good on my record."

"Not if you want to make detective this year," Tyler says with a laugh.

I look between the two of them confused because they clearly know each other.

Noah looks down at me and presses a kiss to my forehead. "Anna, this is Hunter's friend, Tyler. He's a detective out here in Beaufort County."

"Hi, nice to meet you." I wave at Tyler, still embarrassed I was practically humping Noah in front of him. I look up at Noah, wondering if he sent a search party out for me.

He must see the question in my eyes because he starts explaining. "I'll explain it all later. Luckily, Tyler knew this cottage."

I nod and turn back to Tyler.

"Well, I am glad he wasn't here to murder you or kidnap you. I'll just be on my way."

Noah's chuckle against my back sends a warmth through me as we both say our goodbyes.

I turn in his arms as soon as Tyler is out of view.

I go to speak but Noah's lips come crashing down on mine. The fire that was there minutes ago flaming to intense degrees. "Not now," he says against my lips. "I just need to feel you. Know you are okay."

"I'm okay now," I say before sucking his lip into my mouth. He grunts as he lifts me back into his arms and carries me up the stairs of the cottage.

"You made a mess." He laughs against my lips before pulling away to look down and avoid the broken ceramic mug. "It's unlike you."

I pull his face back toward mine. "When I saw you, you were the only thing I cared about."

That statement alone turns him into the dominant man I know him to be. He slams through the cottage door, kicking it shut behind him. He carries me down the hall that leads to the bedrooms but only gets as far as the wall before he slams me against it, his lips devouring my neck, my collarbone, slipping low to brush against the tops of my breasts.

"Fuck, I need you, Mayberry. I need to be inside you now."

Before I can even respond, he uses the wall as leverage to hold me up as he pulls my sweats down with one hand and unzips his jeans with the other.

I don't even have time to respond to his need before he is slamming into me. My back pressing hard into the wall as he pounds with heated force, taking everything I can give him. His lips are sloppy moving from my mouth to my ear to my neck but I don't care. The heat between us has me just as needy and desperate as he is. I claw at his back, pulling his t-shirt over his head.

He growls as I grind hard on to his hips. He bites my neck, my shoulder. Every thrust getting more powerful as we both cry out in feral passion.

His hands move to my hips and before I know it he is slamming me down on his hard cock with such an intense pace, the pictures my aunt had hanging on the wall crash to the floor.

My need for Noah emotionally outweighs my need for him sexually but with every thrust I feel more connected to him than I ever felt before. This is what makes us work, what makes us need each other so badly. Our physical connection makes our emotional connection even stronger.

And with every lick of flame from his body and every

moan from my mouth, we are both saying the things we are too scared to say out loud.

I watch him as he watches himself slide into me. My fingers trail up his abs, outlining each one before making their way up his chest. I circle his nipples with my nails causing him to say indiscernible words as he works us both to the edge. I finally make my way to his jaw and cup his face, forcing him to look into my eyes as I come apart in his hands. He follows at the same time, our gaze never breaking as we both ride out the wave of pleasure.

Only when he finally stops pumping and the pulses of my body slow, does he break our gaze as his lips find mine.

He hoists me back up around his waist, away from the wall as he carries me toward my bedroom. I nod in the direction of the last room.

He lays me down on the bed, pulling out of me, and I moan at the loss of him. He chuckles as he stands up. Pulling his jeans and briefs off. I go to take my clothes off but he tsks me.

His hands find their way back to my body, slowly pulling my pajama bottoms off. He pulls the cardigan off next before making his way to my tank top. He slides his hands over the tops of my breasts, squeezing my nipples firmly. He moves his hands under the tank as he straddles my thighs. His hands caress my stomach and sides before dipping between my thighs, dragging a finger in the mixture of my wetness and his juices. That's when I realize we didn't use a condom.

"Noah," I moan as he works me into another moan.

"Hmm?" he asks with a grin.

"We didn't use anything."

He smiles up at me. "I know."

My eyes bulge out of my head and I try to pull away

from him but his muscular thighs keep me trapped in my position.

"I needed you, babe. I needed to feel all of you."

"But..."

He takes his other hand and slides it from my breasts up to my neck before brushing his thumb over my lip. "We already talked about it. We're both clean."

We talked about it but never agreed to take the risk yet. But before I can remind him of that fact, he hooks his finger inside of me, pressing firmly into my G-spot. My entire body trembles as I feel a gush of heat between my legs.

I whine when he removes his fingers from me and slowly pulls my tank up my body, caressing my breasts, before pulling it over my head.

He leans forward and presses a kiss to the side of my mouth. "Are you upset?" he asks as his growing erection presses into the mound above my soaking pussy.

I shake my head, unable to form any words as he grinds his hips into mine at the same time he pinches my nipple hard between his fingers.

"Good," he says against my lips. "Then I'm taking what's mine again."

I gasp as he slams home, my body crashing quickly into an orgasm with just one intense thrust from him.

He chuckles as I pulse around him, catching my breath from the surprise release I didn't know was there.

He pulls back slowly before driving into me again. My eyelids flutter closed at the intense sensations pulsing through my entire body. Fuck condoms. This right here feels amazing.

I grip the sheets under me as he slowly pulls out. I wait in anticipation for him to use force again but he slowly slides back in. The pleasure is intense as I whisper his name over and over. But I need more, I need to feel his need, not this teasing that is driving me wild.

I attempt to spread my legs wider, to feel him deeper, but he has me caged in. He bends down and laughs in my ear before whispering, "Getting greedy, Anna May?"

The sound of my full name on his lips turns me into Jell-O. My body won't stop radiating pleasure but for some reason it isn't enough. I need more.

I wrap my hands around his ass, pushing him deeper inside of me but he's too strong and holds off on the rhythm, his laughter filling the room.

"This isn't funny," I groan.

"Oh yes it is. You are such a minx. Trying to get more, my wildflower."

"I need it, baby."

"Is that right? You want me deeper?"

I groan in response as he rotates his hips causing the pulsing inside of me to intensify.

"Please," I beg, trying whatever I can to feel more of him.

He sucks my lower lip into his mouth before biting hard. "You asked for it." He chuckles.

Before I can comprehend what he means, he pulls out of me, flipping me onto my stomach. I turn to look at him but within seconds he pulls my hips up while using his palm to press my chest into the bed at the same time he slams into me from behind.

I scream. He is relentless, filling me hard and fast, just the way I was begging him. It doesn't take long for me to find another orgasm. My entire body convulsing with pleasure. I know he is close too by the grip he has on my hip and the groans coming out of his mouth, my name a prayer on his lips. Before he finds his release, he takes his other hand

and presses hard into my clit. I nearly black out from the pleasure just as he comes hard inside of me.

He collapses on top of me, his heart beating hard against my back, his breathing erratic.

He kisses me slowly, peppering kisses up my spine before he pulls off me and flips me over, gathering me in his arms to lay across his chest.

"That was..." he says out of breath.

I prop myself on my elbow and look into his eyes. "Perfect."

His lips crash into mine for a short, intense kiss before he pulls away.

"Was that okay?"

I scrunch my brow. "What do you mean?"

"I was... a little... uh—"

"Rough." I finish his sentence.

"Yeah," he answers as he cups my jaw, his eyes staring into mine.

I trace my finger along his chest. "We've done it before."

"Never like that."

He's right. This time definitely felt different. "I think it's what we needed."

He nods his head as he strokes my back. "I'll be gentler next time."

"Only if I want you to be."

The look in his eyes change to hunger again and I can't help but laugh. "But I think you might need to give my vagina a rest for a few hours."

"Are you hurt?"

I shake my head. "No, but I feel like you're still inside of me."

He presses a kiss to my forehead. "That's how I want you to feel."

We lay there for what feels like hours, enjoying each

other's company, feeling at peace. Until my stomach growls and Noah's laugh fills the room.

"I think we need to get you fed."

"What did you have in mind?" I joke.

He shakes his head as he stands from the bed. "Real food."

He hands me my clothes before he pulls on his briefs and jeans. The letter falls out of my cardigan pocket and he scoops it up before I can take it from him.

"Don't read—" I try to snatch it from him but he pulls away from me and holds it above my head. Asshole.

"Is this the letter Jed gave you?"

I stop trying to reach for it, stunned he knew what it was. "Jed told you?"

He shrugs. "He told me he gave you a letter from Kyle. That's it. And from the looks of the paper, I would say it's pretty old, not a song you wrote recently."

I sit back on the bed and look down at my feet. He has no idea what's in that letter. Hell, he probably thinks it's some beautiful apology and love letter. "It's not what you think."

"What do you mean?"

I shrug and brush back tears that threaten to spill out of my eyes. "It doesn't change anything. Yet it changes everything."

"I'm confused. Is it not closure?"

I shake my head before looking up at him. God, he is so beautiful. Inside and out. I can see and feel how he cares about me. How was I so stupid not to see that with Kyle?

Noah kneels in front of me. "That ghost is in your eyes again, Mayberry."

I try to look away from him but he won't let me. I have no idea how to explain that letter to him. How to tell him I was a fool from the get-go. How all that letter did was make me feel like I wasted years on a man who was never worth my time.

"Baby." Noah grabs me off the bed and settles me into his lap. He wraps his arms around me, holding me as tight to his chest as he can. "Talk to me."

I take a deep breath before speaking. "That letter... that... it let me see him."

"What do you mean?"

"I'm not crying over him," I manage to get out. "I'm crying over the time I lost mourning him."

I can feel the tension in Noah's body. His need to protect me from everything is tangible and I know when he reads that letter he won't be happy.

"Let's eat," he says with unease in his voice.

We walk into the tiny kitchen that barely fits us both. I pull some cold cuts from the fridge I picked up yesterday and make us each a sandwich. We sit at the tiny dining table by the window that looks out over the sand dune. We eat in silence, the letter sitting on the table between us. I know he is brewing from the few words I said about the letter. And I am just waiting for him to ask about it. But I really don't know what there is to say.

The only reason I've reread the letter so many times was to find some kind of redeeming quality about Kyle. But with each read-through, my hatred only got worse. His apology was a cop-out. An excuse to get me back.

I don't know how to tell Noah what the letter says. I can't summarize the awful shit inside of it. "Read it."

He looks at me with surprise.

"I can't tell you what's inside. It's just better if you read it."

"Are you sure?"

I nod and look out the window watching a storm cloud move in. Rain sprinkles the windowpane and I watch the drops fall as Noah reads the letter. I don't dare look at him. Don't want to see the rage I know will be on his face.

His chair scrapes against the linoleum floor as he stands. He walks out the front door, slamming it behind him. I look out the window and watch as he storms across the dune and down to the beach. I can see lightning in the distance. Idiot just ran out on to the beach in a damn lightning storm.

I knock my chair over as I run after him. I grab an umbrella from the stand by the door before I run into the rain and down to the beach.

The letter is in his hand as he falls to his knees on the beach, screaming at the top of his lungs. Thank God for the storm. There are no people out here to watch his crazy.

I run up to him, pulling on his arm as he finally quiets down. "Noah, you need to get off the beach. You could get struck by lightning."

He looks at me and stands, towering over me as I fail to cover us both with the umbrella and let it fall to the ground. "If he was alive right now, I would kill him."

"Noah."

"That asshole does not get the final word."

"Noah."

"I don't like that he can still hurt you even when he isn't here."

"Noah, please," I urge, gripping on to his wrist for dear life.

"He never deserved you."

"I know."

"Then why did you say it changed nothing and everything."

I gather my thoughts as I search his beautiful blue eyes. "Because it made me realize the last seven years was a waste. And all my doubts I had about falling in love again weren't needed. Because he never loved me. He never loved me the way he said he did. And all the fears that were holding me back from getting closer to you didn't matter anymore. You and me, Noah. We are right. We are. We just are. And I won't hold myself back from loving you anymore."

His eyes brighten at my words before a haze of lust covers them. "Anna."

His mouth is on mine. But this kiss isn't passion and lust. This is a different kind of kiss. A kiss I can feel all the way in my bones.

A crack of thunder overhead breaks us apart.

Noah laces his fingers with mine. "Come on, let's get inside before we catch a cold."

5

NOAH

SOMETHING CHANGED. AND I CAN'T PLACE IT.

The feelings inside of me I've never had before.

A burning need to protect this woman in front of me. I can feel it through my entire body. A connection on the deepest level.

How did one letter change everything between us?

And those words she said.

I won't hold myself back from loving you anymore.

They caused a fire in my heart.

I want to love her.

I am one step closer to opening my heart completely to her.

I just need the closure she finally got.

But I know every day I spend with her, the guard around my heart breaks down more and more.

She gives me butterflies.

She makes my heart sing.

I only wish I was as good at words as her.

The screen door blows shut behind us as we walk in from the rain. The wind is picking up from the storm causing the shutters on the outside of the house to rattle.

She shivers from the wet cold enveloping her. "I should latch the shutters."

I wrap my own wet arms around her. "How about you get out of your wet clothes and into the shower. I'll get the shutters."

She looks up at me and for the first time since I met her, there isn't a trace of a ghost in her eyes. I press a kiss to her forehead and walk her down the hall to the bathroom.

I turn on the water before I move closer to Anna. I pull the soaked cardigan off her, followed by her sweats. She grips my forearms as she steps out of them and I fight the urge to fuck her again as my gaze travels to her nipples pressed hard against her wet tank. I pull it over her head and open the door to the shower and guide her in.

"I'll go close the shutters."

She bites her lip and I know she wants me with her but she slowly nods and closes the shower door behind her.

I head outside and quickly secure all the windows as the thunderstorm picks up its fury. As I walk back up the steps of the porch, I pick up the umbrella Anna dropped on her way in. As I go to close it, I see the rain-soaked letter stuck in the spines of it. I carefully peel it out before closing the umbrella. I set the letter on the coffee table. I don't know what Anna wants to do with it, hopefully destroy it.

I walk down the hall, picking up the pictures we knocked down earlier and rehang them on the wall. I smile at a picture of an older woman with graying red hair, her arms wrapped around a young Anna with a guitar in her arms. Her wild red curls blow in the wind, covering half her face but the smile that peeks through is enormous.

There is another picture of Anna and her sister as teens sitting on the porch. Anna once again with a guitar, her sister painting her nails. I place it back on the wall before making my way to the bathroom.

Anna is still in the shower, singing softly in the steam. Her voice is one of the most beautiful I have ever heard. Haunting, melodic, sad.

I strip my jeans and shirt off and step inside the modest shower. Anna jumps and stops singing as I slide in behind her. "You could have kept singing."

"You scared me."

"I've never heard you sing before." I step farther into the stream of hot water, my body moving flush against Anna.

"Yes you have," she says as she places her hands on my chest.

I shake my head. "Only in the recordings. You never sing for me."

She rests her head against my chest. "I just—I don't like singing in front of people."

"Even me?"

She looks up at me, biting her lip. "I—okay, I will."

I smile down at her. "What were you singing about?"

She shrugs as her arms wrap around my waist. "Just finding words to a melody I came up with this morning." I run my fingers through her hair as she speaks. "It's a mess now. The song. But it's about moving on after regrets."

I reach for the body wash behind her and raise a brow when I see it's the kind she left at my place.

"I picked some up on the way here."

I lather up a sponge and run my hands up and down her body. The movements must relax her because she begins to hum.

As I slide my hand down her back, her fingers trace circles around my chest and that beautiful raspy voice sings the most haunting melody.

I forget I was even washing her as her voice gets louder, echoing off the walls of the enclosed shower.

I'm in a trance. Blown away from not just her sound but

the words she sings. A song about lost love and heartache. Fighting for a future without the pain of regret.

My hands wrap around her face as she meets my eyes on the last note of the song.

"I haven't sung that in years."

I can't even answer her. I am still in awe of what I just heard.

She giggles as I stare at her. "Are you that surprised?"

I blink a few times before pressing a quick kiss to her lips. I murmur against them, "No, I just never thought I could be so enthralled by a song before. I didn't want it to end."

She smiles against my lips. "I liked singing for you. It gave me a confidence I haven't felt in a long time."

"You can sing for me whenever you want, Anna May."

She wraps her arms around my neck and pulls me into her, kissing me slowly, deliberately. "I could get used to this."

I pull away slightly. "Kissing me? I think we both feel that way."

She laughs as her lips brush against mine. "No, Noah. Falling for you."

My hands slide to her hips as I pull her into me, kissing her deeply.

I could get used to this too.

AFTER WE STEPPED out of the shower, I told Anna to take a nap while I planned dinner. There wasn't much in the house so I made a quick trip to the store. I check on her before heading back into the kitchen. She barely even moved while I was gone. I smile as I watch her sleep. She looks peaceful, relaxed, like she can finally breathe for the first time in seven years.

I scramble around the kitchen looking for pots and pans. Everything in here is dated and old. I feel like I am cooking in Dottie's kitchen. My grandma never cooks, always orders takeout or has dinner with her neighbors. I don't even think she has looked at her cooking utensils in years. So I can easily manage since I do it all the time at Dottie's.

I find a few candlesticks in a closet and set them on the dinette just as a pair of arms wraps around me from behind.

"You didn't have to do all this," she says.

I might have gone a bit overboard with the salad and garlic bread and lobster ravioli but I wanted today to be special for her. I bought firewood and started a fire to warm the house up a bit since the storm brought in a cold front.

"I wanted to," I answer as I turn her around to face me. She looks adorable in the pajamas she has on.

"What?" she asks as she looks down at her outfit. "I had nothing else to wear. These are all old clothes I used to have here. I had to wash them in the sink to get the mustiness out."

"It's cute," I say as I tug on the oversized t-shirt she has on to bring her lips to mine.

"It's crazy how this stuff used to be tight on me. I never thought I would see the day where it was too big." She pulls on her shirt to cover the bit of stomach that was showing where she tied it. "I'm glad you didn't know me then. Or you never would have kissed me."

I rub my hand over the scruff that is growing on my face. "Anna, baby, it doesn't matter what you look like."

She rolls her eyes and tries to step away from me but I hold her in place. "I've seen the pictures of you but your body had nothing to do with what I saw. It was the happiness on your face, the way your eyes shined with laughter. Your smile makes me weak in the knees."

"You wouldn't be saying all that if you knew me back then."

I grip her chin. "Trust me. I would have. Don't get shy on me now, Mayberry. I know the confidence you have. The way you show it in the bedroom. You can have that anytime. Just believe in yourself. No one is judging you by your weight."

I drop my hands to her ass, gripping it firmly. "I don't care how much you weigh. You look fucking fantastic now. And if you had a little more here," I grip her ass hard before running my hands up her stomach, "or here," my hands move to her breasts, groping them under her shirt. She lets out a mewl and I grin. "Or even here. I wouldn't feel any different about you."

"How do you always know the right things to say?"

"How do you always know the right words to sing?"

She smirks. "Fair enough."

I hate how self-conscious she is. I know it was hard when she was younger and I am not lying when I say I would be attracted to her no matter what she looked like. I am lucky she looks like a fucking siren now with her hourglass shape. A temptress in disguise. I just want her to feel comfortable and confident like she is with me when we're naked.

I change the subject because I know it will take time for her to gain her confidence. "Let's eat."

"Okay."

I pull her chair out as she goes to sit down. The table is small but I manage to fit all the dishes on the table. I chuckle as she dives into the pasta.

"Oh my god, this is fucking delicious. I didn't realize how hungry I was."

"Thanks."

She grins at me after swallowing a piece of garlic bread. "Look what happens when you actually have a kitchen. You made it seem like you didn't know what you were doing."

I shrug. "I knew what to do. I just didn't care. I survived just fine."

"And now you care?"

"Now I have you."

Her cheeks blush and I want nothing more than to wipe everything off this table, set her on top, and make the rest of her body blush as I devour her for dessert. But I restrain myself even though my dick is begging for it.

"So how did you find me here, Noah?"

I set my fork down and take a sip of water. "It wasn't easy. I got lucky, really. I looked for you everywhere, Anna. I went to the daisy field. Everywhere in town your sister and parents said you might be. I called Seraphina and even Liam. No one had heard from you. It wasn't until my conversation with Jed that I remembered you telling me about this place. Of course, I had only a vague recollection of where it was. When I talked to Tyler, I mentioned the color and he knew this place."

"It kind of stands out a bit." She smirks.

"Yeah it does. But I was willing to drive up and down the entire Carolina coastline looking for you."

She grabs my hand. "I'm glad you found me."

"Now tell me about this place. I saw the pictures of you on the wall. Probably would have been a lot easier to find if I just talked to Jess."

Anna sips on her wine before answering. "Jess wouldn't have known."

"She's been here though," I say.

Anna nods. "She has, but no one knows I own it."

I raise a brow at her and she continues. "It was my

great-aunt's house. I used to come here for a few weeks every summer with my sister. She hung out on the beach all day. I learned music. Aunt Sheila was the one who bought me my first guitar. She was a musician herself. She taught me everything. Tempo, melody, songwriting, guitar, piano, saxophone."

"You play saxophone?"

"Trust me when I say you don't want to hear me try." I laugh as she tells her story. "Aunt Sheila got me into music. Taught me how to find the passion behind a song. She was my mentor and my best friend growing up. She passed away ten years ago. I was surprised as hell when a lawyer showed up at my apartment on campus. She left me this house. I came here all the time when I needed to get away from school. I wrote some of my best music here."

"When you were in the band with Kyle?"

She nods. "Yeah. I wrote all the songs. I never let anyone come to this place. No one in the band ever knew about it."

"You said Jess wouldn't have known you were here?"

She eats the last bite of her food and sets her fork down. "My parents had a falling out with Aunt Sheila when I was sixteen. They wanted me to be a scientist or a doctor. I wanted to pursue music. She was my dad's aunt and they never had a good relationship. But they let me and Jess come here because it gave them time to take a trip every year. Once I told them I wanted to be a musician like Aunt Sheila, they stopped talking to her. She didn't have any other family, no kids, just the ones she taught music to. So the last few years of her life she spent mostly alone. Whenever I was able to make it out here, she would be so happy.

"I never told my family she left me this place. And they never asked the lawyers from what I know. They probably assumed it was sold on behalf of the executor to her estate."

I clean up our plates and carry them to the sink. "When was the last time you came here?"

Anna brings our glasses to the sink then leans against the counter. "I'm going to need a lot more wine for that conversation."

She helps me clean up from dinner. She washes the dishes while I dry them. We make small talk while we clean. I don't want to pressure her into talking about what I am sure is going to make her upset.

The storm outside quieted down for a bit but a huge crash of thunder outside makes us both jump. Within minutes, the power goes out.

The fireplace gives off enough light for us to see but the rest of the house is completely dark with the shutters closed.

Anna passes me the bottle of wine. "Go sit down. I know there are candles here somewhere."

I sit down on the couch and find it as uncomfortable as hell. I move around and fluff the cushions but no matter what I do, I sink into the bottom.

"I wouldn't sit on that couch." Anna laughs.

"I realize that now. But I don't think I can get out. I think it's eaten me alive."

Anna sets down a basket of candles on the floor and helps pull me out of the human eating couch.

"I swear that couch has been here since this place was built in the fifties." She opens a chest by the front door and pulls out blankets and giant floor pillows. "I much prefer to sit in front of the fireplace on these."

I laugh as she hands me a leopard print blanket. "Are we gonna sit on this or fuck in front of the fireplace? I mean it's not quite a bear skin rug but it's close."

She punches me in the arm before setting everything up in front of the coffee table. "My aunt had eclectic taste. What can I say?"

I watch her as she sets candles up around the tiny living room. I can't help but stare at her ass the whole time. Even in those five sizes too big pajama pants, I know what's underneath. I might not have been joking about the blanket.

She shakes her ass as she lights the last candle, knowing full well I was taking in the view.

I pull her to the floor in front of me, caging her in with my legs. I wrap my arms around her middle as I suck on her earlobe. "I like this."

"Hmm?"

"You and me here. Alone. Like we have our own little world."

She turns toward me and smiles a sad smile. "I'm happy you're here to make the memories fade."

"What happened?"

She reaches behind us and grabs the wine I poured for us. She must see the letter on the table because the light in her eyes fades a bit as she grabs it.

She swallows down half her glass of wine, her fingers fumbling with the letter. Mine rubbing up and down her legs. "I haven't been here in seven years." She takes a deep breath, her fingers tracing the words on the page. "I brought Kyle here when we graduated college. He was so thrilled to finally see the place I talked about. He knew about it when we were kids and knew I came here to write songs. But I never let him see it.

"I was so in love with him. I thought we should celebrate graduating by making love and listening to the waves break on the shore. We spent a lot of time here that summer. He proposed here. He suggested we move in here after we got married. Of course in those fifteen months between his proposal and the week before the wedding, things changed drastically. We rented a house in our hometown. He started working for his dad. Stopped playing music. Told me to stop my dream. I never understood why until I found out he cheated. Honestly, it wasn't really until this damn letter."

She folds it up and crumples it into a ball. "I should have known when he started having an affair. It was when everything changed about him. After he died, I tried to escape sometimes and come here but I couldn't write music here any longer. It was as if the magic of this place was gone. I never really understood. I thought it was because he proposed here and it all turned out to be a lie.

"But as I sat here for two days, my mind played conversations over and over in my head. Conversations with him. Conversations with Becca. And then I remembered a comment Becca made once about this place. The fact there wasn't a coffee pot. Back then I assumed I told her about that. But I don't think I ever did. There were times Kyle had to go away for business trips. Becca sometimes would say she was headed to the beach. I never put two and two together. Not until I read this.

"I searched the house for anything that might give me proof she used to come here with him. I found nothing. But I just know, I know that was why I could never write here after he died. His ghost haunted this place as much as it haunted my heart."

My hands clench around her as I hear her say more words that prove Kyle was nowhere near deserving of her. And honestly, I almost want to kill Becca too.

Anna turns in my lap and kneels in front of me. "Having you here cleanses this place of those ghosts, Noah. Being with you, making new memories. I can hear the music again. Feel the melody in my fingertips. You gave it all back to me, Noah."

I watch as a tear slides down her cheek and brush it away. "I just want to give you what you deserve."

She smiles at me before turning back to the fireplace.

She opens the letter one last time before throwing it into the flames.

She stands in front of me, her hands clasping the rings around her neck. "I have one last thing to do. Will you come with me?"

I nod as I move my wine glass from the floor to the coffee table and stand. She grabs my hand as she walks to the door.

"Babe, it's still pouring rain out there."

She looks me in the eyes, a desperation there I haven't seen before. "It's time I finally do this."

I have no idea what she means but I would follow her through any storm.

We walk down the steps of the porch and into the rain. We cross the sand dune and fight the wind as we make our way to the crashing waves.

"I've let this control me for too long. Let the past direct my life. Take me on a path I never should have gone. It needs to be done. I need my life back."

I watch her as she unclasps the rings from around her neck. She holds them in her hands, giving them a silent prayer before she throws them both in the roaring waves.

She grabs my hand, holding it hard as she watches the wave recess into the ocean. She takes a deep breath before she turns to me and smiles.

I know whatever she was holding in is gone. The ghosts of her past left to sink to the bottom of the ocean.

When we finally make it inside, she grabs my soaking shirt and rips it over my head.

I see a fire in her eyes.

A need burning deep.

A hunger I know how to fulfill.

I pull her shirt over her head and she pushes down her pants. Her fingers go for the button of my jeans and has them off within seconds. I lay her down on the leopard print blanket as I worship her body in front of the roaring fire. I make her come again and again. My own needs forgotten. But when our bodies finally come together as one, it's love we are making. And for the first time in five years, the idea doesn't scare the shit out of me.

6

ANNA

I wake up to a very hard body pressed against my back with a very large dick pressing into my pussy. I hook my leg over Noah's hip as he slowly enters me.

Last night on that blanket, Noah showed me pleasure I never felt before. And when he finally was inside of me I knew it was different.

Just like now.

This isn't a rush to the finish line.

This is slow and steady.

This is devotion and adoration.

This is everything I need.

I turn in his arms, wanting to look into his eyes when we reach the precipice. And when we do, it's the most beautiful thing I have ever experienced.

He presses a soft kiss to my lips and pulls away, his forehead resting against mine.

I love you, Noah Taylor. The words are on the tip of my tongue but I hold them back. I don't even know why. Everything that was holding me back from opening up my heart is gone. I don't fear love anymore because what I had before wasn't love. But with Noah, it's hard to believe it's not.

"What's going on in that head of yours?" Noah asks me.

"I wish we could stay here longer."

He brushes a piece of hair behind my ear. "Why can't we?"

I run my fingers along his chest. "You have to go back to work."

His hands find their way to my ass, pulling me closer to him. "I asked my boss yesterday if I could take the week off. He wasn't too happy but he approved it. Man's been bugging me for years to use my vacation time I've racked up."

I throw a leg over his hip as I grip his face. "Really?"

"Yeah baby."

I press my lips to his as I feel his dick stir beneath me. "Maybe we should get out of bed so we don't spend the whole day in it."

He licks up my throat before biting on my ear. "Would that be so bad?"

"We can't just have sex all day, Noah."

He chuckles into my neck. "Baby, that's where you're wrong. I don't need to be in bed to find a way to have sex with you all day."

I roll my eyes and push away from him, slowly climbing out of bed. "Prove me wrong then."

Noah jumps out of the bed. I have no time to react before he has me pinned against a wall, both of us laughing.

"GIRL, YOU HAD ME WORRIED SICK!" Seraphina shouts into the phone.

I pull the phone away from my ear as I stand on a sidewalk outside of a clothing store. "I know Noah let you know I was fine, so calm down."

51

"How was I to know he didn't just tell me that and he is really a serial killer?"

"I think you have been watching too much Investigation Discovery lately."

"Oh come on, you know it keeps me entertained. Anyway, what the hell happened?"

I sit on a bench outside the ice cream shop next door. This is going to be a long talk. "You better be sitting down for this."

I hear her fumbling around in the background. "Hold on a sec, let me grab some popcorn."

I roll my eyes at her waiting until she gives me the go to talk. "Kyle was a dick."

"No shit. I could have told you that."

"He wasn't always that way, Sera. He was great for a while."

"Fine. He wasn't always an asshole but I told you before you even agreed to marry him I wasn't getting good juju from him."

I snort. "Sera, you say you don't get good juju from a lot of people. And when you do get *good juju* it's usually only for the night with some guy with a hot bod."

"Ugh. Whatever. So tell me what set fire to your feet so you had to hightail it out of dodge."

I take a deep breath before I start. "Kyle cheated on me. A lot. In fact, he was having an affair with Becca. And—"

"Shut the front door. I knew something was happening between them."

"Sera, you weren't even around when it happened."

"Juju."

I shake my head as I tell her the rest of the story. The letter, Becca's child, her nonchalance over the whole thing.

"That fucking bitch. I knew something was off with her."

For years, Sera has been trying to warn me away from Becca. She has never been a fan, mostly because Becca was a bitch when she found out I made a friend in college who was my new best friend. The two of them never got along.

"It is what it is. I can't change the past."

"How are you holding up with all this?"

I play with the fabric of my ripped jeans thinking about everything. "It ripped me apart. Seeing Becca's son's eyes and knowing the truth. I felt so betrayed. I was ruined. Running was the only thing I could do. But I'm managing now."

"Where did you go?"

I never told Sera about this place. And I still want to keep it my secret. "I just got in the car and drove. Went to the coast."

"How did Noah find you?"

"Well he is a cop; he has his ways." Not a total lie.

"You don't usually want someone around when you run away."

"Yeah, well I needed him when I didn't know I did."

Sera exaggerates a gasp into the phone. "Are you telling me you aren't as cold-hearted as you pretend to be?"

"Only around you," I joke.

"So how has this affected you and Noah?"

I bite my lip thinking about the last twenty-four hours we spent together. Me pouring my heartache and pain into every word I said. And he was there for me, listening, holding my hand. "It's been good," I whisper.

"Good? You got to give me more than that!"

I sigh, trying to put it all into words without giving away too much. "He's just been there. Listened. Supported me. With him, I don't have to try."

"Mmhmm. I see."

"See what?"

"You're in love with him."

"I—I'm..." I don't know why I'm keeping it from her or trying to make up some excuse. I am in love with him. There is no denying it.

"That bad, huh?"

"Fine," I groan. "I'm in love with him. Okay?"

Sera laughs into the phone. "And how does that make you feel?"

"Are you my therapist now too?"

"I'm kidding, Anna. You sound happy despite all the shit you just found out. And that makes me happy. So what are you guys doing?"

"Well I ran here with no clothes so I am buying a few things. Noah wants to take me on a proper date tonight."

"Make sure you buy some fancy lingerie."

"Newsflash, Sera, he's seen me naked."

"Yeah, but fancy lingerie does something to a man."

I shake my head at her. "I'm going to go. Need to be ready in a few hours."

"Have fun tonight! And green lace will look best on you!"

I hang up my phone laughing. I am not buying fancy lingerie for Noah.

Noah brought my overnight bag when he came here, but I wanted something new for tonight. I end up buying a few shirts, a pair of jeans, and a gorgeous white and yellow floral wrap dress. I drive back to the cottage excited for our date tonight. I park my car in the street and gather my bags as I head down the boardwalk to the cottage. I nearly drop everything when I see Noah standing shirtless outside. And it's not his body that has me in awe.

He is power washing the house, bringing out the vibrancy that it once had. I notice the broken boardwalk below my feet is repaired and the steps leading to the porch look new. I was only gone a few hours but Noah has made this place feel like it did when my great-aunt lived here.

Noah turns off the machine when he sees me. His smile wide. It makes my knees weak. Because I love this man more than anything and I need to tell him.

"Hey Mayberry."

"You did all this while I was gone?" I gesture to the boardwalk under my feet and the house.

He shrugs. "I know this place means a lot to you. And it needed some repairs. I want you to feel that inspiration here that you used to feel. And I thought if the house looked new again, you would feel it."

This time I do drop my shopping bags as I cut across the grass and throw my arms around him. He's sweaty from the heat of the sun but I don't care. My lips are on his neck, his face, his mouth. He lifts me up, pulling my legs around his waist.

"Thank you," I whisper as I pull away, resting my forehead against his.

"Anything for you."

I want to say those three words again but I still hold back. An inkling of fear holding down my emotions.

7

NOAH

I sit at the dinette set as I wait for Anna to get ready. I made us a dinner reservation at a seafood restaurant overlooking the waterway and marsh between the islands. It's our first official date. I feel bad I never took her out anywhere before. Our relationship has been spent mostly in private. Our dates on either one of our couches. I'm not complaining about it either. For some reason it felt right that way between us. We were comfortable at home, allowed to spill our secrets without anyone interrupting.

But with the time I have spent with her at this cottage, I felt I needed to do something special for her. Her heart's been dragged through hell the last few days and I want to pull her away from all of it.

I hear the bedroom door open and watch as Anna walks out. She is fucking gorgeous. Her body wrapped in a floral dress that hugs her body in all the right places. Her wild red curls full and beautiful. She put on a bit of eyeliner, making her green eyes pop. She kept the rest of her face fresh so I can see the freckles spattering her cheeks.

I walk to her, my eyes focused on her lips, covered with a pink gloss, and I want nothing more than to suck it off. We are attracted to each other like magnets, both of us reaching for the other at the same time. My hands go to her face and I pull those delicious lips into my mouth, kissing her with a fervor only she awakens in me.

I pull away and she takes her fingers to my mouth, wiping the gloss from my lips. "You are covered in lip gloss."

"I don't care."

"Let me fix mine and then we can go," she says as she turns.

I pull her back to me, giving her one more brief kiss. I can't keep my hands off her. "You look beautiful, Anna May."

She blushes. "Thank you. You don't look so bad yourself."

I look down at my outfit. A navy button-down that I had brought for dinner with her parents and a clean pair of jeans. Nothing special but I like that she likes it.

When she is finished fixing her lip gloss, we walk out the door. She locks up the cottage and we head to my car. We drive in silence to the restaurant, enjoying the presence of each other's company.

We are seated outside looking over the water. She sits next to me so we can both take in the scenery. I can't take my eyes off Anna as she watches the birds dance along the shoreline. My feelings for her are strong and undeniable. With every day we spend together, I find myself forgetting more about my past and looking forward to the future. A future with her.

Those twenty-four hours of not knowing where she was, had me at a loss for words. I couldn't place the feeling. My heart was heavy, my mind a wreck. I promised myself I would never let a woman control my emotions this way. But with Anna, it's so easy to let her in. Easy to let my past be the past. Easy to see myself falling for her.

And I am falling for her.

She is this beautiful, talented woman.

Her energy is addicting.

I can't keep myself away from her.

"It's creepy when you stare at me like that," Anna says as she turns toward me and away from the water.

"I just want to make sure you are okay."

"I am. You make it okay, Noah."

I smile at her as she takes me in. But I can see the hesitation still there. Her hand goes to her neck, reaching for the necklace she threw in the ocean last night.

The waiter interrupts us and her hand goes back to her side. We order a bottle of wine and a plate of oysters.

"I can't believe you are going to make me eat those," she says.

"You spent so many summers here and you never had oysters?"

"Once. And trust me, that was enough."

I smirk at her. "You know they are an aphrodisiac?"

She bites her lip before she smiles back at me. "Do you really think I need an aphrodisiac with you?"

I reach my hand across the table, grabbing hers. "Oh I know you don't."

"Then why the oysters?"

"I love them. Trust me. If you try them my way, you'll like them too."

She raises a brow at me. "Doubtful."

"You know your taste buds change."

She sips her wine. "My taste for men might change too."

I move my hand to her thigh, higher than some would deem appropriate. "Doubtful."

Her cheeks flame to my favorite shade of pink just as the waiter brings out the oysters.

"So, how am I supposed to eat this?"

I show her the best way to eat raw oysters. A little bit of lemon and a little bit of horseradish. I swallow one down and I watch her as she watches it slide down my throat.

"You swallow it whole?" she shrieks.

"Yeah."

She shudders as she prepares one in front of her. "The last time I had one I chewed it and it was so gross."

"Don't chew. Swallow." I lean into her ear and whisper, "I know you're good at that. It's one of my favorite things about you."

Her cheeks turn pink again and I press a kiss to one. "Just try one."

She loosens the oyster from the shell before she tosses her head back, swallowing it down.

"What do you think?"

She shrugs and then grabs another off the plate causing me to chuckle. "You're right, they aren't terrible if I swallow. I'll remember that later."

I throw my head back in laughter. I love spending time with this woman. She makes me feel carefree and it's a feeling I could get used to.

We spend the rest of dinner laughing and joking. The mood light and refreshing.

When we get back to the house, I want nothing more than to rip her dress off and show her how much I need her. But she has other plans.

As we step onto the porch, she twirls, her skirt raising giving me a glimpse of green lace panties. I try to wrap my arms around her but she dodges me.

"Not yet, mister." She points toward the west side of the house. "The sun is about to set and I love the changing colors of the sky. It's when I find the most inspiration."

She heads inside while I sit on the railing of the porch

looking over the marshland to see the sun. Anna comes out with a guitar and sits on the steps of the porch.

"This was my aunt's. You asked what was in the other room before and I lied when I said storage. It was her music room. One of my favorite places. It's where I learned to play piano and guitar. Every night we would sit out here and play music as the sun set. Sometimes the neighbors would come by, sometimes it was just us and my sister. We would play everything from folk to rock to bluegrass."

I move next to her and sit beside her as she strums a few notes on the guitar.

She turns to me. "Thank you for bringing back the peace this place once had."

I lean in and press a kiss to her curls before she starts playing a song. My hand drifts up and down her spine as her raspy voice caresses the wind. The song is a beautiful love song that I've never heard before. I can only guess it's an original.

I listen to her play for almost an hour as the sun finally sets behind the trees. She sets her guitar down and faces me.

I press my lips to hers and pull her up. I grab my phone out of my pocket and turn on some music as I lead us into a slow dance on the porch.

Her hands wrap around my neck, playing with the hairs at my nape as we sway back and forth. The salty breeze of the ocean floating between us.

I get lost in her eyes. I can see why this place was so important to her. Can see what it does to her. There is a calmness and serenity to her. I bring my lips to hers, I can't help it. My feelings are strong and overpowering and I want nothing more than to love her.

She pulls away from me, searching my eyes. "Noah, I— I, you make this all seem right. I don't know what I would have done if you weren't here."

"I would have found you no matter how long it took, Anna May."

Her hand sweeps down my cheek, brushing over my lips before trailing down to my heart. "I love you."

My heart aches at those words at the same time a fire erupts inside of me. I can't hold myself back this time as I attack her lips with need and hunger. I pull her legs around me and set her on the porch railing as I kiss down her neck, between her breasts, and back up.

I want to say the words to her. To tell her I feel the same way, but my heart is fighting it, telling me this can't be real.

I drop to my knees in front of her, hoping I can show her how I feel until I can find the words.

She groans as I pull her panties to the side, swiping my tongue through her wet heat. I grip her hips to keep her from falling off the railing of the porch as I devour her. I slide a finger inside, curling it until I hit that spot that makes her moan.

"Fuck, Noah."

I grin into her pussy as she moans exactly when I knew she would. I suck her clit into my mouth as I insert another finger inside of her, working her to the edge before slowing back down.

Her legs wrap around my back, urging me closer. "I need you, Noah," she groans as she throws her head back.

I suck her clit into my mouth one more time, bringing her right back to the edge before I pull away from her completely.

"Why did you stop?"

I grin at her before throwing her over my shoulder and carrying her into the house. I stomp down the hall into her room and throw her on the bed. I climb over her, undoing the tie on her dress, exposing her body and the sexy as sin forest green lace lingerie she has on.

"Fuck," I moan, rubbing my hand over my mouth.

She wiggles the dress off herself before scooting up the bed and spreading her legs wider.

"You like?" she rasps.

I pounce on her. This woman is so fucking sexy and she doesn't even realize it. But in the bedroom, all her reservations disappear. She becomes my wildflower.

Her hands go to the button of my pants while I slide mine under her ass pulling her closer to me. When she gets my dick out, I pull her all the way on to my lap. I can feel the warmth of her pussy through the lace of her panties. I lift my legs so I can shove my jeans down past my knees. She unbuttons my shirt, licking her way up my torso. She rips my shirt off just as I pull her panties to the side, driving hard into her heat.

Her legs straddle my thighs as she rides me hard. She braces herself on my shoulders, her nails digging into my back with every thrust.

My hands dive into her thick curls, bringing her lips to mine. One hand slides down to her hip, helping her pick up the speed of our movements.

"Noah, oh my god, Noah."

I know she's close. I shift my hips to hit her right where I know it will bring her over the edge.

I look into her eyes just before we both come and I see everything in them.

I see the ghosts of my past disappearing.

I see the woman I love.

I see my future.

"Anna," I shout as we both find our release.

Her lips are on mine and I fall backward, her body lying on me. I manage to kick off my jeans that were still around the bottom of my legs.

I roll us to the side so we are lying face to face. I brush a wild curl off her face and cup her cheek. "I love you, Anna May Cooper."

She smiles as she presses a kiss into my hand. "I love you too."

I never thought I would find someone like her. Someone that made me forget all the shit that happened in the past. All the shit that made me want to never feel like this again. But letting myself go, letting myself love her, it feels like the best thing in the world.

I slowly remove the lingerie she has on. Giving her body every ounce of attention it deserves before I make love to her over and over again.

8

ANNA

"If you keep biting on that lip, I won't have anything to kiss later," Noah says to me as we drive to my parents' house.

We just dropped Jed's car off at his house and now I am in the car with Noah for the fifteen-minute drive over. I was glad he wasn't in the car with me from South Carolina because I bit off every one of my nails and bit the inside of my cheek so hard it started bleeding.

I know I am going to have to tell my family the truth. The rumor's out. Everyone knows that Becca had a kid with Kyle. But I need to let them know everything. They deserve it.

I tried to convince Noah to let us stay one more day in the cottage but he said we needed to spend a day in Hartswell. I knew he was right but I loved the time we had together at the cottage. The day after we went to dinner we spent between the sheets. We watched the sun rise and set and spent some time outside, but most of the day was spent in the arms of each other.

It felt good to give in to my feelings. To let myself finally tell him I loved him. And instead of being scared when it happened, waiting for him to pull away from me, he didn't. He showed me what those words meant to him. And when he told me them in return, my heart nearly burst.

This feels like love.

Not what I thought was love with Kyle.

This is a feeling I never felt before and it had me high as a kite yesterday.

But today I am scared as shit. I don't know how my family is going to react. Especially when they find out how much of a dick he was and how much I put up with.

I still wonder why I didn't break up with him sooner. Why I didn't let myself think about how his behavior changed.

Every mile we get closer to my parents', the panic starts to set in a bit more. All the thoughts I let disappear when I was with Noah at the cottage come flooding back. My breathing gets heavier as I try to find a way to calm down. My thoughts turning to Noah, wondering if this is all a dream. If I'll wake up and he will be gone.

I don't even notice the car pull over to the side of the road until Noah is gripping my cheeks. "Baby, it's going to be okay."

I start to sniffle. "I need to tell them everything, Noah. How are they going to react when they find out what I put up with? What I hid from them for years?"

Noah brushes a tear from my cheek. "They won't think any less of you. You did nothing wrong. They already know the worst parts of it all. They are just going to want to make sure you are okay."

I nod as I try to find my breath.

"You are strong and resilient. It's going to be okay."

I take a deep breath as I find a bit of peace with Noah's

touch. But then Becca's face floats through my mind. "What about Becca?"

"You don't need to talk to her today if you don't want to."

"What if she finds out I am back at my parents'?"

"I won't let her through the door."

I smile at him as I slowly calm down.

"Mayberry, you got this."

He squeezes my hand as we sit on the side of the road for ten minutes. When I feel calm enough, we pull back on the road and head to my parents'.

Noah opens my door for me, leaning his built frame over me in the car. "You want a few more minutes?"

I shake my head just as I see my sister walk out the front door of the house. "I can do this."

"I know you can," Noah whispers as he presses a kiss to my forehead.

He helps me out of the SUV as my sister approaches. She flings her arms around me the second she is next to me saying she is sorry over and over again.

I look at Noah but he looks away. Jess must have known. She must have known and never told me.

I pull away from her, accusation in my eyes. "You knew, didn't you?"

"I'm so sorry, Anna May. I should have told you. But I couldn't find the strength or courage. I didn't want to break your heart. I didn't—"

I hold my hand up in front of her. "How long?"

She looks at the ground, avoiding eye contact.

"Godammit Jess, just tell me."

"When he was about a year old."

I scream so loud I know the neighbors are looking out their window. Noah runs up to me and wraps his arms around me from behind. "You knew all this time. You knew and you didn't tell me?"

Jess starts sobbing. "I didn't want to destroy you. God, Anna, you were already so broken after losing him. I didn't know you even knew he had an affair. Maybe if you had told someone that, told me that, I would have told you about Becca's kid. But—"

"Don't you dare blame me for keeping that a secret. You should have told me. Becca was my friend. You knew I still talked to her. You knew—"

"I tried to tell you."

"No you didn't. You were a selfish bitch and kept it to yourself. When you knew that was one thing I should have fucking known."

"I fucked up, Anna May. I know. I've been kicking myself all week for not telling you sooner. Not giving you any kind of warning."

"You're right, you should have told me."

"I'm sorry."

"Me too," I say as I pull out of Noah's arms and head into the house, leaving my sister outside.

"Anna May," my mom says, wrapping her arms around me as soon as I step through the front door.

"I'm sorry for running away, Mom."

"Honey, you don't need to apologize for anything."

I hate to ask the question but I need to know the answer. "Did you know, Mom? Did you know like Jess did?"

She grips my shoulders. "No, honey, I had no idea."

I bite my lip, holding back tears as I feel Noah place a hand on the small of my back.

"Come on. Let's go sit down and talk. Your father is making some snacks. Do you want something to drink?"

"Vodka."

"Okay honey," she says, not caring about my need for booze.

We walk into the kitchen and take a seat at the large dining table where Connor is already sitting. My dad sets a plate of shrimp cocktail down before wrapping me in a hug.

"Anna May, we were worried sick."

"I know. I'm sorry."

"I'm just happy you have a man who would go to the ends of the earth to look for you."

It warms my heart to hear my parents approve of Noah. Our dinner we had here was one thing, but to get their approval after a bit of turmoil is even better.

"Where were you?" Mom asks as she sets a vodka soda in front of me. "Noah wouldn't tell us."

I give a glance of appreciation to Noah before taking a sip of my vodka. I guess now is as good of a time as any to tell them about Aunt Sheila's cottage. I take one more large sip of my drink. "I went to Aunt Sheila's cottage on Old Island."

"What?" my dad questions at the same time my mom says, "But I thought that place was sold by the executor of her estate."

I shake my head. "That's what I told the lawyer to tell you. She left it to me in her will."

"Why wouldn't she have said anything? Why didn't you tell us?" my dad asks.

Noah grabs my hand under the table. "You were so upset with her when I told you I wanted to go to school for music. You all stopped talking. I felt like I ruined your relationship with her. We were the only family she had and I ruined it. I didn't want to make things worse. So when she passed and I found out she left me her cottage, I kept it a secret." I take a sip of my drink as I continue. "It was a special place to me. And I wanted it to stay that way. I went to see her a lot when I was in college. I'm sorry I never told you guys. But she encouraged me to follow my dreams. She taught me so many things, not just about music but about life. I wanted it to be my secret. It was my sanctuary. At least it was until Kyle died."

"We understand," my mom says as she looks at my dad.

He nods in agreement. "You know we are proud of you and all you have accomplished. We never meant to hurt you like that when you were younger."

"I know. And I got over it quickly. Besides, I still went to college for music. You couldn't stop me."

My dad laughs. "We definitely couldn't."

I look at both my parents as I hear Jess sit down in the living room. I know she needs to hear all this even if I am pissed at her. "Jess, you can come in here. You deserve to hear this too."

She slowly gets up and takes a seat next to Connor.

"I ran into Jed when I ran away from the engagement party. He gave me his car when he saw how desperate I was. I didn't really understand, but he gave me a letter. And when I read that letter, I understood more than I could have ever thought."

I explain to them the real Kyle, the one he kept hidden from us all. The man I fell in love with wasn't the man everyone knew and loved. I told them about the night Kyle died, the fight we had when he told me he had an affair. I told them I never knew about Becca and how it wasn't until the day of Jess' engagement party that I found out the truth about everything.

My parents cry as I tell them everything I have kept hidden for years. They tell me they wish they had known. Wish I had told them so they would have understood better about why I stayed away.

My mother is not too happy with Becca. Pissed that Becca would treat my mother like a saint. Acting like everything was the same as it was when we were kids. She felt betrayed and that is not a feeling my mother takes lightly.

An hour later I am finally able to get some time alone with Jess, thanks to Noah distracting my parents. We sit outside on the front porch, watching the kids across the street play in their front yard.

"I need—"

"I'm sorry—"

We both say at the same time.

"Go first," she says to me.

"I shouldn't have said those things to you. You aren't a bitch. I just—it hurt knowing that you knew and didn't tell me. God, so many things would be different if I had known."

"I never meant to hurt you, Anna May," Jess says as she grabs my arm. "I thought I was helping by not letting you know what Becca did. In hindsight, it was wrong and I should have told you."

I sigh as I look over at her, taking a sip of my drink. "I just wish I didn't lose all this time with you. With Mom and Dad. And I'm not blaming you for that. It's my own fault. I shouldn't have been the selfish one. I should have come home. I should have told you all sooner."

"You were hurting. None of us blame you for that."

"It's been seven years, Jess. Seven years I've lost out on." Tears stream down my cheeks as I talk. "God, I don't know why I was so stupid. Why I let this all go on for so long. I should not be blaming you for my mistakes, Jess."

My sister wraps me in a hug, crying with me. "But we have each other now. We have our time back."

I cry into my sister's shoulder; happy she is optimistic. I've missed her over the last seven years. Our few strained phone conversations were not enough to make me feel like we had a relationship. But now that I am putting everything behind me, I know that I can finally have that relationship with my sister I used to have.

I pull back from her and wipe my tears. "I'm sorry I ruined your engagement party."

She laughs. "Please. You did not ruin it. You know I never would have wanted such a stifling party but I had to do it for Connor's parents."

"Well I am sure I made a great impression on them."

"Who cares?" she says, throwing her hands in the air. "I don't. Plus, now Connor and I can have the party we wanted to have. At a bar. With our friends."

"I hope I'm invited," I tease.

"Only if you promise more drama will happen!"

I roll my eyes at her as I punch her in the arm. "Oh I will find a way, brat."

Jess laughs until her face turns solemn. "There is something else I need to tell you."

My smile fades as I see her serious expression.

"Becca told me something the other night. She came over here trying to... I don't even know what. Cause more problems, I guess."

I try to calm the anger in my veins, but the fury is red hot. "Whatever Becca said can't be true."

"I hope it's not. I really do. Because I don't think we'll be okay if it is."

A million thoughts fly through my head about what the hell Becca could have said that could be any worse than what she already did.

"Remember that night I got assaulted?"

I nod, not liking where this is going. Jess was wrecked after that, who wouldn't be. It took her almost a year to get back to herself. And it hurt so bad that I wasn't there for her when it happened. That I wasn't there to stop it.

"Becca said it was Kyle."

I knock my glass over that is sitting next to me, the rage inside of me burning like a supernova. I brush the ice off the steps and into the yard. "What the fuck, Jess?"

"I'm sorry. I had no idea. I didn't—"

"What are you talking about? One, this is not your fault. Don't apologize for being assaulted. Two, it wasn't Kyle."

"But—but she—" Jess quivers.

"He wasn't there that night. I know for a fact. We were on a date, remember? You begged me to take you to that party but I told you I wouldn't and I told you not to go. Of course you didn't listen because you are you. And you know I kicked myself so much for not showing up after our date. Do you remember that? Remember why I wouldn't go?"

Her eyes go wide as the memory hits her. "It was your anniversary."

"Yeah and Kyle was with me all night. In fact, he was the reason we didn't go to the party, even after I heard that you went. He wanted our night to be special. But when we found out what happened, it was both of us that came and got you and took you home." I grab her hands as the tears fall down her cheeks. "Becca is a worthless piece of shit in my eyes now, Jess. She's manipulative and hurtful. And she would say anything to get you on her side."

"Anything else you want to say about me?"

My eyes snap up when I hear Becca's voice. My fist clenching hard against the wood of the porch. Jess must see my rage as she grabs my clenched hand.

"Calm down, Anna May," Jess whispers.

I push to standing. "I'm not going to fucking calm down."

"Look at you finally showing some grit," Becca says.

And by the way she is stumbling, I am guessing she is drunk.

I walk the few feet to her and get in her face. "Grit? I don't need to show grit around you. I need you to get the fuck out of here."

"Anna, can't we just talk?" she slurs and stumbles into me. That's when I notice the black eye she has.

"I have nothing to say to you."

"But I'm sorry. I'm so sorry. I should have told you."

I stand my ground in front of her, controlling my anger as best I can. "You should have told me a lot of things. But you didn't. And most of what you did tell me was lies."

"That's not true. I—"

"I don't want to hear it, Becca." I hear the front door slam behind me and turn to see Noah storming down the stairs, my parents and Conner standing next to Jess.

I throw my hand up behind me, signaling Noah to stop. I love the man but he needs to let me fight my own battles.

"Please, Anna."

"We both know you are full of lies. And I quite frankly don't want to hear any more of them fall out of your mouth. Stay away from my sister, stay away from me. Get off my parents' property and get out of my life."

I turn to leave but she pulls on my arm. I go to throw a punch, not giving a shit she already has a black eye but Noah stops me.

"Not worth it," he whispers in my ear.

I throw one last glare at Becca and walk into my parents' house, my sister right on my heels.

I look out the window and I see Noah talking to her. Connor is next to him on the phone as my parents walk in the house.

Jess grabs my hand and whispers in my ear. "Thought you would like to know I gave her that black eye."

I turn and look at my sister, not quite sure if she is serious. But the look on her face tells me she really did.

I grin at her as I drag her to the kitchen. "I think we both need a shot."

"Amen, sister."

9

ANNA

THE DRIVE BACK TO ASHEVILLE HAS BEEN PEACEFUL. I feel like I've gotten the closure I need to move on. I can finally rebuild my relationship with my family. I can let myself love again.

I look over at Noah as he drives. His aviator sunglasses covering part of his face just make his jaw more pronounced. I look at his biceps as he turns the wheel. I can't say it enough, but he is the perfect specimen of a human being. The cop you see in those memes on the internet.

And he is all mine.

He looks over at me and smirks. "Want me to take my shirt off?"

"Yes." I smile back at him.

He laughs so loud I can feel it vibrate inside of me.

"I love you."

He looks back over at me, pulling off his sunglasses. "I love you too, Anna May."

He reaches over and squeezes my thigh as he pulls onto our street.

I lean over to kiss him on the cheek but his words stop me.

"What the fuck?"

I look up and there's a huge "For Sale" sign in front of the duplex where I live. "That motherfucker."

Noah pulls into his driveway and I jump out of the car before it's even in park. I stomp over to the sign and pull a sheet out of the document holder. There are pictures of the inside of both sides of the duplex on the document. I was not home when those were taken. I kick the "For Sale" sign. "Motherfucking asshole."

"Whoa there, karate kid." Noah pulls me back. "Knocking this over isn't going to help you."

"I know."

"I'll call Carson."

"Thank you."

Noah takes the one sheet out of my hand and whistles. "This is priced high."

"Really?"

He nods. "Might take time to sell. Depending on the buyer." He glances back at the sheet. "You sure your land-lord didn't leave you a message?"

I throw my hands on my hips and glare at him. "I'm positive. Not to mention he was in my place taking photos without my permission!" I point at the photos that clearly show the décor of my house.

"Fuck. Let's talk to Carson. He might have some advice regarding the legality of all this."

I humph as I storm to the door, forgetting I didn't even grab my purse. I turn back to the car but Noah is already there grabbing my purse and my weekender bag. He meets me at the front door and I grab my purse, searching for my keys.

"I only have a few hours before work. I need to find a

place to live." I shove the key into the door and walk through. Throwing my bag on the ground. "I need to call my neighbor. See if he knows more. And what about showings? My landlord needs to inform me if people are coming over. What if I am in the shower? Shit, I need to straighten this place up."

I look over at Noah who is shaking his head and chuckling. "Babe, your house is always clean. You don't need to straighten it." He sets my weekender bag down and walks over to me grabbing my shoulders. "Talk to your neighbor. But your landlord can't legally show this place without letting you know."

I look into his eyes and let out a breath I didn't know I was holding. "Okay. But I need to find someplace to live. Soon. Maybe I can move in with Seraphina or Liam temporarily."

"No."

I raise a brow at him. "No?"

"You are not moving in with another man."

"In case you weren't aware, Liam is gay," I say as I roll my eyes.

"Are his roommates?" Noah asks as he pulls me in closer, his grip on my shoulders firm.

Well shit. How am I supposed to lie to him about that? "Umm, one is."

"And doesn't he have three?"

I shrug.

"You're moving in with me."

"Excuse me?" I try to pull away from him but he has me locked in his arms.

"It's the easiest solution."

"One, we just started dating—"

"Months ago," he cuts me off.

I ignore him. "Two, you don't get to tell me what to do."

He lifts the left side of his mouth into a grin. "You sure about that?" he leans in closer whispering into my ear. "You let me control you in the bedroom all the time."

My cheeks flame at that because it's true. But beside the point. "Three..."

He pulls me in so I am flush against his body, one hand holding my ass, pressing my hips into his. The other on my neck forcing me to look him in the eyes. "Baby, you don't have a three. Just give up. Say yes."

"You didn't even ask me so I can't say yes." I retort. "And besides I do have a three, it's—ugh—this is a bad idea."

He smirks at me. "How so?"

I bite my lip searching for an answer. In all honesty, I would love to move in with him. See how this relationship unfolds. I am in love with him so naturally this is the next step but I don't want to admit that the real reason is that I am scared. Scared about what could happen. Scared he could break my heart.

"Baby, I know you're scared."

Okay, so maybe moving in with him will be okay since he can read me like a book.

"It is scary. It's a big step. But I love you and if us living together means I get to spend even more time with you, then I am willing to do it. Jump off that diving board into a pool of fear. Because I think it will be worth it in the end."

Why does he have to be such a sweet talker?

His lips brush over mine. "Will you move in with me?"

I look into his eyes and find sincerity and understanding. My heart is bursting out of my chest as the anxiety recedes. If I move in with him I get to look into these eyes every morning when I wake up and every night when I fall asleep.

I press a brief kiss to his lips. "Okay."

He smiles, his grin taking up his whole face and I can't

help but smile too because I love putting that smile on his face.

"AND BREATHE IN," I say with a deep breath. "And out into warrior two pose."

It's Monday morning. Three days after Noah asked me to move in with him. We moved some of my clothes over yesterday since we both didn't have to work. But since he had picked up a shift on Saturday night and I worked til four in the morning, we spent most of yesterday sleeping.

I still don't know what to think about moving in with him. I wonder if it's too soon. Actually, I know it is. But he brings up a good point which he would not quit telling me yesterday when I kept asking him if he was sure if he wanted to do this. He said if I get an apartment in this neighborhood I will be lucky. But I will probably end up twenty minutes from him and with our work schedules, we will either never see each other or I'll be at his place so often it would be like we live together.

I know that would be what happens but I still worry. I haven't been in this position in over nine years. Kyle and I lived together our senior year of college and then got an apartment in Hartswell when we moved back after we graduated. Besides Kyle's indiscretions, I did love living with him. Waking up next to him every morning, making breakfast together, having dinner together. It was the domestication I always wanted.

My chest grows heavy with anxiety. Is that the life I want again? Will my freedom be taken away if I settle down?

"One more deep breath." Yoga is supposed to be relaxing yet all I can think about is Noah. And I am doing a shit job of teaching today. "Now twist your body forward, bend that right knee into a low lunge. Deep breath in and out, try to drop your elbows to the ground, feel that stretch."

Noah will never be the man that forces me to change my ways for him. I know that. He is dominant as hell in the bedroom but he lets me make my own decisions everywhere else. Even though I know he wants me to be more confident, he doesn't push me more than I am comfortable. And I want to be more confident. You'd think losing fifty pounds would bring out confidence but all it did to me was make me more insecure.

Although, if I am honest with myself, the wringer that Kyle put me through made me insecure. But I promised myself last week on that first day alone at the cottage I would put thoughts of Kyle behind me. Live life with a fresh start, a new outlook. I know I can't let my past control me anymore but is it wrong to completely ignore what I've learned from it?

"Bring that right leg back, shoulders square, and into downward dog. Breathe in and out. One more time in and out into sphinx."

I focus on the rest of my yoga class, using my breathing to calm my anxiety and find my center, just like yoga is supposed to do.

When class is over, I step into the office and make myself some coffee.

"So what happened when you went back to Hartswell?"

I jump at Seraphina's voice. "I didn't hear you walk in."

"Well?" she asks, ignoring me.

"Oh you know. Apologies were made. I feel like I mended everything with my sister. My parents are happy that I am happy. And Becca showed up and I nearly punched her in the face."

"Why didn't you?" Seraphina says with a grin.

"Because Jess punched her in the face a few days beforehand."

"Dang, I wish I'd been there to see all this."

I look at her with a raised brow.

"Okay fine, no I don't because you know I would have killed that bitch. God," she sighs as she flops into her office chair. "I cannot believe she did that to you. Well, I can because I always thought she was a bitch but I didn't think she would do it to *you*."

I shrug. "What's done is done and all I can do is move on from it."

Sera sits up a little straighter in her chair, leaning forward, her ice blond hair falling over her shoulders. "Did you just say you are moving on?"

"Yes?" I answer confused.

"Well heavens to Betsy, Anna May Cooper is finally moving on after seven years of living in misery."

I roll my eyes. "If I had something to throw at you right now, I would."

"Does this have anything to do with Mr. Handsome, Muscular Cop?" she asks, raising her brows up and down in suggestion.

I bite my lip as I look down at the floor. "Maybe."

"Maybe?" she shouts in question. "Girl, you better tell me everything."

"I told you what happened."

"No, you told me about Kyle. You didn't tell me anything after I made you admit that you were in love with Noah."

I look at the clock on the wall. The next class starts in two minutes. "Look at the time. I need to get the next class started."

I turn to leave but she bolts out of her chair. "You stay," she tells me before walking out of the office and into the studio, telling the class we are starting with ten minutes of meditation.

When she walks back into the office, she shuts the door behind her. "Did you tell him?"

I think about all the concerns I had about telling Noah I loved him. Everything I was holding back because I feared the rejection I was expecting. But when he showed me what those words meant, when he said them back to me, the thought alone is making me melt into a puddle right now.

"Well from that look on your face I can tell you did. Let me guess, he said he was in love with you too."

I smile at her and nod.

"I knew it. You two are so smitten with each other. Now tell me, did you buy green lingerie like I told you to?"

I laugh at that. "I wasn't planning on it. But you put that damn thought into my head and then I saw this beautiful set, so I bought it."

"Ha! I knew it. Let me guess, it turned his brain to mush?"

I bite my lip and nod. "He just about lost it."

"Works every damn time."

"But it put me back some so I need a raise," I joke.

She opens the office door. "I'll think about it. We should go buy more today after lunch! Now get out there and teach your class!"

As I teach my next two classes, I feel lighter. The thoughts weighing me down before having cleared. I know this move with Noah is the right one. And once I tell Seraphina, she is going to flip.

I WALK through Noah's front door with another bag of my clothes, the obscene amount of lingerie Sera made me buy tucked inside. Although I am excited to put some of it on for him.

I find him sitting on the couch, studying for his exam. I drop my bag and lean over the back, kissing him on the cheek. "Hey babe."

He smiles up at me before pulling my mouth to his for another kiss. Before I know it, he is pulling me over the back of the couch and has me flipped onto his lap. "That's better," he says.

I giggle as I let him kiss me, the best welcome home kiss I have ever gotten in my life.

"How was your day?" he asks as he pulls away, pushing loose curls from my face.

"It was good. My first yoga class in over a week, felt a bit rusty at first."

"I would like to watch you do yoga." He grabs my ass hard. "See this ass bent over in those yoga pants."

"Such a perv."

"Mmm." His lips are on my neck.

I push him back. "I need a quick nap before I go to Jimmy's."

"I'll take one with you."

I climb out of his lap. "Nope. Because then we won't be napping."

He smirks. "Is that a problem?"

"Yes! I need some rest before my shift so I don't fall asleep." I start to walk toward the stairs that lead up to his bedroom, grabbing the bag of clothes as I go.

He stalks behind me. "Then you should have slept at your place."

I push him away as his hand glides down my back. "And you need to study. You have two weeks until your exam, Detective."

He growls at me and scoops me up before I have time to protest.

I YAWN as I look at my watch. It's been relatively slow tonight and the fact I didn't take a nap is making time drag.

I shouldn't have called Noah, detective. I know how much he likes it when I call him that. So my nap time turned into an hour and a half romp in the sack making me almost late for work.

I only have two tables left for the night but one of them has been here for two hours and they don't look like they are leaving anytime soon.

I text Mason. We were supposed to write some new music tonight but I am too tired to do anything but crawl into bed and sleep.

By the time my last table leaves, it's nearly eleven. I was supposed to be the early cut tonight but I wanted that tip from that table. A bunch of rowdy college kids that would not stop flirting with me. Fortunately, they weren't cheap when it came to tips and left me a nice chunk of change.

I grab my bag and say goodnight to my manager and head outside to my car. Somehow I make it home without falling asleep.

I park my car in my driveway and grab my mail. I throw the mail on the kitchen counter and head to my music room to put my money away in my safe before heading to Noah's.

Picking my mail back up, I try to go through it but my eyelids are heavy. I see a large envelope, the only thing that doesn't look like junk, and grab it before walking out my door and locking it behind me.

I walk into Noah's house, the lights are all out except for

the one on the entry table. I shut it off as I quietly tiptoe upstairs.

I throw my bag on the floor next to my side of the bed. I really need to shower but exhaustion is taking over. I collapse onto the bed in my dirty clothes and shut my eyes.

I wake up a few minutes later to Noah taking my clothes off.

"The gate is closed tonight, Noah."

He chuckles into my neck. "Noted. But you smell like stale beer and French fries."

"Fuck. I'm sorry. I was just so tired."

"I've got you, babe."

He takes my clothes off and pulls me into him, my back to his chest, as I fall into a deep sleep.

10

ANNA

My phone ringing wakes me up. I blink away the
sleep, looking at the clock telling me it's after ten. Having a
week off work is exhausting. Who knew that a week of
sleeping in would mess up your entire sleep schedule?

I stretch my hand out to the nightstand looking for my
phone but I can't find it. I peer over the bed and find my
purse on the floor.

What the hell is it doing there?

That's when I realize I am lying in bed naked. I flip
through my hazy thoughts of the night before. I remember
stumbling through the door and passing out in bed. Then I
remember Noah telling me I smelled.

I grab a piece of my hair and smell it. Luckily it isn't as
repulsive as my clothes must have been. I find one of Noah's
shirts laying on the end of the bed and throw it on before
lugging my purse onto the mattress.

There is a large envelope inside but I toss it on the bed
and dig for my phone. When I finally find it, I see I have a
missed call from Jimmy's. I listen to the voicemail to find
out they want me to work a double. I groan because I
despise doubles as a server. Bartending always goes by

quickly but a double serving makes me want to gouge my eyes out with a spoon. I could use the money though after a week off.

I call them back and let them know I will be in by noon. Then I grab the mysterious envelope from the bed. The return label says Nashville Songwriters Association. I have no idea why I would get something from them. I contemplated sending the money in for a yearly membership since it's an international organization but never got the courage.

I slide my finger under the seal and pull out a stack of documents. One of them welcoming me to the organization. The second one is a congratulations letter for being accepted into a two-week songwriters' workshop.

I have to pick my jaw up off the bed. I never applied for this. I knew about it but I was too scared to put myself out there. Hell, I've only been comfortable playing music the last few months with Mason.

Fucking Mason.

And I can guarantee Mason had everything to do with this.

I skim through the rest of the information. Acceptance forms, housing requests, brochures.

I climb out of bed and stomp down the stairs in search of Noah.

I look everywhere for him. Inside, outside, the damn basement figuring he is working out since he does it all the time. Not that I am complaining.

I can't find him until I finally hear the sound of a drill coming from the sun porch he never uses.

When I walk through the door, my jaw drops again for a second time this morning. Noah must have gone to my house this morning because he is in the process of hanging records and guitars on the wall that came from my music room. The windows that used to be hazy and dirty are now sparkling clean letting in so much light.

"What are you doing?"

He jumps at my words. "Mayberry, I didn't realize you were awake."

"What is all this?"

He sets the drill down and walks over to me. "I wanted you to feel like this was home. So I thought the first thing to give you that feeling was to bring your music here."

I smile at him. This man knows the exact way to my heart. I almost go to kiss him until I remember the papers in my hand. "Thank you."

"Anything for you."

"Anything?" I ask, standing taller and taking a step toward him.

"Yeah babe."

"Anything as in you would pay for me to be a part of the Nashville Songwriters Association and submit an application for one of their workshops," I say with accusation in my voice.

He grabs the back of his neck. "Ughh—"

"It was you!"

He holds his hands up in front of me. "Listen, I only did it because Mason told me about it. He said he talked to you and you turned him down. He said this was the best thing for you whether you realized it or not."

"What about what I think is the best thing for me!" I yell as I take a step closer to him.

"Anna, come on. I just thought it would be good for you. I'm sorry if you didn't get in or whatever it is that's upsetting you."

I scoff at that. "Upsetting me? You think I am upset that I didn't get in? No, I didn't want to enter this because it's too much pressure, too much intensity. I could be thrown into a group of the greatest songwriters in the world and laughed at. Don't you think that is humiliating?"

He steps toward me, arms outstretched trying to comfort me. But I step back. "I'm sorry. It was wrong of me to do that. I thought you were good enough. Mason thought you were good enough. We thought if we paid for your membership and applied for the workshop, you would be happy. We thought you would get in. I'm sorry."

I scrunch my brow at him. "Wait, you're sorry because you thought I didn't get in. Is that it?"

"Yeah babe. I really thought you would get in."

I scream and growl at him like I am having a temper tantrum. "Well I'm not pissed that I didn't get in. I'm pissed because you did this behind my back."

He grips the back of his neck as he takes a deep breath. "Okay, I'm sorry. I shouldn't have done it."

"No, you shouldn't have!"

"But I do think you are good enough for it. Maybe the next one you should apply for."

I hold back a laugh at that. "I don't need to."

"Yes, you do."

"No, I don't because I got into this one, you dumbass. That's why I'm so pissed. What if I fuck this all up? What if I am the worst one there?"

"Wait, you got in?"

"Ughh," I growl. "Yes."

This time I don't stop him as he lunges for me. "I knew you would, babe. I knew you would. You are incredibly talented and deserve every accolade you get."

I let him hold me, my arms pinned to my sides as he praises me. "I'm still mad at you. You should have told me."

"Would you have let me send it in if you knew?"

Okay he has a point. "No."

He smirks at me. "Well then I'm glad I did."

"What if I fuck this all up?"

"You won't, Mayberry. You won't."

I finally relax in his embrace. Because I believe him. I believe that he believes in me.

He presses a kiss to my forehead before moving down to my lips.

"I'm still mad at you," I say as I try to pull away.

He bites on to my lip and sucks it hard. "Good. Because I would love to have make-up sex."

Fuck it. I drop the papers in my hand and let him show me just what make-up sex looks like.

11

NOAH

"You need to relax," Anna says to me.

"I'm trying."

She snorts. "No you aren't. The test is in two days. You spend every waking minute trying to memorize everything you already know."

"I can't fail this again."

"You won't."

I groan as I drop my pen from the notes I've written over and over. "I just want it to be over."

Anna moves behind me and starts rubbing my shoulders. "You are so tense. You need to step away from this for the rest of the day. Relax. Meditate. Do something."

"I don't meditate."

"Maybe you should," she says as she hits a knot in my shoulder. I moan at the relief. "Mmm. I know just the thing."

"I don't think I want to know."

She leans over me, her red curls falling over my shoulder before she presses a kiss to my cheek. "We're doing hot yoga."

"No."

"Oh come on. It will feel good and relax your mind."

I pull her hands off my shoulders. "I don't do that shit."

She walks in front of me sitting on the table on top of my notes, propping a hand on her hip. "You do realize that is one of my jobs."

"And you're great at it," I admit.

She leans in close so our lips almost brush. "You'll get to see my ass bending over in leggings, just like I know you want to."

The thought of that round, luscious ass bent over in my face is enough to make my dick stir.

She smirks at me. "See, I knew you would want to if it was for that reason."

"I haven't agreed to it yet."

"Maybe not out loud. But your face sure did."

I grip her hips and pull her off the table and onto my lap. She yelps as I do it. "I'll go if you let me pick out your outfit."

"Fine." She sticks out her hand and we shake on the deal.

"I CAN'T BELIEVE you made me wear this," she groans as we get out of the car in front of the hot yoga studio.

"You own it."

"Well I bought it on a whim. I never actually wore it."

"Good, then I feel lucky."

She punches me in the arm before we walk into the studio. I hold the door for her so I can see that fine ass move in those tight as sin white leggings. She has a matching white sports bra on. I wouldn't let her wear a shirt which she protested as she tried to cover her stomach. But it was when I told her she looked sexy and good enough to eat that she eventually moved her arms and uncovered her stomach and agreed to keep the outfit on.

We put our things into a cubby and she grabs me a yoga mat from the pile in the corner. She opens the door to the studio and within seconds, I am sweating. "How hot is it in here?"

She sets her yoga mat down and then takes mine and lays it next to hers. "One hundred and three degrees."

"You expect me to survive in this?"

She pinches my cheek. "Toughen up buttercup. Besides you can always take your shirt off."

I know she said it because she wants to look at my abs. So I pull it over my head and give her a wink. She shakes her head and turns to her mat, stretching her legs out before the class starts.

That's when I look around and see that the entire class is women and every single one of them has their eyes on me.

The teacher starts the class and it whips my ass. I never realized how difficult yoga could be. I give Anna more credit than I've ever given her for this. I don't know if it's the heat or the fact I need to work on my flexibility but I feel like I have never exercised a day in my life.

I look over at Anna as she giggles at me. I keep on though as I move from position to position. I have no idea what the names are that the instructor is saying half the time. But my favorite is when we are bent over at the waist. I cheat and look up to see Anna's perfect peach of an ass in my face. My dick twitches and I have to fight it to calm down because everyone will see it in the basketball shorts I'm wearing.

By the time class is over I feel like I ran a damn marathon. We ended in lotus pose and I fall back and collapse onto the mat. My body is drenched in sweat and I might be hallucinating. I close my eyes and take a deep breath.

"You gonna make it?"

I open one eye to see Anna hovering over me. Little does she know that position has her tits on glorious display as they fight their way to stay escape her bra. "It's questionable."

She laughs as she grabs my hands. "Do you feel more relaxed?"

"I'm not sure I can feel anything right now."

"Well then I guess it worked."

She attempts to pull me up and I pull her on top of me instead. "I can't move."

"You seemed to have enough strength to pull me on to you." Her eyes light up.

"Gravity."

"You are such a liar."

I pull her mouth to mine until someone clears a throat behind us.

Anna jumps off me and apologizes to the instructor profusely. I laugh. She was already flushed from the heat of this room but now she is as red as a tomato.

I push up off the floor and grab my mat and Anna's and head to the door with her on my heels.

"Oh my god, that was so embarrassing."

I roll her mat up and hand it to her before spraying mine with disinfectant and putting it back in the pile. We grab our things and head out the door as I grab her hand. When we get to my SUV I pull her into a kiss.

"Thank you."

She looks at me quizzically, her fingers tapping along my still bare chest. "Did you like it?"

"Hell no." I laugh. "But I did it. And I do feel better."

Her face breaks into a huge grin. "You are gonna do so well on that exam. Don't worry about it anymore."

I kiss her forehead. "I won't." And I mean it. I have been stressed about this for months but her encouragement and support has me feeling so much different than I was feeling weeks ago. "Now let's get home so we can both shower."

12

ANNA

I PLAY A FEW CHORDS ON THE PIANO REPEATEDLY trying to find the right melody for the song in my notebook. But nothing seems to sound right. I smash my forehead to the keys.

I have only a few days left to submit my paperwork for the songwriter's workshop and I still don't know what to do. I know I want to go. I know it will be the best thing for me. The exposure I need to have a chance at making it as a songwriter.

But with the way my writing has been over the last week I don't feel worthy of the workshop. I can't find my rhythm.

Literally.

And my harmonies sound more like squealing tires.

I'm stressed over moving out of my house, and I still haven't talked to my landlord. All my calls go to voicemail and he hasn't called me back. I even reached out to the realtor and she can't get a hold of him either. She made promises to me that they would inform me of any showings and offers but she didn't know what legal documents my landlord put together to end my lease.

I was able to talk to my neighbor and he didn't know much either. But George had called him and informed him of the building going up for sale. But he was not given any notices about moving out either.

But the thing I am most stressed about is my relationship with Noah. I shouldn't be stressed. He is amazing. He listens, he comforts me, he makes me want to pursue all my dreams. And of course, the way his body fits with mine is better than anything I have ever experienced. But I still worry something will go wrong. I worry we are moving too fast. Most of all I worry that he isn't ready for this. I know he loves me but I still think he is waiting for his ex-wife to return.

I take a deep breath and release it through my closed lips, the vibrations giving me no creative juices. I put my right hand on the keys and play a few notes with my head still resting in the middle of the keyboard.

"Is that a new song writing technique?" Mason asks with a laugh as I hear him close the door behind him.

I'm sitting in one of the recording rooms in the dark, except for the three candles lit on the piano. I'm trying to come up with three new songs to bring to the writing workshop just in case I do accidentally send them in.

I know, I can't make my mind up on anything.

I groan as I answer Mason. "If it is, it isn't working," I mutter into my chest.

I feel Mason sit next to me at the piano. His fingers glide effortlessly over the keys, a gentle, soothing melody brought to life.

I slowly lift my head as he plays the familiar melody. I hum along to a song we wrote together months ago until I finally find the words in my throat. He joins me during the chorus, our words battling back and forth in a song about love and hate.

When the song comes to an end he wraps an arm around my shoulder. "Trouble in paradise? My brother being a dick?"

"I don't think he knows how to be," I answer truthfully.

Mason snorts. "Maybe not to you."

I stretch my fingers out in front of me, flexing the muscles before placing them on the black and white keys. "I just can't write and I don't know what to do about Nashville and I'm worried I'm moving too fast with Noah."

I don't mean to say that last part but it comes out anyway.

"Trust me, you aren't moving too fast with Noah."

I look over at Mason. "You don't think it's too early to move in with him?"

"One thing I know about Noah is that he never does anything irrational. Never makes decisions he hasn't thought long and hard about. If he wants you to move in with him, he means it one hundred percent."

"Are you sure?" I ask with hesitation.

Mason wraps an arm around my shoulder. "He loves you, Anna May. I don't think I have seen him love anyone as fiercely as he loves you." He pauses and I look over at him. He laughs silently like he is remembering something. "You know when you came to our parents' house at Thanksgiving, I told him to make his move or else I would make you mine. The fact that he didn't and I took you on that date just for him to realize what he wanted proves to me that his decision didn't come lightly. He didn't think he deserved you. Even though he wanted you. So I know that whatever you guys are doing together is the right thing."

I nod my head. Hearing the words from Mason help. I needed that extra bit of belief from him that what me and Noah are doing is the right move.

"Now that we can move on from talking about your

annoyingly perfect relationship with my old as fuck brother, what is this 'I don't know what to do about Nashville'? You are going. That's all there is to it."

I laugh at the sternness in Mason's voice.

"Anna, you have been given the opportunity of a life-time. To be in front of musicians, producers, and song-writers who are living the dream you have. The same dream they once had. If you don't go, you'll never make it. If you do go, you might not make it either but at least you went and found out. But I can guarantee that once those people listen to the words you put on paper, hear the sound of your voice, there is no doubting that you will make it."

I slouch forward and throw my head back. "You make it sound so easy, Mason. But I can't even write a song right now."

"So who cares? Isn't that the whole point of this thing?"

I shake my head and play a few keys. "I need to bring three incomplete songs."

Mason grabs my shoulders and pulls me to face him. "Exactly, Anna May. Incomplete. You sitting here trying to finish a song doesn't make it incomplete. Bring it how it is. Raw. Unbridled. Itching to become a hit."

I bite my lip as I meet his eyes. "It's so hard."

"Stop being a perfectionist."

I punch him in the shoulder. "I can't just stop."

He rubs his shoulder and laughs at me. "How about this? We find a way to relax your mind. Then we come back here and figure out the songs you want to take with you. We can even work on them. And then we put the damn papers in the mail because you are going. I'll make Noah drag you there."

He has a point. But like usual, my fear is getting the best of me. I have over a hundred unfinished songs I can bring. But my fear of rejection is causing the anxiety to roll in like

99

a wave. Relaxing is probably the best thing I can do for myself. If I could just figure out a way to relax.

"Yoga?" I ask him. Since it's the only thing I have found that's brought me inner peace in seven years.

He gets up off the bench, pulling me with him. "No fucking way. I heard what you had Noah do. I am not doing that."

"It worked."

He opens the door to the recording room and walks to the front door of the building. "We'll be back in a few hours, Lyn. I think the guys are stopping by to jam. But other than that, there isn't a recording blocked out until seven. I'll be back by then."

I wave to Lyndsey the receptionist, as I follow Mason out of the studio.

"OH MY GOD. You are going to pay for that, mister!" I shout at Mason as he cuts me off on the go-kart track causing me to fly into a stack of hay bales.

I never thought when he told me I needed to relax that he would take me racing. I figured a walk or a drink. But this? I haven't laughed this hard in a long time. It was everything I needed to get out of my head.

I reverse the go-kart and get it out of the haystack and slam on the gas to catch up to Mason. He is pretty far ahead of me but I cannot let him win. Not after he cheated to get past me. This is our fifth and final race. When we started, he said best out of three but when I beat him in all three of those races, he said we were doing five. I brought it up to him that he can't beat me in a best of five because I already bested him but I think the poor guy just wants to win one race.

I shift the gear in my go-kart and speed up to the fastest speed it will go. I turn the corners hard, making up time as I close in on Mason. He must hear me behind him because he speeds his car up too. Too bad he doesn't know the trick I know on the gearshift to make these things go faster than intended. I am so grateful I worked at a go-kart park when I was in high school.

He goes to take the corner ahead of him and he drives too wide. I take my chance and slam harder on the gas, taking the turn so tight I think I might flip but it gives me the power I need to zoom past him and fly toward the finish line.

I park the kart, unbuckle, and climb out, jumping up and down as I watch a not very happy Mason pull up next to me.

"You cheat!"

I laugh at him. "You can't cheat at go-karts. It's all skill. You are just pissed you got schooled in racing by a girl."

He shakes his head at me as he pulls his helmet off. "Please, we aren't twelve."

"Then why are you so upset?" I make puppy dog eyes and speak in a little kid voice. "You gonna cry now?"

"Fuck off." He laughs as we head to the gate. "At least you are relaxed now."

"I am."

"Damn, Mason. You got completely shut out by a girl."

Butterflies erupt in my stomach when I hear Noah's voice. I turn around and those butterflies make their way to my center, heat flooding me. I don't think I will ever tire of the day I see Noah in a police uniform. All his armor adds extra bulk to him but I think it makes him look sexier, more intense.

For the last few weeks we have been living together, I made it a point to try and be home before he gets home from work so I can see him in uniform. But this week his boss switched him back to morning shifts so he can be rested for his detective exam next week. Now our schedules overlap and it's been four days since I've seen him in his sexy as sin uniform.

I bite my lip as I think about taking that uniform off him piece by piece when Mason starts talking. "Fuck off, Noah. I knew I shouldn't have texted you."

I look between the two brothers. "You texted him?"

"Well I didn't think you would beat me since I come here a lot. Thought you might need to release the rest of your pent-up energy on him when I beat you."

I laugh as Noah wraps his arm around my shoulder. "Oh I have pent-up energy alright, but it has nothing to do with that race." I slap my hand over my mouth. I cannot believe I said that in public. If it was me and Noah, I wouldn't have cared. But I never talk that way in front of others.

Noah growls at that comment as his hand trails down my back and grabs my ass. He leans in and whispers in my ear, "I'll take care of that, baby. Don't you worry."

He looks up at Mason. "So how does it feel to get beaten by a girl again?"

Mason cracks his knuckles. "I really should not have texted you."

"I'm glad you did," Noah says. "Because now I can celebrate with my girl."

"You've been beat by a girl before I take it." I say to Mason.

"No one ever beats me. Ever."

Noah cuts in. "Except Rosie. She schooled you every time around that course."

"The only one. Now I got this one too." He laughs. And

I am happy the memory of his sister brings a smile to his face.

"If it makes you feel better, Mase. I did work at a go-kart track in high school."

Noah bursts out laughing. "Picked the wrong thing to help her relax, Mason."

Mason shakes his head. "Whatever. I'm glad that helped Anna. Now go do things I don't want to know about with my brother. We can pick up on those songs tomorrow."

"Thank you, Mason. I didn't know I needed that."

"Anytime," he says with a wave as he walks out to the parking lot.

Noah grabs my hand, pulling me into him. "Ready to go home?"

I nod because I want nothing more than to strip that uniform off him.

13

NOAH

I wipe the sweat from my brow as I hit mile eight of my run. I needed to get the tension out of my system.

Today is the day I find out the results of the detective exam. My sergeant says there is no way I didn't pass. In fact, he already has a position waiting for me as Detective Taylor.

I never thought this day would come. That I would finally reach this goal I didn't think I would achieve after we lost Rosie. But here it is. I might have failed this test twice already but this one feels different. Everything feels different. I don't know if it's because of Anna or if I have finally put my past behind me. Of course Anna has a lot to do with that.

I round the corner of the block and slow down to a brisk walk to cool down. I check my watch. I only have an hour before I have to head to the police station and find out. I run inside and take a quick shower, the cold water cooling me down but doing nothing for my nerves.

I pull the nicest suit I have out of my closet. I slowly button up each button on my shirt before tying the black tie around my neck. I slip the navy-blue suit jacket on and step into my bathroom. I comb my hair back and take a deep breath.

I got this.

I pat Brutus on the head as I walk out the door and slide into my cop car. If I pass I won't be driving this vehicle anymore. It almost feels bittersweet.

As I pull into the station I have a handful of texts from my partner.

Niko: I hope you failed. I don't want a new partner.

Niko: Everyone around here sucks.

Niko: I can't believe you are leaving me.

Niko: I hate you.

Niko: All jokes aside. You got this, man. Congratulations.

I smile as I read his texts. I will miss that kid. Of course I will still see him around and will work with him on cases as needed. But I'll miss the relationship we've built the last few years together as partners. Of course, If I do get this I'll also have a new partner and a new relationship to build. But I am glad I have the department at my back. I originally was going to be a county detective as it is hard to get a spot with APD but someone retired last month and they haven't filled the position. My sergeant tells me the department wanted it to be me but I think he is lying.

Me: You'll probably get stuck with a rookie. Sucks to be you.

I laugh as I walk into the station. He was a rookie when we became partners after my old partner retired and I gave him a ton of shit. It's only fair he gets to do the same now.

I head into the small conference room I was told to go to. I am the first one here and I tap my foot anxiously on the ground as I wait for my sergeant or the chief of police to walk in. My phone buzzes in my pocket. It's a text and a picture from Anna.

Anna: Can't wait to celebrate with you tonight. I love you.

The picture is her holding a pair of handcuffs.

Fuck me.

My dick stirs in my pants just as the door opens to the room and the chief of police walks in. I force my dick down as I stand and shake his hand.

"Noah Taylor, I never thought I would see the day that you finally made the decision to become a detective."

I shake his hand and we both sit down as my sergeant walks into the room followed by Sergeant Willows, head of the detectives. "It was a long time coming, sir."

"And he deserves it more than anyone. One of the best cops on the squad." Sergeant Ames sits down with a folder in his hand and a box. "Want to do this or shall I?"

The police chief gestures for Ames to continue. "Officer Taylor, it is with great honor I present to you your new badge." My breath catches in my throat as he opens the box and hands me the gold emblemed badge. "Congratulations. We are proud of you, Detective Taylor."

I blink back tears, not letting them fall as I grip the badge in my hand. I make a silent prayer to Rosie, letting her know this is all for her.

The police chief clears his throat. "Noah, you had some of the best scores I have ever seen anyone have on this exam. I know you will make a huge difference with the department and with the city of Asheville. It's with great honor I offer you a position here with us at Asheville PD as a detective."

I grip his hand in a firm handshake thanking him for everything, the opportunity, his trust in me, the job. He goes over the expectations and everything I need to know, what the next few weeks will look like as I adapt into my new role.

BY THE TIME I get home, I only have a few hours before the party starts. Niko and my brothers planned a celebratory party for me because they all said they knew I would pass. And I am excited to celebrate with them. The huge weight that I've had on my chest for years is finally gone. I did all of this so I can protect others from what happened to Rosie. And I know she is looking down on me, happy that I made detective.

I set my keys and phone on the kitchen counter before letting Brutus outside. I shout out Anna's name but don't get a response. Her car was in her driveway so I know she is around. Maybe she is at her old place, packing up a few more things to move over.

I head next door and walk in, shouting her name again so I don't scare her but she doesn't respond.

"Excuse me, sir, but I believe you just broke into this place. I can arrest you for that."

My face breaks into a smile as I turn around and find her in the hallway. My dick hard as a rock with one look at her.

She has on the damn cop costume she wore last year for Halloween. The dark blue of it making her green eyes pop. But that is not what I am focused on. My eyes move to her voluptuous tits that are barely contained in the dress. And I know her ass looks even better in it. She even has the knee-high boots on and the garter belt. I grin at her as I assess her. Last time I couldn't touch but this time she is all mine.

I take a step toward her but she holds her hand up in front of me. "Stop right there. You are under arrest."

I don't stop. I slowly walk toward her as she swings the handcuffs in her hand.

"I told you to stop. If you don't stop resisting, I will use force."

I can see her breaths picking up the closer I get to her and I know how turned on she already is. "I'm sorry, officer, but you don't have any jurisdiction here."

"Is that so?" she asks me, her voice husky. She props her hand on her hip and I bite my lip at the sight of her.

I reach her and grip the wrist the handcuffs are in. "This is a crime scene and only detectives can be on the scene."

She lets go of the handcuffs, letting them fall to the ground and presses her hands into my chest, gliding them up to my neck. She stands on her tiptoes and brushes a quick kiss across my lips. "I'm so proud of you."

My hands go directly to her luscious ass but she pulls them away. "Well Detective, the crime scene is secure. I'll just be on my way."

She turns around and bends down, directly at the waist to pick up the handcuffs. It gives me a direct view of her pussy. My little wildflower is not wearing any underwear.

My hands are on her ass in seconds, pulling her against my hips so she can feel how hard my cock is. I dip one hand underneath the skirt, slicking my fingers through her center to find her already dripping for me.

She stands up and I wrap my arm around her front. "You are in violation of the law, officer. I am going to need to arrest you."

I grab the cuffs out of her hand and lift her up. She squeals in my arms and rubs her ass against my dick. I walk her into the bedroom and throw her on the bed. I take my suit jacket off, followed by my tie.

She flips over on the bed and stares at me as she spreads her legs.

I grab the handcuffs and crawl over her, gripping her arms, dragging them above her head. "You have been a very bad cop. What shall your punishment be?"

She moans as I lick up her neck and bite on her earlobe. She struggles against me as I pull her arms up to her headboard, clasping the cuffs around the top and to each wrist.

"Those handcuffs were supposed to be for you," she rasps.

"Mmm. I like them better on you." I slowly move my hands down her body, twisting her nipples through the costume. My hands find the way to her thighs and I spread them even further apart. She is glistening and I cannot wait to taste her.

I lower my head as I lick up her thigh, her whimpers making my dick raging hard. But I need to taste her first. My tongue drags through her center before I suck on her clit.

"Fuck, Noah."

I chuckle into her heat, knowing the vibrations will only make her more turned on. I lick and suck and bite on her until she is almost to the edge before I pull back. I unbutton the buttons on her costume slowly, teasing her with my hands as I move up her body. Once the costume is open, I peel it to each side of her, revealing her sexy, plush body.

My mouth goes for her nipples, sucking and nibbling on them as she moans my name. Her hips buck into mine and I know she is close again, looking for friction to get her off.

I slide my way back down her body, my fingers sliding between her folds, teasing her entrance before pulling away again.

"Dammit, Noah. I am so close. Just—just—"

I blow cool air on her clit as my finger teases her again

and she groans so loud I feel the vibrations in my dick. I give her one last lick before pulling off the bed.

She is flushed all over and from the look in her eyes she likes this game as much as I do even if she doesn't want to admit it.

"I wish I could take a picture of you like this," I tell her, my fingers wet with her juices coming to my mouth. "You taste just as good as you look."

"Maybe you should just finish what you started."

I smirk at her as she struggles on the bed. I slowly unbutton my shirt, pulling it off before I take off my pants and briefs. My dick is in my hand and I stroke it as I watch her squirm.

She bites her lip and I know how badly she wants me. I crawl back onto the bed, slicking my fingers through her heat once more. I use her wetness to coat my dick as I stroke it in front of her. Precum drips from the tip and I grow harder with every stroke.

"Noah, please." Anna's begging makes me even harder.

"Do you want my dick?"

Her legs spread wider on the bed, letting me see her pussy that is begging for me. "Fuck yes. Just put it in me, please."

I laugh wholeheartedly at that. My fiery, redheaded vixen.

I move up the bed and tease her entrance with my cock. Her eyes roll back in her head at the briefest touch of pressure. I lean over her, holding my palm to her cheek. "I love you."

Those words alone make her face soften just as I claim her mouth with mine. She tries to grind her pussy into me but I am just out of her reach. I let go of her mouth as my hands caress her body again, making her squirm from my touch. And just when she thinks I'm not going to give her what she wants, I slam into her hard.

She feels like fucking heaven. I pull out slowly, relishing the feel of her heat on my dick. I continue my slow movements in and out of her, bringing her pleasure to the edge but not letting her fall off it.

She says my name over and over again as her head twists back and forth on the pillow. Her fingers gripping the bedspread, her knuckles white.

Her eyes are closed as I get up on my knees and pull her into me, hard. Her eyes fly open as I do it and I press my thumb to her clit pushing her over the edge she so badly wanted and needed. I feel her pulse around me as I slam into her over and over. The angle intense, as I get deep into her.

She won't stop screaming my name and I know her orgasms keep coming, over and over again. "Too much, too much."

I lean forward again and whisper, "This is what you get for being a dirty cop."

I pull back and flip her over, her arms twisting above her head as I pull her to her knees. I grip her hips hard before slamming into her from behind. Sweat dripping down my forehead and onto her back. She looks over her shoulder at me. "I'll be dirty again and again for you, Noah."

Those words only increase my speed as she screams my name. This sex is intense and wild and reckless but I don't care because I feel closer to her than I ever have before.

I reach around her and squeeze her clit one more time just as I release my seed into her. I pump into her a few more times both of us riding the wave.

I collapse on to the bed next to her and she flips over to face me. I cup her cheek and bring her lips to mine. She swings her leg over my hip, grinding into me and I laugh. "Not enough for you, baby?"

"I can never get enough of you." Her eyes honest and sincere as her words.

I find the key to the handcuffs on her nightstand and unlock her wrists, rubbing them as I free them.

"Can we do that again?"

I laugh as I pull her on top of me. "I'll do that with you for the rest of my life."

14

ANNA

I can still feel Noah between my legs as we drive to Jimmy's for his party. Hell, I'll be able to feel him for days.

When I texted him that picture of the handcuffs I didn't think it would have led to sex as rough and reckless as that, but holy shit was that amazing. I could get very used to that.

Noah glances over at me as he parks, a knowing smirk on his face.

"What?"

"You're beautiful. You know that?"

I grip his hand. "I love that you tell me that every day."

He leans over and I think he is going to kiss me but he pulls on the clip in my hair. I reach to stop him. "Oh my god, Noah, I have sex hair. You didn't give me enough time to fix it."

"We were already late."

I cross my arms as I turn to him. "And whose fault is that?"

"Baby, I can't help it that your pussy tastes that good."

I roll my eyes at him and go to get out of the car, trying to wrestle my wild hair back up.

Noah chuckles at me as he gets out of the car and walks around and opens my door the rest of the way. His hand is back in my hair, pulling it down.

"Noah, stop."

"Baby, sex hair is better than the marks on your neck."

I push him away as I pull the visor down in the car and check my neck. Sure enough there are light bruises and bite marks on my neck. "Motherfucker. Do not tell me you did this on purpose!"

"You are the one who teased me with handcuffs and made my dick hard right before I had to talk to the chief of police."

I blush. It took me almost an hour to send that picture to him. I might be wild and free in the bedroom but sending him that picture made me feel a little bit dirty.

He leans into me, kissing up my neck and I try to push him away. "Don't you even think about leaving more."

He chuckles into my neck. "Mayberry, I'll leave more later but not where you think."

The words send chills down my spine as I think about all the places this dirty man could leave his mark on me.

He pulls me out of the car and we walk hand in hand into Jimmy's. It feels weird walking in here as a patron and not an employee. But if it wasn't for this place, I never would have laid eyes on Noah. He was my neighbor but I didn't know him. I started to learn about him when he came in here with his police squad.

The place is decorated with "Congratulations" signs and balloons. His partner comes up to him first and wraps an arm around him, pulling him into a tight hug.

"Congrats, brother. You did it."

"Thanks, Niko."

"And fuck you now that I have a new partner."

They both laugh at that before Niko pulls me into a hug

too. "Thanks for making this guy less mopey and annoying than he used to be."

I laugh as Noah curses at him. We make our way around the room greeting everyone I know and Noah introducing me to people I haven't met from the police department.

I grab a beer and sit at an empty table. I love watching Noah in his element. It's what made me start to have feelings for him in the first place. When he would come here with other officers. So carefree and happy, not the same man I would watch from my front porch.

I smile now as I watch him laugh with his friends. Making detective was a big deal for him. I know he wanted it more than anything but his fear kept getting the best of him. I hope I am the one that put that fear of his to rest. Because he has helped me overcome so many of my own fears. I never thought I would see the day where I felt happy and content. Sure I get nervous about my music and silly things like that. But at this moment in my life I feel at peace with everything. And I know it's because Noah helped me get there. I never thought my heart would love as fiercely as it is now and I don't ever want it to stop. I could see my forever with Noah.

The thought jolts me as Carson sits next to me. "You make him happy."

I look over at Carson and raise a brow.

"I've never seen him this happy before. Not even when he was married to Claire. She treated him like shit a lot. He never saw it but I did."

I don't know what to say to that because I never knew her and I am not one to judge on the stories I hear from other people. But what I do know is I will never walk away from him like she did. "I love him you know."

Carson nods and takes a sip of his whiskey. "She did too."

"Don't compare me to her," I say defensively.

"I'm not. I just don't want you to break his heart."

I look over at Noah and smile as I watch him throw his head back in laughter. Enjoying the view of his perfect body in his tight jeans and tight black shirt. "I don't want him to break mine."

Carson grabs my hand and squeezes. "He won't. I'm glad he has you. I mean that, Anna. You've let him be the man he used to be before life wore him down."

"I just want him to be the man he wants to be."

"And that's why you are perfect for him. I'm glad he has you." With that, Carson walks away leaving me slightly confused.

Mason takes his seat quickly and sets a shot glass of tequila in front of me. "Carson giving you a hard time?"

I blink at him and shake the thoughts from my head. "Ugh no... maybe... I'm not really sure."

"He just wants Noah to be happy." He pauses. "And you make him happy. Don't listen to Carson. He is going through some shit right now. He's turning into a dick."

"Is everything okay?" I ask, honestly concerned for Noah's brother.

Mason shrugs. "Him and Tiffany are having some trouble is all."

"That sucks. They looked so happy last time I saw them together."

"Yeah well I am sure this will be short lived like usual."

"This happens often?" I ask as I adjust myself on the chair.

"More or less. He is boring, let's not talk about him." Mason quickly changes the subject. "Did you submit your paperwork and pick out your songs?"

I smile at that. "Yeah I did. I'm all set. I can't believe I'm doing this!"

Mason raises his shot glass to me. "Anna May Cooper, you are the best damn songwriter on this planet. You are going to blow them away!"

I knock my shot glass against his and down the tequila.

"You still have a crush on my girlfriend?" Noah asks as he walks up to us, his hand landing on my shoulder.

Mason guffaws. "Dude, can't you let it go? That was so long ago. And she is clearly head over heels for you."

My cheeks flame. I still find it weird Mason had a weird crush on me back when I was in The Sparrows. Noah leans over me, tilting my head back and kissing me.

"I'm head over heels for her too."

"Ugh, you guys are gross. I'm outta here."

Noah fist bumps his brother as he leaves and Noah pulls me to my feet. "Did you want to go?"

"We just got here, babe. I'm fine. You celebrate."

He presses his forehead against mine. "I love you."

I grip his shirt in my hands. "I love you too."

15

ANNA

I WALK INTO MY HOUSE AND HEAD STRAIGHT FOR MY music room that is slowly being moved over to Noah's house, our house. I open my safe and pull out the envelopes labeled rent, bills, and Nashville. As I stare at the envelope marked Nashville I wonder if I even want this anymore. I can write songs here, record them at Mason's studio. But it won't be the same exposure. Nashville is still my ticket to get what I want in life. To be a songwriter. To put hits on the radio.

I am torn between staying here and my dreams of Nashville. I like my life here. I've fallen in love when I never thought I would be able to. I feel like I have a family here.

But could I do it? Walk away from the life I have built here? A life I never thought I could have. Could I walk away from Noah?

The truth is I don't think I can. And now I am torn between following my heart and following my dream.

At least I have the songwriting camp coming up next month. But what if I find out I love the city and I want to stay there? Or what if they want me to stay?

I put the money away and head to my room, stripping out of my clothes and jumping in the shower.

If Noah wakes up, he will probably wonder where I am. But I can't see him right now. I can't let him see me torn up like this. I'm sure he has the same thoughts too. I see it in his eyes sometimes. I can tell he means it when he says he loves me but the hesitation that is buried deep in him still shows through. Is he worried I will leave him too?

I WAKE up in the most uncomfortable position on the floor of my music room. Sheet music is spread around me and my guitar is somehow half under my back. I groan as I get up feeling like I pulled a muscle.

The smell of coffee infiltrates my nose. I know I didn't set the auto start on the machine last night. After I got out of the shower I was still so torn about sleeping here or going to Noah's that I decided to work on music. Obviously that didn't work too well for me.

I push all the sheet music into a pile and put my guitar back in its case before making my way to the kitchen. Noah is sitting at the table sipping a cup of coffee.

We are supposed to finish moving the rest of my stuff over to his house today. One of the reasons my head was a mess last night.

And after that there is a family dinner at his parents' house. Another reason I really need to get my head clear.

He rises from the table when he sees me walk in. His arms are around me and I instantly feel better. That should be answer enough for me.

"Hey." He kisses my forehead. "I was worried when I woke up and you weren't next to me. But I came over here and found you passed out in your music room. Figured you must have had some inspiration last night and fell asleep. I didn't want to wake you."

I walk over to the coffee pot and pour myself a cup. "You should have. I woke up in the worst position." I grab my back and try to stretch it out.

Noah's hands are on me instantly. "Want me to give you a massage?"

I scoff at him. "No, I should try yoga. If you give me a massage you will probably have my clothes off within five minutes and then none of my shit will get moved."

He laughs. "You're probably right. You still want to move everything today? If your back hurts I don't want you to injure yourself more."

I wave him off. "I'll be fine. Besides the realtor told me there would be showings this week and I would prefer to be gone before all that happens."

"Okay, babe. Well why don't you start your yoga and I'll pack up the kitchen."

"Okay."

An hour later I feel refreshed and relaxed. The yoga helped clear my mind and the stress from my body. Even now as I watch Noah pack my things with care I know I am making the right decision. I love him. I love him more than I've ever loved anyone. There will come a time when I have to figure out what's more important, my dreams or my heart, but right now I am sticking with my heart. Besides, maybe I will be able to have both one day.

"I can't wait for your house to finally look like a home," I tease him.

"Our house, Mayberry."

I smile at him, a warmth flooding my body at his words. "Our house."

"It could definitely use more plants. The one you

brought over already made me feel like my house was a home."

"And just think you can get rid of that nasty old leather sofa in your living room and we can use mine."

He stops what he is doing and stares at me. "My what? That sofa is not going anywhere."

I roll my eyes at him. "It's going to the curb. That thing is hideous. And uncomfortable. Don't even try to fight me on that."

"It's not hideous."

I shake my head as I reach for Noah. "The thing looks like it's twenty years old."

"It's well loved."

"It's gone."

He scowls at me. "If I didn't love you, I might call this whole thing off."

"Good thing you do love me." I wink at him as I head to my room to pack.

We spend the afternoon moving furniture and boxes across our driveways. I managed to win on the couch debate when Asher came over to help move heavy furniture. But Noah being the stubborn man he is, didn't get rid of his awful couch. Instead he moved it into the basement because he decided he would need a man cave at some point.

I manage to set up a lot of my décor in his living room, bringing the room to life. I adjust the succulents on the mantle when he comes into the room wrapping his arms around me.

"Thank you."

I look over my shoulder at him. "For what?"

He rests his chin on my shoulder. "For making this house a home."

"It's just a few decorations but it makes a difference."

"No. You. You make this house a home."

I turn in his arms and see the sincerity in his eyes. And love, so much love for me. I kiss him. I never thought I would find a love like the one he gives me.

"Ahem." Asher clears his throat. "I know that you are old creepy horn dogs but can you not do that in front of me."

"Says the guy who tried to kiss me at my job." I laugh.

Asher's face goes red. "I thought we said we wouldn't talk about that again."

"We must have forgotten," Noah says as he grabs my hand. "Come on, we should head to Mom and Dad's."

The three of us pile into Noah's SUV and head into the mountains. It's a peaceful drive, one that I should take more often. The thoughts I had early filter through my brain as I get lost in the views overlooking the smoky mountains.

I've grown accustomed to being here. Living in Asheville has helped me find a lot of the peace I was searching for over many years. Maybe this was supposed to be where I ended up. In the beautiful lush mountains surrounded by creeks and rivers. A place that I can easily call home. A place that feels like home.

The fears I have about leaving Noah and chasing my dreams seem almost resolute. Why can't I have both? Why can't I live my dream here?

Noah reaches over the console and grabs my thigh, giving it a tight squeeze. I look over at him and smile as my hand covers his. He faces the road but I can't take my eyes off him. This perfect man. A man I never thought could be mine. He is loyal and protective. He loves fiercely and hard. He is not one to take me for granted or throw me away when something better comes along. He could really be the forever I never was able to have.

He glances back at me and smiles. My heart beating hard in my chest as I take in the beauty of that smile. A smile I see so often now. A smile I used to force out of him. A smile that always deserves to be on that face.

We pull into his parents' driveway and I suddenly have the answers to all the questions I have kept locked inside of me. I don't need Nashville to chase my dreams because leaving Noah behind would be harder than anything I have ever done in my life. He is my forever.

Noah opens my car door and takes my hand as we walk to his childhood home. I remember the first time I came here. I was so worried about meeting his family, worried they wouldn't like me. But I've been here three times for family dinners since Thanksgiving and I have never felt more accepted in my life. This too feels like home.

Marlene answers the door and pulls me into a giant hug. "Anna May, I am so happy you are here. Come inside, let me take your coat. Would you like a glass of wine?"

"Gee Mom, I'm glad you're happy to see us too," Noah mutters.

"Oh hush, child. I am always happy to see you. But you know that so I don't have to say it. Make sure you hang your coats up. Asher, do not throw it on the chair!"

I laugh as I look over the arm Marlene has on my shoulder as she steers me into the kitchen. Sure enough Asher is picking his coat up off the chair and grabbing a hanger from Noah.

Dottie is in the kitchen talking up a storm with Carson, Tiffany, and Mason who are already here. As soon as she sees me, she slams her glass on the counter and runs over to me. "My favorite daughter-in-law. I am so happy to see you."

I freeze in her arms as she says it. That thought just a bit terrifying. It was hard enough to get me to agree to move in with Noah. The thought of marrying him a little too much, even if I think he is my forever.

"Dottie. She's just my girlfriend."

Dottie gives Noah a smirk and raises her brows at him suggestively. "Well, last time I saw her she wasn't anything, so I am happy to see she is now your girlfriend."

I pull away from Dottie and accept the glass of wine Marlene has poured for me.

"But since in a few short months she has become a girlfriend then I can only assume it won't be long until you tie her down."

My eyes bulge at that and not at the thought of Noah putting a ring on my finger. It's at the knowing look Noah shoots me as she says it and I know he is thinking about when he tied me down with handcuffs.

"Dottie, no one gets engaged that quickly anymore," Carson cuts in. I can't help but notice the look Tiffany shoots him as he says it. Maybe that's part of the troubles Mason was talking about.

"Well if Noah is as studly in the bedroom as he is in real life, then a couple romps in the sack and Anna might get knocked up and then a wedding," Dottie fires back as she pretends to hold an imaginary shotgun, firing it off.

My cheeks are bright red and I chug half my wine. Asher is cracking up next to me and Noah punches him in the arm.

"Alright, no one is getting engaged soon." Marlene ends the conversation. "How about we all go sit out on the balcony and celebrate my oldest son's promotion while the sun is still shining."

Everyone agrees and heads to the stunning deck that overlooks the western view of the mountains. If we sit out here long enough, we will be able to see the sky turn orange to pink to red as the sun sets.

Noah grabs my ass as we all file out the door and I swat

him away. "Do you think I should tell Dottie how I really like to tie you down?" he whispers in my ear.

I turn around and bring him to a halt before we make it outside with the others. "You better not say one word about that to anyone. Especially your brothers."

Noah leans down, pressing a kiss to my neck, trailing kisses up to my ear. "You are too easy to rile up, Mayberry."

I push him away. "You know when the right time to rile me up is and it's not here."

He grins at me and I flip him off as I turn around and take a seat outside with the rest of the family.

16

NOAH

I SEARCH THE INTERNET, PAGE AFTER PAGE OF POLICE reports, social media sites, and newspaper articles looking for anyone that matches the description the two victims gave us on the case I'm working on. My new partner and I have spent the last week collecting as much information as we can on the case. I'm trying not to struggle with it since it hits so close to home but I am making do.

Luckily my new partner is not a dick. He's been on the force for about eight years longer than me and has been a detective the last seven years. He is full of knowledge and can read people better than I have ever seen. He also consistently teaches me. He never gets pissed when I don't know something or the textbook procedure I know isn't quite on par with how they do things. I feel lucky I got assigned with such a great guy and he doesn't seem too pissed with me either. Unlike when Niko first became my partner and I was pissed with him half the time for his immature attitude.

"Yo rookie, it's after seven. Shut it down. We will get back on the case tomorrow." Detective Marcus Rodriguez tells me as he turns off his desk lamp.

I look over at my partner and nod. Both of us put in a

ton of effort, both willing to work late but he always makes sure we don't spend all night here. I also have to get used to the fact I'm considered a rookie again.

"Yeah okay," I answer and file the papers on my desk.

"A couple of the guys want to meet at Jimmy's for a drink, you want to come?"

I grab my gun out of my drawer and put it in my chest holster. "Sure. Could use a drink after looking at that screen all day."

We both head out of the office and walk across the street to Jimmy's. Normally I would want to go home but since it's a Wednesday night I know Anna is working and after the day I had I want nothing more than to see her.

A few of the other detectives are sitting at a round table in the back corner. They have two pitchers of beer and are cracking jokes. Marcus and I take a seat in the empty chairs. There are extra glasses on the table so I pour both of us one.

"Hey rookie, so glad you could join us. Surprised they don't have you on toilet duty tonight," Jon says, one of the younger detectives.

Stew hits him upside the head. "You were the only rookie we gave toilet duty to because you made a mess in the bathroom."

"He is just glad he isn't the rookie anymore. Although he is still a dick," Marcus jokes. "Glad he isn't my partner."

"Fuck off, Marcus. You got to deal with a rookie now."

Andrew, one of the older detectives, cuts in. "Noah is far from a rookie. He is one of the best cops APD had. He also passed his exam with higher numbers than all of you, so cut him some slack. I am sure within a year or two he will be better at his job than half of you combined."

Marcus slaps me on the shoulder. I'm stunned Sergeant Willows told him that.

"Damn, here comes that hot waitress. I would like to

take her for a spin. You think she wants to come to this gun show?" Jon asks as he flexes his not impressive biceps through his dress shirt.

"Unlikely. I'm sure someone that sexy doesn't go for assholes like you, Jon," his partner, Elliot, fires back.

"Oh come on. That ass is dying to be squeezed by these hands."

I look behind me to see who he is looking at and see Anna a few tables over dropping off drinks. I smirk as I turn back around. I cannot wait to see Anna tell him off.

Jon is still going on about her and I would normally be pissed about someone talking about her like that but I know he is an asshat and she would never agree to anything with him. And I am not concerned she would leave me.

Marcus is the only one that knows Anna is my girlfriend since we came here one day last week. He looks over at me and grins when he sees the look on my face.

"Have you all figured out what you want to eat?" Anna asks as she walks up right next to me.

Stew orders for all of us, getting a handful of appetizers to share.

"Anything else?"

"How about your number?" Jon asks as Andrew shakes his head.

I grin as I look up at her, her cheeks flushing. "Umm no sorry."

"Aww come on baby. You don't know what you're missing."

"Probably not a whole lot," she mutters quietly so only Marcus and I can hear her. "I don't date cops."

"Baby, I ain't a cop. I'm a detective."

I can't help but laugh at that. Anna finally looks at me, her eyes going wide, before she turns back to Jon. "Yeah still a cop. Not my type."

I drag my finger up the back of her leg and she shakes me off.

"I'll go put your order in and I'll bring you all another pitcher."

She walks away but not before shooting me a dirty look that only I can see.

"I think I got a chance with her," Jon jokes.

Marcus shakes his head laughing. "If you think you have a chance with her, you are clearly an idiot. You really think she would go out with you?"

"I saw the way she blushed especially right before she walked away. I got this in the bag. She is just playing hard to get."

I am the only one that knows that blush before she walked away was because my hand was dangerously close to her glorious pussy but I am not letting Jon know that.

Andrew turns to Jon. "What makes you think she is playing hard to get?"

He shrugs. "The ladies love me. They all want me."

Anna shows up at that moment with a new pitcher of beer. "I highly doubt all the ladies want you."

Jon looks at her, running his eyes up and down her body. He looks like a predator, not a cop. "Most do."

"Well I'm not most," Anna states matter-of-factly.

"That's for sure," I say.

She glares at me while Jon keeps speaking. "So why not cops?"

"I prefer a real man, not one who thinks he is better than the rest because he as some sort of power."

"Well baby, I'm all man."

She shakes her head and laughs. "Doubtful." She pauses and then a grin takes over her face. "You know I am surrounded by cops all day. You all are always in here. And

I always turn you down. Maybe I should give in, see what it's like. Have one of you prove me wrong."

Well damn, she is feisty tonight.

"See I knew you would give in."

She laughs and tucks the tray she was holding under her arm. "You have two things against you right now so I'm not going to choose you." She looks at me. "Hmm, I prefer dark and mysterious. You look too boy next door."

I bristle at that. I have no idea where she is going with this.

"Hmm." She taps her finger on her chin. "I don't really ever do this but I've had a shitty day and five minutes alone with one of you might make it better."

Stew starts cracking up. "Ma'am you can count me out. No offense."

"None taken," Anna says as she sets her tray down on an empty table behind her. "Now let's see who should it be?"

Andrew speaks up too. "I'm out," he says, raising his left hand. "I'm married."

Anna throws a hand on her hip and pouts. "Well now this is less fun. I'm stuck with two unattractive cops. I guess it will have to be one of you two."

That leaves Jon, Elliot, Marcus, and me. I don't know what she is playing at but I don't appreciate her nods against me. She is going to pay for that later.

Marcus clears his throat. "How about this? What's your name?"

"Anna."

"Well we always like to give the rookies a hard time. I think you should take the rookie out for whatever you have planned."

Her smile lights up her face and I have to tell my dick to calm down. "Oh kind of like hazing. I like it."

"Except we don't condone hazing," Andrew pipes in.

"Of course not." She looks around the table. "So who gets to spend five minutes with me?"

Jon starts mumbling something about this all being a load of horseshit. And Marcus points at me.

"Hmm. Well I guess you'll do." She grips me by the tie and I will my dick down as I stand up. I don't want to have a semi in front of my coworkers. "I hope you are good at giving foot rubs. I need one more than anything."

The guys at the table laugh as she says it and I think she is about to let me go but she pulls me to the back of the restaurant and through a back door.

"A foot rub, really?"

"I can't believe you let that guy talk to me like that," she shouts.

"Babe, he's a dick. We all have trouble getting him to shut up."

She crosses her arms and glares at me.

I go to reach for her but she holds her hands up in front of her. That's when I notice she is giving me a thorough look over, biting her lip as she takes me in.

"Fuck me," she says before jumping on me, her lips smashing into mine.

Her force knocks me back a few steps into the wall and when I regain my balance, I turn us around so I have her pressed to the wall, my dick rubbing against her center.

"Noah, you look so fucking hot in a suit."

I chuckle into her chest. "You tell me that every day I come home."

"Yeah but I can't get enough," she says as she grinds into me.

"Do you really hate the boy next door look?" I ask her.

She pulls away from me, grinning. "Oh Detective, you know me better than that." She leans into my ear. "I only like one and I think he might need to strip search me later."

My lips find their way back to hers before setting her back on the ground. "I think I could arrange that."

She adjusts her shirt and her pants before heading to the back door. "I need to get back to work."

I pull her back to me, running my hands through her curls. "I messed up your hair."

Her thumb goes to my mouth. "You have some lipstick on you. Of course maybe I should leave it."

I nibble on her thumb and then wipe my mouth. "Better?"

"Yeah." She blushes.

I press a kiss to her forehead. "I love you."

"I love you too."

We walk back into the restaurant. She heads for the kitchen to pick up an order and I go back to my table.

"Did you really give her a foot massage?" Jon asks.

I laugh as I shake my head.

"I'm sure he will be giving her more than a foot massage tonight," Marcus chimes in.

I rub my lips and smile.

"Did you kiss her?" Jon questions angrily.

"Just like I do every night," I say nonchalantly.

Marcus slaps his hand on the table cracking up. The rest of the guys must have figured it out too because they are all laughing as Jon stares at me in disbelief.

"Next time you want to talk about a girl like she is a piece of meat, Jon. I suggest you know who she is first," I order.

"Who she—?"

"That's my girlfriend. And I don't take too kindly to assholes talking about her like that."

Jon's face turns red and he quickly leaves the restaurant without saying a word.

"Classic, Marcus. Classic move." Elliot chuckles just as Anna comes back with our food.

She smiles at the guys then leans over and kisses me in front of them.

17

ANNA

I wipe down bottles at the bar. It's a Friday night at The Beer Garden and it's been crazy. Spring is in the air. It's early March but temperatures have been hitting the seventies during the day making all the college kids crazy. At least spring break is next week and most head to the beach.

I slump against the bar, sipping on some water, feeling like I've been at this for days when it's only been four hours.

"Don't die on me now," Liam says as he makes a pitcher of margaritas for a table of sorority girls.

"I'm getting too old for this."

"Girl, you ain't even thirty, you can do it."

I set my water cup down and stand up, ready to take the next order. "Yeah, well I only have a week left until then."

"And then just two days until you leave for Nashville!"

My heart skips a beat at that. I still can't believe I let Mason and Noah talk me into it. I was so close to throwing that letter in the trash can and I didn't. And now that I am leaving in a week I don't know if I have butterflies or raging fear in my stomach.

"Excuse me."

I turn around and find an older man waiting for a drink. My mind getting the best of me again. "Oh gosh, I am so sorry. What can I get you?"

He looks me up and down and it gives me chills. This guy is a total creeper. Probably only here to hit on the young, drunk girls.

"I'll take an old-fashioned."

"Bourbon preference?" I ask.

"Top shelf."

"Coming right up," I say as I walk away.

I grab our top shelf bourbon and a shaker. I mix muddled cherry juice with simple syrup and a dash of bitters. I pour it into a glass of ice followed by the bourbon and garnish it with a cherry and orange slice. I bring it back over to him and take his money. When I bring back the change, he continues to stare at me.

"Can I get you anything else?"

"Maybe a sweet taste of that pussy."

I stumble back a step. I look for Liam but he is at the other end of the bar. I'll have to take care of this on my own.

I reach for his drink. "I think you've had enough. You should leave."

He grabs my wrist hard. "The only way I'm leaving is with you coming with me."

I try to make eye contact with one of the bouncers but they don't notice.

Suddenly the man's face is pushed to the bar, his drink knocked over and spilling onto his face.

"The only person she is going home with is me."

I breathe a sigh of relief at Noah's voice. He picks the guy up off the bar, pulling his arms behind his back. He nods at a bouncer, who starts to walk over to us.

Noah whispers in the creep's ear, loud enough for me to hear. "And that pussy of hers is sweet as hell but you will never get to taste it."

My cheeks flame at those words because I know he wanted me to hear them. Noah talks to the bouncer asking him about getting an ID before the bouncer grabs the guy and tosses him out.

I walk around the bar as Noah makes his way to meet me. "You didn't have to do that."

He wraps me in a tight hug. "Yes I did."

"I had it under control."

He grips my chin and I get lost in his eyes. The blue of his eyes glow with a need to protect. "I know you did, baby."

I shake my head at him as I try to get out of his grip.

"Hey," he says, pulling me back into him. "I just worry about you here sometimes."

"I'm fine. I'm behind a bar. The girls that serve need to be careful. Not to mention there are at least five bouncers working at night."

He presses a kiss to my forehead. "There is just a case that has me on edge, babe."

I wrap my hands around his back. "The one I saw on the news."

He nods. "I just want to protect you."

Those words make those butterflies I always get around him flutter to life. "I know."

"I had a tip he might be here tonight."

A chill goes down my spine. "You think it was him?"

"Nah. Doesn't fit the description. But he was a creep and he deserved to be kicked out."

I smile at him as I pull away. "Well I need to get back to work. You gonna be my personal bodyguard tonight?"

I finally look at what he is wearing. Jeans, t-shirt, boots, baseball cap. Very civilian.

He grins at me. "At your service."

I reach up and press a kiss to his lips. "I love a bodyguard, Detective."

His eyes smolder at those words knowing just what they do to him.

He pulls me back to him, whispering in my ear. "You are asking for trouble later by saying those words."

My hand glides up his thigh and over the bulge in his pants. "I like trouble."

With that, I walk away but not before he smacks my ass. I laugh as I walk to waiting patrons wanting drinks.

The rest of the night goes by smoothly. Noah sits at the end of the bar drinking water with lime, surveying the crowd. I just survey him.

"HAPPY BIRTHDAY, YOU OLD ASS BITCH!" Seraphina shouts as we all cheer with a round of tequila shots.

I wanted a low-key birthday. Nothing crazy. And with the serial rapist that Noah is trying to find, we both thought it best we have it at home. Not that I am worried about being attacked when I have my hunky bodyguard around and I am surrounded by all my favorite people, but it is safer for all of us.

And I am happy that Noah is home too. Do I find it extremely sexy that he is a detective? Hell yeah, just ask my panties. But I worry about him. He got thrown into his job immediately. And it comes with a lot of danger. Not that his job as a police officer wasn't dangerous before but as a detective, he sees a lot more. But I know he loves his job and I am happy to see him so excited every day he comes home from work.

I take my shot of tequila and go to suck on a lime but Noah presses his lips to mine as my own personal chaser. I laugh as I pull away. He is so drunk right now and it's adorable. "You know you are supposed to chase the shot with a lime."

"Mmm," he says as his hand snakes up my thigh and under my skirt into my panties. "But you taste so much better."

I swat his hand away and walk over to a chair by the firepit. Mason is sitting next to me with a guitar in his hands. He starts playing a song I wrote and I look at him dubiously. He hums the first few notes and I shake my head.

Although I have gotten much more comfortable with writing and performing. I still only do it at the studio. Or in front of Noah. But there are about fifteen people here. That will be the biggest crowd I've played to since I was in The Sparrows.

"You know you are going to have to sing in front of people next week," Mason says as he stops playing.

"I know."

"Then it's good practice."

"But they will be strangers, it's easier."

He shakes his head at me and laughs. "I read over the entire agenda for this workshop. The first day is a welcome party. They won't be strangers when you actually play."

I bite my lip as my hand goes to my neck. It still feels like something is missing there without the rings. Seven years of grabbing onto those things created a bad habit I can't break.

I look over to Noah whose eyes are locked on mine. He smiles at me and there is something about that smile that brings a sense of peace to me.

I look back to Mason. "Okay."

He fumbles with a guitar pick in his mouth and it falls out. "You shitting me?"

I shake my head, letting my hair fall into my face. "No. But you better start playing before I change my mind."

He strums the first few chords and I hum along to the melody. I hide my face behind my hair, using it as a shield to protect me from the rejection I am scared I'll receive. But as I sing the first few lines of the song and make it to the chorus, my voice gets stronger. I realize everyone who was talking has stopped and when I look up all eyes are focused on me.

It brings me a feeling I haven't felt in years. Gratitude, excitement, acceptance. The feelings I used to feel on stage come to life and I let my voice carry itself across the flames of the fire. I pour my soul into the song, letting the lyrics warm my soul like the fire in front of me warms my body.

When I sing the last note, I open my eyes and everyone is staring at me with their mouths open.

"Holy shit," Mason says before Liam starts clapping and Seraphina squeals.

I don't even realize tears are falling down my face until Noah is in front of me, wiping them away. I look into his eyes and I smile the biggest smile I think has ever crossed my face.

"I did it," I say and Noah nods at me mirroring his grin with mine. Then the thought hits me square in the chest. "I'm going to Nashville. And I am going to do the same thing. And I am going to surprise the shit out of all those songwriters and musicians."

"Yeah you are, babe. Just like I said you would."

Mason grabs my shoulder breaking my gaze from Noah. "I—I don't even have words. Holy shit, Anna May. Fuck that was—that was something else."

Sera runs over to me, her squeals high pitched in my ear. "I haven't heard you sing like that ever, Anna. That was even more intense and raw than you ever sang before."

"It was captivating," Carson says as he walks over to me too.

Pretty soon everyone is surrounding me. Praising me for my song and my voice. I have never felt so elated in my life. I have never felt like the path I am on is the exact path I should be on.

The party continues long into the night. Mason and I play a handful of songs together along with some of his friends and Darnell.

By the time I stumble up to bed with Noah, I feel like I am on cloud nine. It could have been all the lemon martinis but I don't think I have ever felt this happy, this complete ever in my life.

As me and Noah crash into bed, I realize for the first time I am excited about my future.

I ROLL over and groan at the headache pounding away at my brain. I reach out for Noah and wrap myself around his back, one leg hooking over his hip.

He slides his hand up and down my thigh before mumbling. "Do you feel as shitty as I do?"

I giggle into his bare back, pressing kisses on his shoulder before making my way to his ear. "I think we drank enough for the next year."

"Maybe two," he mutters.

I hear him digging around in his nightstand drawer before he moans as he flips over to face me. He goes to kiss me but I pull away.

"I don't think you want to kiss this mouth right now. It

tastes like day old tequila, lemons, and cotton."

He chuckles as he pulls my mouth to his anyway. "Mine is worse," he says against my lips.

He isn't lying.

But I deepen the kiss anyway as I feel his dick stir against my thigh. I grind my hips into him but he pulls away.

"I never gave you your birthday present yesterday. Everyone got here too early."

He reaches behind me and grabs whatever he must have grabbed out of his drawer.

I freeze when I see a box that looks suspiciously like a ring box.

He must see my hesitation. "Don't worry, baby, it's not a ring. If I was going to propose, I would have made sure it happened." I smile at him as he hands the box to me. "I just thought you might want this. Need that feeling back."

I look at him curiously as I pop the box open to find a piece of raw stone on a silver chain.

"You still reach for that necklace around your neck. I thought I could replace it with something better. Especially since I know you are going to get nervous when you're in Nashville." He takes the necklace out of my hand and clasps it around my neck. "It's aquamarine. It's the stone of the ocean. I thought it would remind you of being at the cottage."

A tear crests my eye as I stare at the beautiful aqua blue stone. "I—I don't—thank you Noah. I love it."

"I love you."

"I love you too."

I wrap my arms around his neck, dropping the box behind him as he slides into me, showing our love over and over.

BY THE TIME we finally make it out of bed, it's after two in the afternoon. With Noah getting promoted to detective, he has the weekends off except for the one weekend a month where he is on-call.

We head into the kitchen and start making chicken and waffles. Breakfast and lunch in one. Brutus is on our toes waiting for us to drop something when the doorbell rings.

"I'll get it," I tell Noah since his hands are covered in egg and flour. I kiss him on the cheek and head to the door.

Brutus is already up on the window seat, barking at whoever is at the door. He jumps down and I hold him back as I put my hand on the door handle.

"Brutus, sit." He does a horrible job at listening. I open the door and step outside, closing the door and Brutus behind me.

Standing on the porch is a woman I have never seen before. She is petite but tall, strawberry-blond hair falling in perfect waves over her shoulders. She is dressed in what looks like designer clothes with oversized sunglasses covering her eyes.

"Can I help you?" I ask.

Even though I can't see her eyes, I can tell she is assessing me by the way her head drops slightly to take me in. That's when I remember I never put pants on when we came downstairs. I am just wearing one of Noah's Asheville Police Department shirts.

I watch her pink lips move as she speaks. "I'm sorry, maybe I have the wrong house. I was looking for Noah Taylor. But he doesn't have a dog."

My heart starts to beat rapidly in my chest as I put pieces of information together. I think of all the conversations Noah and I have had. It hits me hard in the chest. I'm almost afraid to ask. "No, this is Noah's house. I'm sorry but who are you?"

She takes off her sunglasses and stretches out a hand to me, her dark brown eyes seem as if they are looking right through me. "I'm Claire, his wife."

I wash my hands off, wondering who the hell Anna is talking to outside. Brutus is going crazy, barking up a storm.

I dry my hands and walk to the door, yelling at Brutus to lay down. I open the door and my heart drops to my stomach just as I hear Claire say, "His wife."

Anna backs into my chest and I wrap an arm around her before she can run. "I—I'm sorry, his what?" she stutters.

"His wife."

I hold on to Anna tightly, knowing her gut reaction is to hightail it out of here as fast as possible.

"You're not my wife anymore, Claire."

She smirks as she pulls a stack of papers out of her purse. "According to these, I still am."

I freeze when I see her pull divorce papers out of her purse. Divorce papers that I never got back when Carson found her and sent them out. Carson informed me that I could still file without her consent. And considering the circumstances of our divorce, of her disappearing with nothing but a note, the judge granted the divorce. Legally we are divorced. She just doesn't know it.

"No, you aren't." I feel Anna stiffen in my arm and I wrap my other around her, trying to calm her down.

"You scared that your new plaything is going to walk away?" Claire hisses at me.

I am scared of that but I won't let Claire know. I am also scared about the way my body is reacting to seeing her again. I force out words as my body fights the need to wrap Claire in my arms because I finally know after all these years she is okay. "You need to leave, Claire."

"I don't think I do. Because according to these papers I never signed, this house is mine too."

Fuck. How the hell am I supposed to get her away from here?

"Why don't we take this inside, Noah? Have your little lover put some clothes on."

"Fine," I acquiesce. I don't want to cause a scene with all the neighbors that are around.

I open the door behind me and pull Anna inside. Claire follows right on our footsteps.

"Wait here," I tell Claire before I drag Anna and a growling Brutus upstairs.

I shut the door to my bedroom and turn around to see Anna red with anger. "What the fuck was that, Noah?"

"I don't know. I don't even know how she found me."

Anna grips her hair as she stalks toward me. "You didn't even defend me. You just let her talk about me that way. A plaything? Really Noah?"

I rub my face in frustration. "I was in shock, okay? I didn't know what to say."

"You could have told her I was your fucking girlfriend. That I live here with you! That we are building a life together!"

145

That's when I realize the mistake I made. I didn't defend her. "Anna," I grovel. "I'm so sorry. I was shocked. You need to understand that. You aren't my plaything or whatever the hell she called you. You are my future. I fucking love you. You know that. Can't you see that?"

She goes to rip the necklace I gave her off but I lunge for her and stop the movement. "Please don't. I love you. I will fix this."

"She needs to leave," Anna commands.

"She will be gone so quickly." I kneel in front of her, gripping her waist, fighting tears that threaten to break free. "Just please don't leave, Anna. This is all a mistake."

Anna peels my hands off her and crosses her arms. "I thought you were divorced."

"I am," I say as I look up at her, still pleading on my knees. "She never returned the papers. She was sent multiple letters for multiple court dates, she never showed. The judge still filed the divorce."

Anna nods but turns around grabbing clothes and changing into them. "I need space. But she better not be here when I get back."

Before she can reach the door, I grab her wrist.

"Please don't, Noah. I can't—I can't do this." Tears fall on her cheeks and I pull her into a hug, holding on to her as tightly as I can because I am afraid that once I let go, she won't come back.

I pull her head back and smash my lips into hers. As much as she kisses me back, pours her love into that kiss, I can't help but feel like it's a goodbye.

"SO WHO IS SHE?"

I'm sitting at my kitchen table, staring at the remnants of the breakfast Anna and I never finished making as I grind my teeth.

"Oh come on. You don't want to tell me?"

I clench my fist as I finally look at her. "My girlfriend."

"It's awfully hard to have a girlfriend and a wife at the same time."

"Cut the shit, Claire. We are divorced. You failed to contest any of it so it was finalized."

She shrugs her shoulders and smiles like a snake, a smile I have never seen before. "Unfortunately for you, I did contest the divorce but for some reason those letters from my lawyer never appeared before the judge."

I have no idea what she is talking about. My brother and I spent a year trying to find her and when we finally did, spent six months trying to get her to sign the divorce papers. "What are you talking about? The divorce was never contested."

"Maybe you should talk to brother dearest. He probably hid them. He never liked me."

She is crazy. I think she has lost it. My family loved her. They were just as devastated when she walked away as I was. "I'll talk to him. But right now, I need you to leave."

"I'm not leaving, Noah."

"Why are you here then?" I ask, holding back every urge to literally pick her up and toss her out.

"I needed time to think. Our marriage was falling apart. We were in two separate headspaces. And I just needed time." She stretches out her hand to grab mine but I pull it away. "I never should have left you. I love you, Noah."

I watch a tear slide down her cheek and fight the urge to make it better. I loved Claire. I loved her so much it took me five years to get over her. It took Anna to get over her. But I cannot have her here messing with my emotions. "It's been five years, Claire. Five fucking years," I grit.

"I know. I'm so sorry." She starts crying and this time I reach for her hand out of habit. "I should have come back sooner."

"I've moved on."

She grips my hand tight, her nails leaving marks in my skin. "Give me a chance. Please, Noah."

I pull my hand away from hers. "I can't."

"Why not?"

"I can't walk this path with you again. You tore my heart apart, Claire. I spent years trying to figure out why you left. Why you walked away from me with nothing but a note. And I can't let you do that again."

"I won't."

I shake my head and stand, moving behind the dining chair and grip the back. "That's not what I mean. I won't let this happen. That woman who ran out of here. I love her. I love her so fucking much. I can't lose her."

"But what about me?"

"What about you?" I growl. "I don't care, Claire. I don't. You left me. You walked away. And when I got those divorce papers and the judge filed them, I thought it meant I would never see you again."

She sniffles but it sounds insincere. I walk to the front door of my house and yell. "Get out, Claire."

She stands from her chair, grabbing her designer hand-bag, and meets me at the front door. "I'm still your wife," she mutters.

"No, you aren't." I grip the back of my neck. "I'll call Carson. Get this figured out."

She goes into her bag and finds a piece of paper and a pen. "Here's my number, baby. Call me."

I crush the paper in my hand, angry over the endearment. Before I can push her out the door, she wraps her arms around my neck and presses her lips to mine.

And I make the mistake of not pulling away, not pushing her off me. Because the kiss brings back so many memories. Memories of the ten years we had together before she threw it all away. I don't even realize I'm kissing her back until she moans into my mouth.

And that's when I realize her lips aren't the ones I want on mine. They are thin and sticky, not the plump ones I dream of. Her nails sharp as they dig into my skull, not the soft, callused hands that caress my body every night. And when I open my eyes, I see strawberry-blond hair, not the fire of my fierce wildflower.

I push her away and wipe my mouth, appalled at myself for letting that happen. When I look at Claire, that snake-like grin is back on her face. "I'll see you around, stud."

She walks out of my house and to her car. My heart and head battling over the reaction to her old nickname for me.

When I see her pull away, I slam the door and grab my phone to call Carson. I want nothing more than to run to Anna but I know her. I know her better than anyone and I know right now she needs time.

I WALK into Carson's office and collapse into one of the chairs facing his desk.

"That bad, brother?"

I rub my hands over my face, trying to find some sort of comprehension as to what the hell just went on in my life. The woman who I thought I loved for ten years strolls back into my life expecting to pick up where we left off. And the woman who now owns my heart has walked away. Even if she said she only needed space, I could tell by that kiss that she was giving up on me. Giving up on us.

"I fucked up."

Carson takes his glasses off and folds his hands over his desk. "Clearly."

I lean over, elbows on my knees as I stare at the Turkish rug on the floor of Carson's office, memorizing the pattern on the edge of the rug.

I hear Carson get out of his chair and see his feet in front of me. "I can't help you if you don't tell me what happened."

I look up to see him leaning against the front of his desk, arms crossed. "Claire showed up on my doorstep this morning."

"Excuse me?" Carson coughs. "Did you just say Claire?"

I nod as I lean backward against the chair, throwing my head backward. "Anna answered the door. In my t-shirt."

"Well Claire is no longer your problem, Noah. That divorce was settled. She isn't tied to you anymore."

"Not according to her."

"She isn't your problem."

"Well she caused enough other problems."

Carson sighs. "What did you do?"

"Claire is different. She's changed. She isn't the girl next door anymore. She acted like a snake. She insulted Anna."

"And?"

I let out a long breath. "I didn't defend her."

Carson whistles. "Mistake number one."

He knows me well enough to know that I can't just let one bad thing happen when shit goes south. It always spirals into a giant snowball. Making my life a mess that takes too much effort to crawl out of.

150

"Anna left."

"Permanently?"

I shrug. "I'm not sure. We fought. I begged her to stay. She said she needed space."

Carson bites his thumb. "I see. And knowing you, you let her go?"

"I know how her brain works. She runs. When things get tough she runs away."

"You didn't chase after her?"

I groan. Maybe I should have this time. "No. I didn't. I let her go because I know she needed that space. But when she kissed me, it felt a whole lot like goodbye, Car."

"Doesn't she leave for Nashville tomorrow?"

I nod. "That's what worries me. She runs when her heart is broken. And now she is ready to go to this workshop and I'm not sure she will come back."

"Did she say anything to you about leaving?"

"She said she would be back."

"Well that's good news."

I shrug.

"So now lay on mistake number two," he says, crossing one leg over the other.

"I blew up on Claire. She was spouting this nonsense about court documents and her contesting everything." I look up to meet Carson's gaze. "She says she had contested the divorce."

"She didn't show up for one court date."

"I told her that. She was so pissed at me. Like it was my fault she left and that I moved on. I told her to get out. I think she wants to take me to court over all this."

Carson nods as he looks me over. Sometimes I forget I'm older than him because he does seem wiser than me more than half the time.

"And now I am waiting for mistake number three."

"Fuck," I mutter into my palms. Once again scrubbing my face for clarity. "She kissed me."

"And let me guess, you kissed her back."

"It was an accident."

Carson guffaws. "I've never heard of a kiss being an accident. A mistake maybe but not an accident."

"The memories flooded back, man. The good ones. But it didn't take long for me to push her away."

"You know you are going to have to tell Anna that."

"I'm well aware," I growl.

Carson sighs as he takes the seat next to me, throwing a hand on my shoulder. "Look, I can't do much for what's going on between you and Anna. You need to fix that. But you also need to know something." He pauses. "You still have love in your heart for Claire. Hell man, it took you five years to get over her. And it's going to be hard to fight those feelings. Fight off what you have been trying to forget. But you need to if you want to keep the woman that's right for you. Unless you want to make it work with Claire."

"Fuck no," I spit out. "I need Anna. She keeps my heart beating."

Carson smiles. "I know, brother. I know. You are going to have to fight through this. Because this might be a tough battle."

My eyes snap to his and I can tell he his keeping something from me. "What the fuck does that mean?"

He looks over to his office door that is slightly cracked and gets up to shut it. He moves back over to his desk and sits down, rubbing his palms over his face. "I fucked up too."

"What the hell does that mean?"

He takes a moment to compose himself. "I could lose my license for this."

"What did you do?" I growl.

"I did what was necessary to get you out of that marriage."

A million thoughts float through my head. And all of them lead back to Claire telling me that Carson was lying. "She said you were lying to me."

"I didn't lie, per se."

"Just tell me what the fuck you did!" I shout at him. My knuckles turning white as they grip the chair I'm sitting in.

He stands up and walks over to his safe, pulling out a manila folder of documents. "The day the judge filed your divorce, I came back to the office. My secretary left a pile of mail on my desk a few days beforehand but I was so involved in that homicide case, I ignored anything that didn't pertain to it."

I don't like where this is going.

"I finally sifted through the mail. Mostly junk except for one envelope." He opens the folder and slides it to the end of his desk so I can grab it. "She contested the divorce, Noah. But this was after months of not showing up for court dates. The envelope is postmarked three days before the paperwork was filed. Meaning it showed up on my desk the day before the final hearing."

I stare at the signed letter. Dumbfounded. Pissed. Terrified of what this could mean.

"Before you flip off the deep end, this doesn't mean the divorce won't stand. But if she made copies, which I am sure her lawyer did, the divorce can be turned over. And she could own half of what you own."

"Fuck."

"And she could potentially refile for divorce and take you for everything and alimony for negligence on my part because of this."

"Why didn't you tell me? Why didn't you let us work this out with her?"

Carson pinches his fingers between his brow. "She fucking destroyed you when she walked away from you. I never thought that would happen. Fuck, we had a family barbeque the week before and she was telling me how the two of you were talking about starting a family. I was pissed at her, man. Pissed that she tore you apart and made your life miserable. And to this day I still hate her because her walking away made you a shell of a man for five years. All of us feel like we didn't have a brother for that time.

"And then Anna came around. And she changed you. You started to smile again. You shifted into the person you used to be. Hell, you finally put the effort into passing your detective exam. I know you failed it twice."

I look up at him with a furrowed brow. No one knew that.

"Anna brought you back to life and I swear to God I will do anything to keep this document hidden, destroyed so you don't fall back into the man you used to be. But in order for you to do that, you need Claire out of your life. You can't let the ghost of her tie you down, wrap you up in bullshit to make you choose her."

Carson is right. But I just don't know how I am supposed to do this. "What are you going to do?"

"When this showed up in the mail," he says laying his finger on the envelope. "I got a weird feeling in my gut. And you know my gut wins me cases."

I nod. My brother is one of the best defense attorneys in the state.

"I think she is hiding something. I think she was hiding something back then too. I'm going to talk to my P.I., see what we can dig up."

"What do you want me to do?"

"Stay the fuck away from her. And don't you dare use

your resources to try and dig into her life. That could be used against you." He pauses. "And fix shit with Anna."

"I want nothing more than to fix this."

"Good." He pauses. "But you can't tell her about this either. I need strict nondisclosure."

"Then how am I supposed to explain this to her?"

"Find another way."

19

ANNA

I watched Noah leave the house soon after Claire did.

I'm a wreck.

After everything I went through with Kyle I cannot find the energy to do it again.

I know this is different. I know Noah is just as confused as I am. But my heart can't separate my past from the present right now.

I shouldn't have run away. I should have stayed with him. Made that bitch say what she had to say in front of me.

But the fear of déjà vu was taking over my brain. Anxiety weighing down on my chest making it hard to breathe.

The worst part is I need Noah right now. I need him to breathe and he is the one person I cannot be around.

I take the last sip from the bottle of wine I was drinking. I need to get over to Noah's and pack my things for Nashville.

I look around my half of the duplex. Fortunately, I still had a week to move out and could hide out here after whatever the hell happened this morning happened.

I grab the few things I have left here. A bottle of wine, a lone plant on the kitchen windowsill, and a notebook I found in a kitchen drawer. I leave my key in an envelope on the counter and make my way over to Noah's house.

Strange that one conversation led me to think of his place as his and not ours.

I sniffle and hold back the tears.

I run upstairs and start shoving things into my bag, not really caring if I have any complete outfits.

Funny how things change. This morning we were celebrating our love, showing each other how much we love the other, and now I feel like it was all a train wreck.

I'm not sure what's going to happen between us and I don't know what I even want.

My heart is telling me Noah. That it's simple. I need him in my life.

But my head knows it can't go down this path again. Can't be led astray by a man who might not want me completely.

And what is going to happen when I leave for two weeks. Is he going to find comfort in his ex-wife? Or will he be counting down the days until I return?

I bring my poorly packed suitcase downstairs and put it by the door. I head back inside and into my new music room. The one that has brought me so much life. I run my fingers over the records on the wall. Feel the softness of the plants hanging from the ceiling, draping off the walls. I look out into the slowly descending night, the stars not quite visible yet.

Will I be able to come back to this place? This new sanctuary Noah helped create for me.

The heaviness in my chest becomes unbearable so I head outside and watch the sky. I watch the sun slowly fade as the night turns black. The stars finally peeking out behind the clouds. I ask them for answers, for a truth I can't find in myself. But they don't respond as the tears fall silently from my cheeks.

I wake up as the smell of cedar and juniper infiltrates my nose, as I feel the warmth of a body against me. My eyes flutter open to find Noah carrying me inside. He doesn't say a word. And I don't need him to. Because being in his arms has given me the most clarity I have felt all day.

He quickly strips both of us of our clothes and follows me into bed. He presses a chaste kiss to my forehead before wrapping me in his arms, holding me tight, clinging to me as if I'm his lifeline.

He must think I fell asleep because he starts whispering all the words I need to hear in my ear. That he needs me, loves me, would be lost without me. I let him speak all his secrets into my hair as I feel his tears fall onto my shoulder.

I WAKE up the next day still wrapped in Noah's arms. I have no idea how long he cried onto my shoulder. His tears comforted me for some unknown reason as I let myself fall asleep to the cadence of his voice.

I stir and his arms wrap tighter around me. I flip over and face him. His eyes swollen and red and I am not sure he slept at all. I run my thumbs along his lashes and press a kiss to each eye. I move to his lips, coaxing them open, yearning for the feeling he gives me when he kisses me.

One swipe of my tongue is enough for his daze to turn into a burning need. He flips me onto my back, his mouth attacking mine. Trying to prove to me how much he needs me.

But I feel a sadness in his kisses as well. As if he is holding back a secret.

I pull away from him and sit up. "We need to talk."

"I know." His voice cracks. And I know from those two words my heart will crack too.

I climb out of bed and take a quick shower. I don't have much time before I have to leave. I hold back tears as I think about how our morning should have been. Us tangled in sheets, me running late because we can't get enough of each other before I leave. Tears being cried over not seeing each other for two weeks after months of spending every day together, not because our world was torn apart yesterday.

Now I am crying because I am afraid. I am afraid that what he says may be the final words to make me leave this place for good. Leave him for good.

When I walk out of the bathroom, dressed and ready to leave, I find Noah sitting on the side of the bed. His face buried in his hands. My warrior of a man looking defeated and broken.

I walk over to him and place my hands on his shoulders, rubbing the tension out of them, giving him the freedom to tell me what ever he has to say that I know will end us.

"She kissed me," he whispers as he looks up at me.

My heart seizes at the words. I don't want to ask the next question but I need to. "And did you kiss her back?"

I can tell from his inability to keep eye contact with me that he did. The loss I was expecting to feel turns to rage as I step away from him. I try to gather my thoughts but the fire in my veins burns too hot. "All of this, Noah," I say as I gesture around the room. "Everything we built you just ruined with a kiss. God, how can I be so stupid to think that you were over her. That you could love me with every part of your heart. I'm an idiot. I can't do this again."

"Please Anna. It was a mistake," he begs.

"You seem to be having a lot of those ever since she showed up on your doorstep," I seethe.

"She means nothing to me."

"And I don't think I do either."

"You mean everything to me," he says as he tries to grab for me.

"Not enough." My voice breaks.

"Anna, I love you so fucking much. I can't live without you."

"I've heard that before, Noah, and guess what? That man didn't mean it either."

He looks at me with the saddest eyes I have ever seen and I almost go to him, wrap him up in my arms and forgive him for it all. But I don't.

"So this is it? This is the end?" he asks as a tear slides down his handsome face.

I love this man. I love him so much and I don't know if I can step away. "I don't know."

"Please, I am trying to make this right. I don't know what she is doing here. Let me figure this out."

I look at my watch. I need to be on the road so I can get to Nashville in time. "I really just don't know, Noah."

"I'm not him, Anna. I won't do to you what he did." Noah's voice grows stronger.

The thing is I know he isn't Kyle. I know he won't cheat on me. He won't go back to her. I mean it was just a kiss. A kiss I can tell is tearing him apart inside. Yet I can't find it inside of me to let it go.

My hand goes to the necklace around my neck. The one he gave me just twenty-four hours ago. The thought makes my eyes burn as I head to the stairs.

"Anna, I am begging you. Don't end this. Not now."

I turn and look at him, my heart begging me to take his side. But my head has other plans for me. I remove the necklace from around my neck and place it on the dresser by the doorway.

I walk downstairs without another word. Too afraid that if I stay any longer I won't leave at all.

I head to my music room and grab my guitar and sheet music. I look around it one more time, wondering if it will be the last time I step in it.

When I make my way to the door, Noah is standing there my suitcase in his hand. "Let me carry this to the car for you."

I nod, walking past him as he holds the door open for me.

I put my guitar in the back seat as Noah puts my suitcase in the trunk.

I open the door to my car and Noah stops me, wrapping me in a tight hug. "I'm going to make this right, Anna. I promise you that."

I let him kiss my forehead before sitting in the driver's seat. He waves at me as I pull out of the drive and head down the street toward the highway. Toward my dream. Although I am not even sure what my dream is anymore.

I make it around the corner and pull over bursting into tears.

I only hope I can fix my heart in Nashville.

20

NOAH

I ROLL OVER IN BED AND TURN OFF MY ALARM. IT'S JUST past six in the morning. I should get up and go for a run before heading into the precinct but I haven't been able to find the energy. Hell, I have barely slept since Anna's been gone. I think I finally fell asleep due to pure exhaustion just after four in the morning.

I have a gaping hole in my chest. Anna took my heart when she left. And right now, I am just battling to stay above water. It feels like I'm drowning every second of every day. I'm gasping for breath, trying to stay afloat but her loss is too much to bear.

She's only been gone five days but it feels like years. I've texted and called her numerous times despite Seraphina's advice and she won't respond. She only texted me to let me know she got to Nashville safely.

Seraphina was the first person I went to when Anna left for Nashville. I needed advice. I needed to know how to fix what I broke with her. How to make her come back home to me after her workshop.

Seraphina only told me to give her space and time. Not to text her constantly or leave her a million voicemails. She was in Nashville to further her career and she didn't need distractions.

I tried to hold back but it's been hard. I have never felt so lonely in my life. I never understood what it was like to have your heart broken until Anna left.

The past few nights I've sat in her music room trying to feel her presence. I can still smell her patchouli and lemon scent and it brings me a sense of calm. I just hope it doesn't fade before she returns.

Brutus jumps on the bed and licks my face before curling up into my side. He has been just as sad as I've been. He loved Anna just as much as I do. And he has been moping around ever since she left.

I finally make my way out of bed and go through my morning routine. I let Brutus out, eat some breakfast and head upstairs to take a shower. After my shower, I brush my teeth and try not to stare at the dead eyes reflected back in the mirror. I put on my suit and grab my badge and gun out of the safe and head into work.

I'm glad it's Friday. Only one more day of faking my smile and attitude in front of my partner. I look in my rearview mirror, my reflection looks like it's aged years this week. The bags under my eyes prominent, the wrinkles more defined. Luckily I have been able to play it off from working on the case we've been on for the last few weeks. I've made some progress on it, narrowed down a list of suspects only because of my lack of sleep. It's the only thing that distracts me from thoughts of Anna.

The day goes by at a grueling pace. It's like time has slowed. By the time six o'clock finally hits, I am ready for a drink. A lot of drinks.

I forego going to Jimmy's with the rest of the guys. I don't want to have to answer questions. Even though my partner and I have only spent a few weeks together, he knows something is up.

My plan is to head home and change and then head to Mason's studio to get shitfaced with him. Mason has been worried about me ever since Carson told him what happened. Carson wanted him to look out for me while Carson dug into Claire's past. So far he has come up empty-handed.

I pull in my driveway and groan when I see the Range Rover Claire was driving sitting in the street. I should have kept driving. Just gone straight to Mason's studio but I couldn't leave Brutus alone for so long.

I slam the door as I get out of my SUV and hustle to the front door. I hear Claire on my heels but she is the last person I want to deal with.

I make it inside and slam the door before she can sneak in behind me. I hear her yelling at me through the door but I just lean against it and slide to the ground. What has my life become?

I shoot a text off to Carson hoping he can give me legal advice.

Me: Any news yet? Claire is banging on my door and I wish I could tell her to fuck off.

Brutus licks my face and sits in my lap, half growling half whining at Claire's yelling on the other side of the door.

Carson: Nothing yet. Don't talk to her. I don't want her to use anything against you.

Me: No shit, man. I practically had to run into my house. She was waiting in her car outside when I pulled in.

Carson: You could call the police.

Me: I'm not bringing that attention to me. Besides, it's not like I can file a restraining order.

Carson: If only.

Me: I just need to find a way out of this house.

Carson: I'll get Mason on it.

I sigh as I throw my head against the door. My eyes starting to close even though Claire is causing a scene outside. Maybe if I just let her continue, the neighbors will call the cops.

I must doze off because I am startled by my phone ringing. I can still hear Claire outside, she isn't yelling anymore but it sounds like she is pacing, the click of her heels back and forth on the hardwood.

I look at my phone half expecting it to be Claire but it's Mason.

"Hello?"

"You ready for a jailbreak?"

"Fuck man. Get me out of here."

Mason chuckles into the phone as I stand and walk upstairs. "You willing to jump your neighbor's fence?"

I open my safe and set my gun and badge inside. "I'm willing to pretty much do anything at this point."

"She will leave eventually."

"I'm sure."

Mason clears his throat. "Alright well, I just drove past your house and it looks like she is sitting in a chair on the porch."

"I could have told you that." I set my phone on speaker and change into jeans and a long sleeve shirt.

"I'll meet you behind your house. That way you don't have to break the law. I'm kicking my friend Jason out of the car to walk the street, make sure she doesn't walk around to the back when you leave."

I start laughing. The first laugh I've had all week. "Is it just me or do you feel like this is high school?"

"Yeah." He laughs. "It sure does."

"I'll meet you out back with Brutus in two minutes."

"I'll text you if Jason says she isn't on the porch."

I rub my hands over my face as I hang up the phone. I can't believe I am sneaking out of my own house to escape my ex-wife.

I whistle for Brutus as he follows me down the stairs. I let him outside and head back to the coat closet to grab my jacket and Brutus' leash. I don't have a text from Mason so I can only guess the coast is clear.

I see him pull up and I call for Brutus. I attach his leash and head to the driveway. The gate to the back alleyway is on the other side of my detached garage. There is a small chance Claire could see me but I hope she doesn't.

I make it around the garage without her noticing, pull open the gate, and climb into the back of Mason's Bronco.

I slam the door as Mason peels out of the alley. "Dude, this isn't an action movie, you aren't being chased by the cops." I hold on to the seat in front of me as I try to grab my seat belt.

"Totally feels like it."

"If you get pulled over, I am not pulling my badge."

"Whatever, bro."

We drive around the block and pick up his friend. I look at my house as we drive by, seeing Claire banging on my door again. I don't know what the hell is going on with her because she never acted crazy like this. If she did, I would have understood why she left. But this is not the same person I was married to for six years.

I don't talk about anything as we drive to Mason's studio. I know he has a ton of questions. Carson and I haven't told him anything beyond the fact that she is back. I can't let him know about the potential of my whole divorce being redacted.

When we pull up to the studio, I grab Brutus as we get

out of the car. Mason puts the code in for the studio door and I follow him inside.

"I have to check on a recording session but I'll be out soon."

I grab the back of my neck. "Sorry Mason, I didn't mean to pull you from your work."

He holds up a hand. "Don't worry about it. Jordan is working. I was just supervising."

I nod as he disappears into a room. I head to the kitchen area and find a bottle of whiskey. I pour a large serving into a red cup and drink half of it before sitting down on a couch.

Jason cracks open a beer and sits across from me. "I'm not even going to ask, man."

"Thanks."

I text Anna again as I sit on the couch sipping on whiskey and Jason strums a guitar. I'm not surprised when she doesn't answer me back. My eyes drift shut again, the week of no sleep catching up to me.

I wake up to Mason sitting next to me holding the whiskey bottle in his hand. "Hey, Noah. I figured you wanted to wake up before people showed up."

"Thanks." I let Mason pour me more whiskey as I adjust on the couch.

"You want to talk about it?"

That's when I notice we are the only people in the room. Jason disappeared somewhere. I sip on my whiskey as I watch Brutus snore on the floor. "Not really."

"Too bad I didn't mean it as a question."

I sigh and lean forward, resting my elbows on my knees.

"Look, man. I know there is a lot of shit going on. And I probably can't do anything about it. But maybe I can listen. Maybe that will help."

"Have you heard from Anna?" I ask, peering over my shoulder at him.

I can tell by the look on his face he has. "Look Noah, she told me not to tell you."

"I'm your brother," I grit.

"And she is my friend."

I turn back to the coffee table in front of me and sip my whiskey. "I don't think she is coming back."

"She will."

I pinch the space between my eyes. "I don't know, man. She is so mad at me. And she should be. I fucked up. I didn't defend her. I let Claire be a bitch and walk all over her. But I need her, Mase. I need her so much."

"I wish I could tell you she feels like you do but she doesn't."

The thought sends a shooting pain into my heart.

"But it's not because of you. She is doing great. She has her distraction in the workshop. She is building her path, Noah."

"I'm happy for her."

"But I can tell she misses you." He pauses. "I talked to her earlier. She asked about you."

My ears perk at that.

"I told her you looked like shit and were a miserable fuck."

"Not a lie," I mutter.

"She's worried about you. I mean, she didn't say that but I could hear it in her voice."

I tap my foot on the ground. I wish more than anything she would just call me.

"She told me what happened with Claire."

"I apolo—"

Mason cuts me off. "If you were gonna say you apologized, leave it alone. I know you did. And I think she knows you truly are sorry."

"Then why is she ignoring me?" I ask, looking back over my shoulder at my brother.

Mason takes a sip of whiskey and leans back on the couch. He rubs his face before answering so I know I am not going to like the answer. "She thinks you still have feelings for Claire."

"I don—"

Mason holds his hand up. "Calm down. I told her that, but it's hard to see past that sometimes. She loves you more than the world, Noah. Her greatest fear is losing you."

No, it's not. Her greatest fear is I will cheat on her like Kyle did. But I don't tell Mason that. Instead I tell him some of my truth. "It fucked me up, man. Her coming back here. All those feelings I had for her came racing back to me at the sight of her. Anger, pain, love." I pause. "But I don't love her like Anna. God, Anna is my fucking world. I had a hiccup. A moment of shock. And I feel like it ruined everything."

Mason shakes his head. "I don't think it did. She needs time to sort it all out."

I nod because I know that is exactly what she needs. I know it's not helping that I keep texting her. It's not giving her the space she needs to think things over. I vow to stop the texts at this moment.

"Everyone will probably be here soon. Stop moping. Have a good time. Forget about all this for just a few hours."

I throw back the rest of the whiskey in my glass and pour both of us more. "You're right."

I haven't had a night like this in years. As in probably ten years. I'm always collected. Always the responsible one.

But tonight, I have let myself go. Beer after beer, shot after shot. I'm not even sure what time it is or what day it is.

I really hope I don't have to work tomorrow. I forgot why I am even drinking like this.

I stumble over something on the floor but catch myself on a table. I think I was going to get some water. Maybe. Or a beer. Probably water.

But someone changes the music and I stop in my tracks. The raspy voice of my wildflower floods the speakers.

"Have you heard this girl sing yet?" someone shouts.

"Fucking amazing!"

"Have you seen her? She is hot as hell too."

"Maybe she will show up tonight. My dick has needed some sweet pussy."

My vision goes red as I hear these two douchebags go back and forth over Anna.

Fuck. Anna.

That's why I was drinking. I was trying to forget about her.

I blink and try to clear my double vision when I see the two assholes talking about Anna. My fist is clenched and I am ready to knock out this pompous dick who thinks he can talk about her like that.

"Whoa man," douchebag number one says as my fist attempts to hit douchebag number two in the face. But I miss or maybe someone pulled me back. I'm not quite sure.

"Noah." Mason's voice is in my ear. I look down and see his arm wrapped around my bicep.

"What the fuck, man?" douchebag number two says right before he takes a swing and punches me right in the left eye.

"Fuck," I groan as I hold my face.

"You two, get the fuck out of here," Mason shouts.

"What the hell, Mason? He just came at us out of nowhere."

Someone else grabs me as Mason turns to the guys.

"Well you were talking about Anna May like she was some kind of snack."

"She is, man. Didn't you try to hit that?"

I look over at Mason and see him punch his friend in the nose. "No, *man,* I didn't. That's my brother's girlfriend, you idiots."

The two guys look over at me. I am still seeing red even though I can barely see. My left eye throbbing.

"Fuck. We didn't know."

"Shit, isn't he a cop?"

"Get out," Mason orders as he points at the door.

The two guys leave without a word just as a girl walks up to me with a bag of ice. "Anna would have gotten all hot and bothered with you defending her like that."

I grab the ice from where the girl is holding it. I squint up and see Seraphina. "I don't think she cares."

Sera snorts. "Think about it, Noah. That girl is in love with you. That's why she was so mad. And she only runs from those she loves, so think of it as a romantic gesture."

"That's fucked up, Sera," a deep voice says next to me. It's when I realize he was the one who pulled me back, Dee, Anna's friend from college and Mason's business partner.

Mason drags a chair over and pushes me into it.

"It's fucked up but it's true," Sera responds.

"Alright party's over," Mason shouts.

I grab his arm. "You don't have to end it over this," I say, gesturing to my eye.

"I know. But I am going to anyway. Too many people here as it is."

Dee lights up a joint next to me and I couldn't care less about it.

Sera stares at me. "I told you not to text her."

"I haven't texted her since this morning. I'm stopping. I swear."

She takes a sip of water before answering. "I told you not to text her from the get-go."

"It was hard not to."

Mason comes back over to us and sits on top of the table next to us. "That was stupid."

I know he is referring to me trying to punch that guy. "Did you hear what they were saying?"

"Yeah and I ignored it. Anna would never give those two fucktards the time of day."

"I forgot about her. I finally put her out of my mind for the night."

"I don't know who put that song on, Noah. I mean it." He takes a drink of his beer. "I was enjoying watching you be a shit show for once. I knew if you heard her voice you would fall apart."

"This all sucks. God, I wish Claire didn't come back. I wish we could have just kept going on living our lives. I want to marry her. I want everything with her." I realize my drunk ass is saying more than it should but I can't fight the feeling inside of me, regardless if it's drunken thoughts.

"And on that note, we are leaving," Dee says as he grabs Sera.

"What no! I want to hear this."

Dee shakes his head as he pulls Sera away.

Mason stands up and pulls me with him. "You guys stay. I didn't kick everyone out. I just need to talk to my brother alone."

Mason pulls me into one of the recording rooms and pushes me onto a couch. He grabs two beers out of a small fridge in the room and hands one to me. "How's the eye?"

"Hurts like a bitch."

"I bet." He takes a swig. "So, you really want to marry Anna? You just moved in together."

I adjust the ice on my face. "I didn't mean to say that."

"But you meant it."

I nod. We haven't been together that long but I cannot deny the fact I want to spend my life with her.

"I'm glad you found her, Noah. I mean it."

I meet Mason's stare and nod. "I never thought I would find someone like her. I just hope I can get her back."

"You will," he says matter-of-factly. He takes another sip of his beer. "Tell me about Claire. And don't give me some bullshit answer. Carson wouldn't be so locked down on the situation if it was nothing."

I pull the ice off my eye and squint. It's gonna hurt even worse in the morning. "I don't know, man. It's nothing."

"Bullshit. If it was nothing, you wouldn't have me picking you up in an alleyway."

Mason's right but I can't tell him what Carson did. I might be drunk but I have enough clarity to know that.

"I'm not letting you leave this room until you tell me. I won't tell Hunter or Asher. Obviously I won't tell Mom and Dad. But you pulled me into this situation."

I rub my hand over my face trying to avoid my eye. "It's complicated."

"No shit." Mason studies me while I sip on my beer. I put the ice back on my face and wince at the pain. "She looked weird, man."

I look at him quizzically. Claire looked the same to me maybe more put together. She was well dressed and fashionable. It's nothing new, she always looked presentable but she does have an air about her she didn't have before. "What do you mean?"

"Dude, she was driving a Range Rover. Unless she won a bunch of money, she never could afford that with her job."

Claire was a marketing assistant when we were married. "Maybe she got a good promotion."

Mason rests his chin in his palm. "Maybe. But it also

looked like she had a designer bag. She was dressed like she had a shit ton of money. When she left you, she didn't take anything from your joint accounts."

"How do you know that?"

"Carson told me."

I close my eyes and rest my head on the back of the couch. "I don't know. It's weird. Everything. When Carson finally found her after a year, she was living in New Jersey."

"Maybe she moved up to the east side. Found herself another man."

I let out a deep breath. "I don't know. Maybe. We can't find shit on her right now."

"Maybe Carson should have his P.I. look into marriage certificates for her."

"This all sounds crazy. Claire was never crazy."

Mason snorts. "Dude, she left you with a fucking note. If you don't think that's crazy, I don't know what it is."

I sip my beer. "I just want this to be over. I just want to be back in bed with Anna the day after her birthday. Everything was right that morning. Everything felt perfect."

Mason stands and sits next to me on the arm of the couch. "You'll get there again. I know you will."

21

ANNA

I GRIP THE NECKLACE AROUND MY NECK. WE ARE about to do our first showcase of the workshop and I am nervous as hell. There are record executives, musicians, Grammy nominated artists all sitting in the audience at the Bluebird Café. Yes, we have a showcase at the Bluebird. I honestly might shit myself.

I wish I could talk to Noah right now. He has a way of calming me, helping me re-center.

My fingers fumble with the raw stone. When I got to my hotel room and unpacked my suitcase I found the necklace inside. Noah must have put it in when he took my suitcase to the car. It was wrapped inside a piece of paper with a note.

I love you. Knock 'em dead. I'll be waiting for you.
XO Noah

It was a short and simple note but it's given me so much faith in us. Between the note and his endless barrage of texts and voicemails, I know that what we have is true. I know our love will win. But I need this time and space away from him. I need it to balance my life.

And a week without him has only proven that I need him. I need him so badly. He is my rock. My protector. My hero.

"Anna May Cooper, you're up next," says a man wearing all black and a headset.

I shake out my nerves letting go of my necklace and following the man into the back of the building and into a side door in the corner of the room.

The Nashville Songwriters Association didn't want us to watch others perform until we did so we wouldn't get nervous. Of course, this place doesn't have much room to begin with. I don't know if it helped at all because my whole body is tingling.

I watch the young singer ahead of me finish his performance. He is amazing. He is so young, barely twenty but he has a deep southern twang to his voice and he is easy on the eyes. He wants to be a star and I am sure he will get there one day. Most of the people accepted into the workshop want to be songwriters and musicians but there are a few who want to be the ones on stage singing the songs. They all have a one-up on other up-and-comers since they all have an amazing ability to write music.

I take a deep breath as everyone applauds for the last performer. I feel my phone vibrate in my pocket. I shouldn't check it. I should leave it alone but part of me hopes that it will be Noah. I don't care what he has to say but just a few words from him would make me feel better. He stopped texting me two days ago and I worry what the reason may be.

Mason: Don't fuck up.

I laugh as I read his text. It came at the perfect time. The nerves diminish a little as I laugh over his text. I told him earlier that today was the first showcase and he kept telling me not to forget the words to my song.

After today, we have smaller showcases every night depending on if we are invited to them. Artists and record executives will invite you based off tonight's performance if they want to hear more of what we have to offer.

I put my phone in my pocket and am directed on to the stage. Rather than play guitar tonight, my usual choice, I am playing piano. Almost every other person here is playing guitar and I want to stand out.

I don't let myself look at the audience as I walk onto the small stage. The lights are dim but you can still see everyone's faces.

I take a seat at the piano and inhale deeply.

This is it.

This is my moment.

I adjust the microphone in front of me. "Hello, I am Anna May Cooper. This is a song I wrote this week called 'Don't Let Me Walk Away.'"

I had so many songs I could have sang tonight. I could have sung one of the three I brought with me to work on this past week. But instead I chose a new song. A song that came to me as I sat on the floor of the shower in my hotel crying over Noah Wednesday night.

It was the first song I took out of my notebook on Thursday when I went to the workshop. I worked with one other person on it. Not to find the lyrics but just to help with the melody. The mentors told me it was a risk singing the song. That I needed more time developing it. I needed to sing something more universal to catch more attention.

But I knew I needed to sing from my soul. Sing the song that I can feel all the way into the deepest part of my bones. A song I will never sell to anyone but know that it will get me the attention I need.

I take one more deep breath as I play the first few haunting chords of the song. I hum along to the melody, an off key crescendo to bring out the tension in the song.

I close my eyes and let myself sing the words pouring from my heart.

It was a cold December day when you found me
Like the nights I spent crying all alone
I never thought he would haunt me
But the ghosts were real and kept me in the cold

I spent seven years lost out in the wild
Finding the words to feed my soul
But all I came up with was dust and ash
The memories fighting for control

I pound on the keys of the piano as the words echo through the room. I keep my eyes closed, focused on the feel of the music but when I hit the chorus and belt it out, I finally turn to the audience.

Don't let me walk away from you
Don't let me be the one to say goodbye
I never should have left the way I did
I didn't mean to make you cry
I need you here next to me
Instead I sit here alone
I don't know why I walked away without a word
So don't let me walk away from you

I hum along to the melody, let the raspiness build in my throat as I approach the bridge to the song.

I need you now

I need you gone
I would rather be alone
I'm a mess
I'm a wreck
I was the one who never should have left

and I don't know why
I don't know why

So don't let me walk away from you
Don't let me be the one to say goodbye
I never should have left the way I did
I didn't mean to make you cry
I need you here next to me
Instead I sit here alone
I don't know why
I don't know why
I don't know why I walked away without a word
So don't let me walk away from you

My fingers press into the final chords of the song and let them ring out as I sing the last lines. My voice cracking with the pain I feel.

I was the one who never should have left
and I don't know why
I don't know why

I blink as I turn to face the audience, a silence ringing through the room. Maybe I fucked up. Maybe my mentor was right and I should have played something more upbeat. But in my heart I knew the song was right. I feel a tear on my face and I wipe it away. I had no idea I was crying during my performance.

I stand ready to thank them when someone stands up and starts clapping. Soon after another person stands, followed by another. Within seconds the whole room is on their feet. I nearly forget to breathe as I take it in. My hand grips my necklace saying a silent prayer to Noah. Without him I never would have written that song. The sorrowful story of a love gone wrong and the fear to make it right. It was a mix of us and our past relationships. Everything that brought us together.

I smile at the crowd thanking them one last time as I am gestured off the stage. I head to the bar where there is a tiny space in the corner for all the students to stand when we finish.

I order a lemon martini and chug it. My nerves and excitement making me anxious. A few of the other students congratulate me and tell me I sounded amazing.

I order another martini as I listen to the other seven students perform. When they finish the lights come on and everyone starts mingling.

My mentor, a producer by the name of Austin, grabs me and hugs me tightly against his chest. "Well I'll be damned. I was wrong. That was amazing. Astounding. You stole the attention of everyone in this room, Anna May. I was blown away."

I look up at him and smile. It feels like my smile is taking up my entire face. "I haven't felt that kind of energy in so long, Austin. I felt like I was singing with The Sparrows again. That raw, gritty honest singing." I clutch my hands to my chest hoping to calm the beating of my heart. "I just can't believe—"

"Anna May Cooper?" a voice says behind me.

I look up at Austin who is smiling wide at whoever is behind me. I turn around and come face to face with one of the biggest record executives here. "That's me."

"I just want to say I was so impressed by your performance tonight. I read on your dossier that you are just a songwriter but I think you belong on that stage."

My smile breaks a bit at that. As much as my love for the stage seems to be coming back, it's not the life I want to live. "Thank you, Mr. Cohen. I appreciate that. But I had my time on the stage. I would rather just write the songs."

He shakes my hand. "Well believe me, Anna May, if that's what you want to do then I have no doubt you will be doing it soon. I look forward to seeing you later this week."

I say goodbye as he goes off to talk to someone else and I nearly shriek. "Did that just happen?" I ask Austin.

He puts an arm around my shoulder. "Anna May, that really just happened. I think it's time we all celebrated. Let's hit those honky tonks! I am sure my phone will be flooded with requests for you the rest of the night and into tomorrow."

My excitement is overwhelming. I want to call Noah. I need to hear his voice. I need to tell him everything that has happened. But then I think of Claire and my mood deflates. What if he is with her? What if he changed his mind about me?

We end up hitting some of the bars on Broadway. It's about eight of the students, a few mentors, and Austin and his wife. Austin keeps doing a little dance for me every time he gets an email from someone wanting to see me. I shake my head at him and laugh as he does another one. So far at least twenty people want to see me again.

I order another martini, the buzz keeping my good mood up. One of the songwriters, a girl named Ashlynn, pulls me onto the dance floor to dance. I'm not much of a dancer but I laugh and throw my head back as we bask in the high of the night.

By the time we sit back down I feel sweaty as hell. I

drink a huge glass of water as I talk to Austin about some of the details of the week to come. He says my schedule will be insane but that we will see every person we can to get this done. We still have to write two more songs this week as part of the workshop but I am not worried about all the stress and pressure. If it will keep my mind off calling Noah I will be happy.

Ashlynn orders me another martini as my phone rings. I look down to see Mason is calling me, and I excuse myself so I can head outside.

I hit the green button on my phone and before I can say a word, Mason starts talking my ear off. "Anna May, you either bombed completely and are tucking your tail between your legs and heading back home. Or you blew everyone away, like I said you would, and have a million people trying to spend time with you. Hell, you probably already hired an assistant and they are the one that answered your phone."

I laugh at him as a warm breeze floats down the street. I push my curls behind my ear. "Nope, I haven't been able to decide between the ten assistants that want to work for me," I joke.

"I'm guessing you didn't fuck up."

I guffaw into the phone. "Thanks for the motivating text message by the way. Really made me want to do my best."

I can feel Mason smiling through the phone. "I know what motivates you. Tell me what happened?"

I smile having trouble containing my excitement. "Mason, I don't even know where to begin."

"Well, let me guess, everyone was completely silent and in awe of your voice when you finished and then you got a standing ovation. The only one of the night."

I look around confused as to how Mason knew all that

and thought maybe he somehow was there, although I have no idea how that could have happened. "Umm."

He chuckles into the phone. "People were tweeting all about your performance."

"What?" I ask completely dumbfounded.

"Yeah, Anna May. You're kind of a big deal already."

I lean against the building in complete surprise from Mason's words. "I don't understand."

"Not everyone there was in the industry. And I may know someone who knew someone who was there. I saw a video."

"No one was supposed to be recording anything." My heart beats wildly in my chest.

"Anna, you do know what year it is, right? No one follows the rules."

I bite my lip as anxiety starts to take over. "You heard the song?"

"Fuck yeah. It was intense and powerful and unrefined."

I take a deep breath before I ask my next question. "Are you going to show it to Noah?"

He takes a few moments to respond and I worry he already sent him the video. "Only if you want me to."

I breathe a sigh of relief. "Thank you."

"You know, Anna. I think you should let him hear it. Damn." He pauses. "That song was incredible. And not one I ever heard you work on. And by the lyrics, I know you must have just written it. I think he needs to hear it."

I rest my head against the wall and look up at the stars that are almost nonexistent in the light pollution. "I'm not sure if I'm ready."

"For him to hear the song? Or for him to figure out you used it as your way of apologizing?"

I blink back a few tears that formed in my eyes. "Both."

"He deserves to hear it."

"I know."

We are both silent for a few minutes. The only sound is the soft music filtering through the phone on his end and the revelry in the streets on mine.

"I'm proud of you, Anna. Noah would be proud of you too."

"Thank you."

"Keep doing whatever the hell it is you are doing there."

I smile at that. "I'm just writing songs."

"I think you are doing more than that." Mason laughs. "I'll let you get back to your night. Don't party too hard."

"I won't."

"Goodnight Anna."

I contemplate just hanging up but my heart gets the best of me. "Hey Mase."

"Yeah?"

"Tell him I love him."

"You can do it yourself."

I nod even though he can't see me. "I know. But until I find the courage to. Tell him, please."

"He knows you do, Anna."

I can't believe I am going to say this. "Play him the video."

"You sure?" Mason sounds stunned.

"Yeah. And let me know when you do."

"You are an incredible woman, Anna May."

I don't know how to respond to that so I just smile. "Goodnight Mason."

"Night."

I hang up the phone and hold it against my chest. My anxiety creeping up on me. I have no idea when Mason is going to play him the video and I only hope Noah understands where I am coming from with that song.

22

NOAH

I climb into my SUV and yawn. It's after seven in the morning. My body quickly adapted back to normal hours after my promotion. But there was a brutal crime tonight and I had to be at the scene. We got called in around four this morning and with my lack of sleep over Anna, I got about an hour and a half before my phone rang.

Both my partner and I think it might be related to the serial rapist but we can't be sure until we process more evidence. He's never killed anyone before but from all my studying and fifteen years on the police force I know that MOs can change.

I pull into my driveway and grab the coffee out of the center console. I don't need to go into the office until later but I know I won't sleep after this. I need to figure out as much as I can about this case. Find some connection in all the evidence.

I'm so busy looking at my phone when I reach my front step that I don't even notice Claire sitting in a chair, slumped over asleep.

I haven't seen or heard from her since I had to sneak out

of my house five days ago. She hasn't contacted my brother either. His P.I. was at a dead end up until Mason and I gave him that extra information we thought of. And Mason might be on the right path because Carson's P.I. can't find a Claire Taylor anywhere not since she left Asheville five years ago. He even checked under the name he found her using when we filed for divorce, her mother's maiden name but nothing is popping up under Claire Dune either.

I sigh and rub my hand over my face as I set my coffee cup down on the rail of the porch and lean against it. As she sleeps she looks innocent. Like the woman I fell in love with fifteen years ago. The woman I thought was my happily ever after.

She looks nothing like the woman who showed up on my doorstep ten days ago. Her hair is piled on her head in a messy bun. She traded in her designer threads for sweats. Her face is fresh making her look younger than she does when it's covered in makeup.

I contemplate waking her up or going inside my house and leaving her there. I can hear Brutus prancing on the other side of the door waiting for me to come in. I take a sip of my coffee hoping to find an answer in it. I am about to walk inside when she finally blinks her eyes awake.

"Noah, you're here." She looks around as if she's confused about how she got there. "How long have you been standing there?"

"How long have you been asleep on my porch?"

She looks down into her lap and grips her hands together. "I—look I'm sorry about showing up like this. But I have a favor to ask you."

I clench my jaw, annoyed that she didn't answer my question. Even more annoyed by her response. "You have a favor to ask me?"

She nods. Her head still down. "Noah, I need somewhere to stay."

I scoff at that. "Go to your parents'."

"I told you they moved."

I cross my arms over my chest. I cannot believe she is asking me to stay here. "Well go stay with other family. One of your sisters, your brother. I don't care who."

She shakes her head and sniffles. "None of them want to talk to me."

"Because you left them just like you left me?" I accuse. "I looked for you for a year, Claire. I exhausted every resource I had. And so did your family. No one knew where you were. And now you just expect to pick up where you left off?"

"It's not like that, Noah."

"Bullshit. If it wasn't like that you wouldn't just show up out of nowhere expecting your life back and ruining the lives of everyone else."

She peeks her eyes up at me. "I didn't think you moved on."

"It's been five fucking years. How many times do I need to remind you?"

She stands up and grips my hands before I can pull away. "Noah, you are the most loyal person I know. I love you and I know you love me too." Her palm touches my chest. "This heart will never stop beating for me, Noah. I know you too well."

I push her off me, rage boiling in my veins. "I may have loved you back then, Claire. But the love I had is gone." She doesn't deserve to know how long it took me to get over her. To stop feeling loyalty to her. Those feelings I once had are gone and I don't even know if they were ever real to begin with or just her ghost haunting me.

"Noah." I see a hint of malice flash across her eyes but it's gone before I can search for it again. Her tone turns solemn. "Please, I have nowhere to go."

"I told you to stay at a hotel."

I stare at her as she wraps her arms around her middle. "I ran out of cash."

I grip my hair with my fingers. "Unbelievable," I mutter.

She tries to reach for me again but I pull back fast enough this time. "I wouldn't be here if I had somewhere else to go."

I don't want to take pity on her but that look in her eyes is giving me a seed of doubt. Maybe she really is telling the truth. "I need to call my lawyer."

I turn to head into the house and I feel her behind me. "You stay here," I demand.

I slam the door behind me as Brutus jumps on me, welcoming me home. "Fuck," I yell at no one causing Brutus to scoot away.

"Hey buddy." I squat down. "I'm not mad at you."

He slowly approaches me and licks my face and I know he accepts my truce. I walk to the back door and let him out. It's only seven thirty in the morning but I could use a beer right now. Anything to keep my mind off that train wreck on my porch. I need to talk to Carson.

Me: Asshole I need you to call me. 911.

I let Brutus in and lock the door behind him. I don't trust Claire. And with the psychotic way she acted last week I wouldn't put it past her to find a way into my house.

I look at my phone and Carson hasn't seen my message. It's only been a few minutes but he is usually awake at five and to the office by seven or seven thirty.

Fuck it.

I crack open a beer and slam the entire thing. This whole

situation is turning me into an alcoholic. I swore I wouldn't have another drink after Mason's party on Friday since I had the worst two-day hangover in the world but every day without hearing a peep from Anna and the pressure of this case, I find myself having a few drinks every night.

My phone rings and I answer it just as I pop open another beer.

"A little early to be drinking, brother."

"Fuck off, Car. If you were present for the conversation I just had, you would be drinking too."

I hear him shuffling papers around on his desk before he talks. "Alright lay it on me."

"Claire is outside."

"Shit, do I need to stage another escape?"

I snort at that. "Nah."

"Then what's going on?"

I head up the stairs to my room and sit on the edge of my bed. "She says she needs somewhere to stay. Says she has no money."

"Maybe she should sell her Range Rover," Carson says sarcastically.

"Not helping, man."

"I'm kidding. What about her family? Can she go to them?" he asks sincerely.

I take another sip of my beer. "They have all shut her out."

"She deserves it," he exhales into the phone. "Let me guess, she did what she always used to do and gave you the pity eyes and the 'Noah I need you' speech."

I grip the back of my neck and start to pace my room.

"From your silence I will take that as a yes."

The truth is I never realized she did that until just now when Carson brought it up. But as I think back to all the times I gave in to her or we had an argument, it always came down to that. "Fuck."

I hear Carson fumbling with something in the background. "Sorry man. I didn't mean to bring it up that way."

I pace my room as I clench my fist. "I'm such an idiot."

"Look, Noah. You're not an idiot. You loved that woman but she had you wrapped around her finger. And she is trying to weave her way back into your life once again."

"What the hell am I supposed to do?"

Carson clears his throat, his telltale sign for having an idea I am not going to like. "I think you should let her move in."

"What? Are you crazy? And throw my entire relationship with Anna away?"

"Ugh no. Because you need that woman."

"Then what the hell are you talking about?" I yell into the phone.

"We use this to our advantage."

"How is this advantageous?"

He chuckles. "How did you pass your detective exam?" He pauses. "This is like undercover."

"How?"

I can almost hear his smile through the phone. "You let her live with you. Then you have access to all her things. Her purse, her phone, her car. We might be able to find out what the hell she is really here for."

Carson's plan makes a helluva lot of sense but I am struggling with what Anna is going to think about this. Because I know she will be pissed as hell. "What about Anna?"

"I'll take care of Anna."

I grip the back of my neck and finally stop pacing. "You think this will work?"

"It's the best shot we got. Anything to find a way out of releasing those papers."

I nod even though he can't see me. "Okay. I get it. From the investigative side of things, this makes sense."

"I'm glad we are on the same page."

"But I am not letting her sleep in my bed."

Carson laughs hard into the phone. "Dude, you have a guest bedroom. I never would have suggested this if you didn't."

"And you'll tell Anna?"

"Yes. I'll find a way to get in touch with her. Let her know this is just so we can find a way out of this mess."

"I haven't told her about the papers."

"I sure as hell hope not."

"Carson, you can get in a lot of trouble for this."

He exhales loudly and I can picture him leaning his face over his desk. With a sound of defeat, he responds, "I know."

Those two words tell me a whole lot more than I think he knows. "This isn't the first time, is it?"

Something crashes in the background, maybe a glass falling off his desk. "What? Are you accusing me of something?"

I can tell by his defensive attitude this whole thing could put him into a shit ton of trouble. "Nah, man. I was just curious."

There is an awkward silence over the phone. "I need to go. I have an appointment in a few minutes." He pauses. "Just let her stay there. Do what you can to find anything out. And I'll get my P.I. on your house too."

I don't like the idea of someone staking out my house but if it gives us answers I'll deal with it. "Okay, Car."

He hangs up without a goodbye. My mind turning at the thoughts I shouldn't be thinking about him. Is he corrupt? Has he gained all his success through lying and cheating?

I sure as hell hope not.

I grab my beer and head downstairs. I dump the rest of it in the sink before tossing it in the recycle bin.

I take a deep breath as I head to my front door.

I cannot believe I am going to do this.

I pull it open and see Claire leaning against the rail smoking a cigarette. "When did you start smoking?"

She looks at me and then the cigarette before she taps it out on the rail and tosses it into my bushes. "Oh umm recently. Stress and all."

I point to where she threw the butt. "Clean that up. And there is no smoking in my house. You can do it in the back yard by the back of the fence."

Her face turns into a smirk. "Does this mean you are letting me stay here?"

"Unfortunately yes."

"Don't be so sad, stud. This is going to be so good for us."

"Unlikely," I mutter.

She pats me on the cheek. "Let me grab my bag."

I watch as she struts to her car in the street. I have no idea why I agreed to this. What my crazy, asshole brother was thinking but maybe this is what I must do to make this all right.

She heads toward me and hands her bag off to me. I reluctantly take it as I shut the front door behind us. I watch her as she takes in the house. It's not like she hasn't been in here before.

I head down the hall to the guest room as she says, "This doesn't seem like you."

"What?" I ask as I step into the guest bedroom.

"The house doesn't have your vibe to it. It feels kind of bohemian and trendy. Plants, rugs, throw pillows."

"Anna decorated it."

"Hmm," is all she says as she sets her designer purse on the bed. "Do you still sleep on the left side of the bed?"

I look at her quizzically and then realize she thought we were sharing a room. "It doesn't matter what side I sleep on."

"That's sweet of you, stud," she says as she approaches me.

I back away. "Your bathroom is right outside, first door to your right. There should be clean towels in the cabinet in there."

"You mean this isn't your room?"

I scrub my hands over my face. "Look, Claire. It took a lot for me to agree for you to stay here. Don't push it. You know there is no way we are staying in the same room. We aren't a couple, we aren't married. This is me doing you a favor."

She gives me that pouty face again and I think back to my conversation with Carson. "Now I need to get some work done. There is food in the kitchen. If you make something please clean up after."

"Fine," she states matter-of-factly.

"I need to get some work done before I head into the office."

"Want me to make us dinner tonight?"

I pinch my eyes shut, she clearly doesn't get the picture or she is trying to work her way into my life. "I have to work late."

"Maybe tomorrow then?"

"We'll see." That answer seems to be enough for her to leave me alone.

I head back upstairs and to my bedroom. I change into workout clothes and lock the door behind me.

I might have let Claire into my house but I am not letting her into my life. And she sure as hell isn't allowed in my bedroom.

I head to the basement and get a workout in. I could use a nap but there is no way I am going to get any sleep with her around.

23

ANNA

THE LAST THREE DAYS HAVE BEEN CRAZY. I'VE BEEN getting up at six a.m. to do yoga, relax and rebalance before heading into the studio by eight in the morning. I spend ten hours a day working on music before I get whisked away to record companies, small venues, hell, even houses to showcase my songs.

Austin asked me this morning if I could stay another week. Let me know I could crash at his house just so I could get more exposure and not run myself down the last few days of the workshop.

I told him I would think about it. But I don't know if I want to stay. I love Nashville. It feels like a second home. But that's the thing, it's second. My heart belongs in Asheville.

I need to talk to Noah but I am still scared to call him to find out what is going on between him and Claire. Mason assures me everything is fine but I still worry. Even though I know I shouldn't. I didn't ask Mason if he showed Noah the video. I can only assume he hasn't because I know Noah would be calling me the second he heard the song. I should apologize to his face but he knows I express my words better through lyrics.

I slouch down into a chair outside one of the practice rooms. Austin and a few of the other mentors want me to write and record a new song today. They want me to show the big five labels how quickly I can write a song. I think it's stupid. I could write ten songs in a day but that doesn't mean any of them are good.

The ones I spend time on are the ones that make you feel. I know I can write one of those songs in a day but I need to be in the mood. I need the inspiration. I need to feel the music in my bones.

I scratch out lyrics and flip to a new page in my notebook. I've already gone through five pages of scratched out nonsense. Nothing seems to be hitting me in the gut with the words I put on paper.

I reach over for my coffee, the one lifeline I have had the last few days and find my cup empty. I groan and pull myself out of my chair. Might as well get some more if I am going to get this done today. I have six hours and forty-two minutes to write and record a song. My future is grim.

I walk down the hall of the studio we are in. It's huge and owned by one of the best producers in Nashville. There are six separate rooms to record, three practice rooms, a conference room, a large kitchen, and an enormous lounge. It's the kind of studio I wouldn't mind being in all day every day.

I reach the kitchen and slam my mug down when I notice the pot of coffee is empty. The rule is if you take the last cup, you make a new pot. It's even written on a note above the machine and on a note taped to the cabinet with the mugs.

I pull out the coffee grounds and start brewing a new

pot when my phone rings. I pull it out of my pocket and answer without even looking at it. "Hello?"

"Anna? It's Carson."

Why the hell is Carson calling me? Unless something happened to Noah.

"Noah. Is he okay?" I ask slightly panicked.

"Yeah he's fine."

I lean against the counter drawing imaginary circles on the floor with my shoe. I wish it was Noah calling me and not his brother. Carson and Noah have similar voices and the sound of his voice sends a bolt of need through my body. "Why are you calling then?"

He clears his throat before he starts to speak. "Look, I have some not-so-pleasant news. No—"

"He chose her, didn't he? He gave up on us?" I cut Carson off, dropping the empty mug in my hand and let it shatter on the ground.

Carson hesitates before answering. "No. That's not it at all. But I need you to—"

"What is going on, Carson?" I yell into the phone.

"If you quit interrupting me, I'll tell you." He waits for me to say something but I stay quiet. "Thank you. Now listen. I want you to hear this from me before you hear it from someone else. Noah needs some more time away from you."

"What?" I shriek. "He's the one that fucked up. Why does he need space from me?"

Carson sighs into the phone. "He doesn't need any distractions right now."

"And I'm a distraction?" My voice growing louder with every word Carson says.

"More or less."

"Fuck you, Carson Taylor."

"Anna, listen please. This has nothing to do with you."

I scoff into the phone. "This has everything to do with me."

"No, it doesn't. He needs to figure some things out with Claire. Let some dust settle and I am afraid if you are around, it won't."

"He is choosing her?"

Carson sighs again and I know I don't want to hear any more of what he has to say. "This isn't a matter of choice, Anna. This all has to do with some legal things that need to be cleared up."

"You mean like the fact Claire says they are still married?"

I hear him muttering to someone in the background. "Yes. It has everything to do with that."

"It's true then? The divorce isn't real?"

Carson takes a few seconds to respond and I already have my answer. "It's compli—"

"I've heard enough."

I don't even say goodbye as I hang up the phone. I am sick of hearing things are complicated.

My phone starts ringing again but I ignore it. I scoop up the broken ceramic from the ground and grab a new mug and pour myself some coffee.

As I walk down the hall to the practice room, my phone keeps ringing so I turn it off. I do not want to deal with any of the Taylor brothers right now. My heart is cracking.

How could Noah do this to me? How could he just take that woman that shattered his heart years ago back into his life? Did he never stop loving her? Was our love a joke? And he doesn't even have the balls to call me, to tell me to my face this is over.

I slam the door behind me and collapse on to the couch. I press my palms to my eyes to keep the tears from falling.

But it doesn't work. I fold over into the crease of the couch blocking out the world.

I don't know how long I cry or when I fell asleep, the exhaustion from the past week and what happened with Noah taking over.

I feel a hand on my shoulder and roll over. Cole Farmer, the twenty-year-old up-and-comer, is sitting next to me. "You okay, Anna May?"

I wipe away any tears around my eyes as I sit up. "Um yeah, I just fell asleep. Tired is all."

His brow drops forward as he squints at me with whiskey-colored eyes that look almost gold. This kid is going to be a heartthrob. "I was sittin' in the corner when you walked in. You were cryin'," he says with his strong southern twang.

"Allergies," I mumble as I get up off the couch but Cole pulls me back down.

"I might be young but I know when things ain't right, Anna May. You been cryin'. I know those were tears. And I know I'm young. But I've seen my mama go through a fair share of broken hearts. You can talk to me."

I sigh as I lean back into the couch. A thousand emotions are running through me and I really do wish I had someone to talk to. But the only people I have are back in Asheville and I don't want to turn my phone on.

I look over at Cole, his skin bronzed from his time working on a farm back in Texas, his jaw square and little hairs are trying to make their way across it. He may be young but he has a heart of gold. And from the look in his molten eyes, I can tell he has seen a lot in his twenty years.

"Why has your mom had so many broken hearts?" I ask, keeping the subject off me.

He smirks and a dimple pops out on his left cheek. "Ever since Pa died when I was little, Mama spent a lot of her time tryin' to find a love like his. Hasn't worked out too well."

"Why not?" I ask.

Cole shrugs. "Her and Pa were best friends since they were five years old. They became high school sweethearts, married right after graduation. I was born a year later. They were your picturesque small-town love." He pauses, gripping his knees. "When he died, a big part of Mama died too. But she is so young and she just needed that kind of love in her life. She loves too hard. The men she loves are just with her for her looks."

His face grows sad as he speaks and I grab one of his hands. "I'm sure she will find someone one day."

He looks at me and smiles a sad smile. "I hope so." He leans back into the armrest of the couch so he is looking right at me, my hand still in his. "Who made you cry?"

I grab the necklace around my neck out of instinct. I've grabbed it more times than I can count.

"Let me guess," Cole says. "Whoever gave you that necklace."

"It's complicated." I snort, realizing I just gave the same answer I've been given by Noah and Carson.

"Love usually is."

I think Cole's words over. Maybe he is right. Love is complicated. It's not easy. Love is a messy thing. It's the explosion of a champagne bottle that wasn't settled enough. It's your dog that rolls in the mud and shakes it everywhere. Love is messy and hard and complicated.

"You should write about it," Cole says as he nudges my knee with his.

I shrug. "Too soon. The wound too fresh."

"That's the best time to write. Let it pour out of you. Let your heart bleed onto the page."

I bite my lip. My head is as messy as my heart. How am I supposed to find the right words?

"I'll help you."

I look over at Cole and see a flash of sadness in his eyes. Maybe he's been hurt too. He might be young but he's from a small town. He might just understand more than I think he does.

"Okay."

That infectious smile of his takes over his face, his dimples popping out. He swipes his hand through his blond hair before standing up and reaching his hand out for me. "Come with me. I found the perfect place to write here."

I grab my guitar as he pulls me out of the room and through an emergency exit door. "Where the hell are you taking me?"

He looks over his shoulder and winks. "You'll see."

We climb four sets of stairs before we exit onto the sixth floor of the building. He drags me to a set of elevators and hits the up button. I look around and see that we are on one of the business floors of the high rise we are in. The studio takes up half of the second floor. The bottom floor is restaurants and reception. The four floors between the studio and the businesses are a parking garage.

The elevator dings open just as someone starts to walk toward us yelling. I look at the rotund man, his face turning red as he tries to make it to the elevator. He is wearing a security uniform, his shirt buttons popping at his round center.

"Come on," Cole shouts, pulling me hard into the elevator just before the door shuts.

"Let me guess, we weren't supposed to be on that floor?" I ask as I tuck my hair behind my ear and set my guitar against the wall.

A goofy grin takes over his face as he smiles. "Nope," he says with a pop.

I look over at the elevator buttons and see he hit the button for the top floor. I raise a brow at him and he chuckles.

"I was hanging out in the stairwell last week and someone left the floor, I assume to go smoke in the garage. I slid through the door and took the elevator to the top. Once I found the place we are going I knew I needed to come back." He grins at me. "I waited for the smoker again and taped the lock on the door. No one has noticed."

I laugh just as the doors open to the top floor. I follow Cole out the elevator and to a door marked emergency exit. I have no idea where he is taking me as we climb another set of stairs that leads straight to another door.

"Ladies first," he says as he gestures to the door.

I look at him curiously but my curiosity gets the best of me and I open the door.

We are on the roof that overlooks the city of Nashville. I swear I can see miles away. I walk to the edge and peer down, Broadway booming a few streets over.

I start to walk around the entrance block to the nook where Cole is standing with a smile on his face. On the other side is a garden full of plants, a lush oasis in the middle of the city. I walk through the rows of greenery, my fingers brushing over the softness of the leaves and flowers. I can see a few garden beds with fresh fruits and vegetables growing.

When I come out on the other side a few couches are set up with lights hanging around it as well as a guitar and a notebook. I feel Cole approach behind me. "What is this place?"

"I found it randomly. I was having a day when I found

this place. I was looking for an escape and made it to the roof. I've been up here every day since."

I turn to face him. "Who's is it?"

His face flushes a little and I laugh as I see him get shy. "One of the restaurants downstairs. The chef has her own garden up here. Farm to table idea."

"She caught you?" I guess.

"I scared the shit outta her." He grabs the back of his neck and laughs. "But I remind her of her grandson so she let me stay up here. She even comes up here sometimes to listen to me play."

I look around and take in the space up here. It's beautiful. It reminds me of Asheville. The lush greenery bringing a sense of calm to my otherwise fucked-up life.

I take a seat on one of the couches, laying my guitar next to me. I close my eyes as I lean back, finding my center like I do in yoga. I breathe in and out, letting go of everything that happened earlier in the day.

When I finally open my eyes back up, Cole is looking at me.

"You alright?"

I nod. It's true, I do feel better. The open air, the plants, the calmness, it all feels better than being cooped up in the studio. "Shall we write some songs?"

Cole smiles at me as he sits across from me, picking up his guitar. "Let's do it."

I SIT in the corner of a bar in a dive and sip on a gin and tonic. Cole got an opportunity to play here at the last minute so Austin and I decided to come here and watch. No doubt in my mind things will move quickly for him. He is talented and a heartthrob.

We ended up spending hours last week writing songs on the roof of the building. Austin was blown away by what we wrote and kept both of us in Nashville longer. Cole has become such a good friend and an amazing songwriting partner. There is a spark between us when it comes to music and I hope we can write more together in the future.

I am heading home to Asheville tomorrow. And I am not sure what I am going home to. Noah called me a few days ago, the first time I heard from him in over a week. But I was too scared to answer the phone. I didn't want to lose the magic I was feeling with my work.

He didn't leave a message. And I am not sure if that is a good or bad thing.

"You sure you want to leave this place?" Austin asks me, shaking me from my thoughts.

This isn't the first time he asked me either. And even though my heart is broken and I have no idea what is going on with Noah, Asheville still feels like home. I pick at the hole in my jeans. "Yes. But that doesn't mean I don't love it here."

Austin nods as he sips on his beer. "You could make a lot of money here if you stayed."

I look up at him. "I can make a lot of money anywhere. I just write the songs, Austin."

"The labels and producers want you here."

"And I can come back when I am needed."

Austin places his hand on my knee. "Are you going to be okay?"

I haven't told him much. He has figured it out from my songs. "I'll figure it out."

He nods and takes his hand away. "You always know—"

"I can stay with you if I need to." I finish the sentence for him. He's told me that ten times in the last week.

"Ash likes you a lot."

I smile at that. His wife is adorable and amazing. The few days this week I stayed with them in their guest house she was a joy to be around. She always made sure I had food to eat and the quiet I needed to work. Their three kids are a bit rambunctious and liked to watch me play.

"I like her too. She is an amazing mom."

"She's a good wife."

"She is."

He flags down the bartender to order another round of drinks. "Don't let the bad times ruin your spirit, Anna. You have so much to give to the world."

24

ANNA

I THINK I HAVE BITTEN MY ENTIRE LIP OFF AS I DROVE home today. I talked to Noah for the first time last night in almost three weeks. I came back from Cole's show a bit tipsy and the anxiety of what I was walking into today weighed heavily on me.

We both cried when I talked to him. I didn't realize how much I missed his voice. We were both a blubbering mess of apologies and proclamations of love.

But he told me something that has had me anxious all day.

Claire is living in our house.

He didn't want to go into the details and I'm not sure I wanted to hear them.

I still am not sure.

I hung up after he told me. I didn't know what to think.

I couldn't sleep last night so I left early this morning. I said a quick goodbye to Austin and Ashley thanking them for their hospitality before heading back home.

I pull into our driveway a little before eleven and relax when I see Noah's SUV is here. I know this is his weekend on call and I did not want to walk into our home with him gone and Claire knitting on the couch.

I look in the rearview mirror and try to fix my hair. I didn't brush it this morning in my haste to leave and it looks like a mess. I swipe lip balm over my chewed lip and take a deep breath before heading into the house.

I walk across the path to the front of the house and climb the steps. My fingers shake as I grab the door handle. I don't know what I am going to see. I can only hope that the words we shared from the beginning of our conversation last night ring true.

The house is quiet as I walk through the front door. No sign of Noah, Claire, or Brutus. I look around and every-thing looks the same. No signs she is moving in and taking over. I walk past the guest room as I walk toward the kitchen. The door is open and it's clear someone is staying in there and I breathe a sigh of relief. All the flashbacks I was having of Kyle and Becca flutter away, knowing that Noah made her stay in the guest room.

I hear noise coming from the basement so I head to the door. When I try to grab the handle, it's locked. Noah never locks the door when he is down there. I start to panic a bit as an image of Noah and Claire together downstairs flashes across my mind. I put my ear to the door but the only sound I hear is Noah's grunts and the creak of the weight machine.

Brutus starts scratching at the door. He must have heard me walking around. I hear Noah tell him to calm down as I hear his steps as he walks up the stairs.

"Claire, I told you not to bother me when I'm working out." His mumbled words come through the door.

He opens the door and I stumble backward. My eyes going straight to his sweat slicked chest. I follow a drop of sweat as it drips down the center of his shirtless body, running down the ridges of his abs before hitting the edge of his shorts.

I look back up at Noah and meet his stare. His look of surprise quickly turns ravenous. Lust and need beating out of those sapphire eyes I've missed so much.

Words aren't needed as we crash into each other. A tangle of limbs and teeth. My mouth adhering to his in the most needed kiss of all time. He hefts me up, pulling my legs around his hips as he tries to carry me toward our bedroom.

Brutus yips and barks at his feet, no doubt wanting to say hello to me too. But I can't pull myself away from this man.

Noah presses me into the wall in the hallway, his lips going to my neck and ear, whispering a million I'm sorrys and I love yous all at once. I feel his stiff shaft against my stomach as I tell him it's okay and I love you and I'm sorry.

I grind down on his hips and he growls in my ear. He pulls me away from the wall as I pull my shirt over my head.

"Fuck, Anna, I need you right now," he says as he bites on my lip.

"Take me, Noah. I'm yours."

"I need to get you upstairs," he grunts as he pauses on the steps, pushing me back into the wall as he fumbles with the button on my jeans.

I grip his neck, kissing him hard before I push him off me. He stares at me as I unhook my bra, my full breasts teasing him as my nipples harden. I slowly walk up the stairs, swaying my hips as I go. I look over my shoulder and he is watching me with a predatory grin. I smirk at him as I get to the top of the stairs and slowly peel my pants and thong down. I kick them to the side and turn to look at him but he's already on me, pushing me toward the bed.

He shuts the door and locks it and then strips his own

shorts and briefs off. His cock his hard as he strokes it while staring at me. I bite my lip as I scoot back on the bed, spreading my legs for him.

He growls and is on top of me in a split second. His lips kiss me hard. Our kiss needy and wild. My hands grip his neck as his grip my thighs pushing them open. He slides into me with such force I nearly lose my breath.

But this is what we need. A mess of tongues, teeth, limbs, and love.

Grinding and moaning as we give each other what we desire.

An apology in the dirtiest sense as I let him own my body.

When we both find our release, he collapses on top of me, his hands in my hair.

"Anna. Mayberry. I love you. Please don't leave me like that again."

I can't help but laugh. He pulls away from me, a confused look on his face.

"Noah, I was leaving either way."

"We weren't okay when you left. We were in a fight."

I trace my finger down his face, over his slightly crooked nose, across his lips. "Then I guess that was the make-up sex."

I feel his dick stir as it sits inside of me. "Mayberry, that wasn't make-up sex. That was I missed you sex. You might not be able to handle make-up sex."

I giggle at that and his lips fall on mine.

"We need to talk, Noah. You need to explain all of this." My tone serious as I change the subject.

He sighs and pulls out of me.

He rolls onto his back and scrubs at his face.

I prop myself up on my side, leaning on my elbow, as I pull his hands away.

He looks at me and I know from that one look I want to spend forever with this man.

"This is all a bunch of shit. And I feel like no matter what I do, I am going to lose you," he admits.

I grab his hand as a reassurance I'm still here.

"Claire contested the divorce."

"Now? She can't do that."

He shakes his head. "She contested it before the divorce was finalized."

I scrunch my brow. "But I thought you said she never responded to anything."

"Apparently she did."

"I don't get it."

"Carson's trying to figure it out," he says with his eyes closed.

Something about this doesn't feel right. "So why is she here?"

He pulls away from me and sits up, gripping the back of his neck. "She had nowhere else to go."

"So, you decided it would be totally fine for her to stay here?" I bark.

"It wasn't an easy decision."

"Noah, it's a very easy decision. No. You should have told her no." I take a breath trying to calm the anger building inside of me. "And why didn't you ask me? You should have called me, Noah."

He turns to face me. "I called you, Anna. I called you a hundred times that first week you were gone. You didn't answer one of my calls. You didn't respond to any of my texts. What was I supposed to do?"

"You could have mentioned it in anyone of those damn texts and I would have called you," I yell.

"Then what?" he shouts. "You would have called me?

Yelled at me? Broken up with me? Anna, I already felt like I was losing you."

I climb off the bed and head to the dresser. "I needed space Noah. But apparently you thought if I decided not to come back you would have your backup plan here."

"She isn't a backup plan, Anna. She is my ex-wife," he growls.

I put on a bra and pull a shirt over my head. "Who is now living in our house!"

Noah gets up as I pull on a pair of yoga pants. "Why do you think I lock the doors? I do it so she can't get into our space."

I laugh at that as I storm to the closet for a pair of sandals. "She's in our space, Noah. This whole home is our space. Or did you forget you asked me to move in with you?"

He stands in the doorway of the closet, blocking me in. "Don't."

"Don't what?" I ask, crossing my arms over my chest.

"Don't do this again, Anna. Don't leave."

The last two words come out as a whisper. And I almost go to hold him because I can hear the pain in his voice. But then I hear her on the stairs.

"Stud muffin? I got us some lunch. I thought we could have a picnic," Claire singsongs from the other side of the bedroom door.

I look at Noah with disgust. "Seems she is adapting to being here just fine."

I try to push past him but he blocks me in. "Anna."

"Let me through, Noah."

"She means nothing to me."

I look up at him with venom in my eyes and voice. "Apparently neither do I."

I duck under his arm on the doorframe and attempt to

leave the room but he grabs me by the arm. "Don't leave me again."

I look down to where he is gripping my arm. "Let go of me."

He must hear the bitterness in my voice because he lets me go. I grip the door handle and look back at him one last time before unlocking the door.

Claire is on the other side of the landing as I make my way to the stairs.

"Oh hi, Anna. I didn't know you were here." Her voice drips sarcasm.

I shoot daggers at her as I step over the discarded clothing on the stairs and head out the front door without another word.

25

NOAH

I watch Anna walk out the door again and I feel like I lost her for real this time.

"Hey baby."

The sound of Claire's voice jolts me from my trance.

"You naked for me? I can be too."

I grab a pair of shorts out of a drawer and slide them on. "Fuck off, Claire."

"That's no way to talk to your wife."

"You're not my wife." I growl.

"We'll see about that," she retorts.

I push past her and head down the stairs and grab Brutus' leash and my keys. I cannot be around that woman. Anna was right. I should have told her no.

I jump in my car and head to Carson's office. It's Saturday but that man doesn't know how to take a day off. I need him to get this shit figured out fast.

I bring Brutus with me as we head inside. I storm past the empty reception desk and down the hall to his office.

I burst through the door. "We need to figure this shit out."

He looks up at me, startled, from whatever he was

searching through on the internet. "Christ. You could fucking knock."

I pace the floor as Brutus plops down on the expensive carpet. "I don't know why I listened to you. Why I let you talk me into Claire staying at my house."

He turns away from his computer screen and looks at me. "You haven't done your part of the plan."

I grip the short strands of my hair. "I looked through her shit when she left the house the other day but there is nothing there."

"What about her purse?"

"She always has it with her."

"Even when she showers?"

I stop pacing and stare at him. "I've never seen her shower." I sit in one of the chairs in front of his desk. "Fuck. She must only do it when I'm not home. There's got to be something in there."

Carson stands and walks over to the credenza. He pours us each a glass of bourbon and I gladly take it. "Maybe you should go back to your house after you leave for work."

I nod. "I can try. But I don't know what she does when I'm not there."

"We could send Mason."

"I'm not pulling him into this more than he already knows." I sip on my bourbon.

Carson stares at me like he is trying to read me. "You told Anna?"

I groan as I lean over my knees on my elbows. "Yeah. She didn't take it too well."

"Your ex-wife is living with you. I can't imagine she would."

I glare at him. "You told me to do it and you told me you would talk to Anna about it."

"And I thought we would have this figured out before

Anna came back."

"She was supposed to be back a week ago. You know we wouldn't have figured it out by then."

Carson shrugs as he walks over to the window looking out onto the park behind his office. "I told her to stay longer. In Nashville. I was hoping this would all be cleared up by then."

"You did what?" I growl.

He turns toward me, sympathy etched on his face. "I'm sorry, Noah. I didn't want to tell you and piss you off."

"What did you tell her?"

"It's not important," he states.

"It's fucking important, Car. She was already upset when she came home. And then I had to walk around the truth and all it did was piss her off more. She fucking left, Carson. She left and I don't think she is coming back this time."

Carson sits in the chair next to me. "I'll make this right."

"It's too late," I mumble.

I feel Carson's hand on my shoulder as I hold back tears. I am not crying in front of him. But I feel as if my life is falling apart again. But this time it feels worse than when Claire left me.

I GROAN as I roll over and look for my phone.

Carson and I got shit faced after our conversation.

And it was a stupid idea because I am on-call this weekend. If I got called in last night, I could have been suspended.

"Fuck," I groan as I look at my phone. It's my partner. "Hello?"

"There's been another murder."

"Okay. Text me the address. I'll meet you there."

"You sound like shit."

"I'll be there."

I hang up on him and grip my head. It feels like a thousand drummers in my brain, banging against my skull. I sit up and see my bedroom door is wide open. Did I forget to lock it in my drunken stumble up the stairs last night?

I rub my eyes and look around the room. Why the hell is there women's underwear on the floor?

Footsteps sound up the stairs and Anna walks into the room. She stares at me and I stare right back. Did she come home last night?

"I just came to get some things." She pauses. "You look like shit."

I nod as I get out of bed. The urge to puke rising up my throat. I watch Anna as she heads toward the closet but stops in front of the panties on the ground. "What's this?"

Fucking hell.

"What the hell, Noah? You really did decide to move on. Didn't take long."

That's when I notice the bra on the floor too. Way too small to be Anna's. "Anna, I don't know—"

"You don't know what happened?" She spits in my face. "Let me guess. You got drunk last night with your ex-wife and then fucked her in our bed."

She storms into the closet and walks out with a duffel bag. She starts shoving clothes from the dresser into it. "Dammit, Noah. I just needed space. I needed to think and you do this to us."

I can hear her voice waver as she is on the verge of tears. But I also know I would never touch my ex-wife. And I sure as hell know I didn't have sex with anyone last night. I was too drunk for my dick to do anything. I get up and walk over to her. "Anna..."

She puts her hand in my face. "Don't, Noah. I can't take this again."

I grab her despite her protests and wrap her in my arms. Her tears fall and she struggles against my arms.

"I loved you, Noah. I loved you so much."

I don't miss the past tense of her words. The words breaking my heart into more pieces than it was already in. "I didn't do anything."

She pushes off me. "The evidence says otherwise."

Claire walks through the door wearing one of my t-shirts. She has a plate of food in her hand and a glass of orange juice. "Hey babe. Thought you would want some breakfast after last night."

Fucking psychotic bitch.

My eyes dart to Anna who is taking in the entire scene. Her lip quivers as she picks the duffel up off the ground.

"Oh hey, Anna," Claire says with a hint of pride in her voice. "I didn't realize you came to get your things."

Tears stream down Anna's face and I try to grab her but she backs up before I can touch her. She shakes her head at me and mouths a fuck you before she takes off down the stairs.

"Anna," I shout as I take off after her, pushing Claire out of the way. I run out into the front yard, aware I only have on boxer briefs and watch as she struggles to throw the bag in her car. "Please, listen to me."

She slams the back door and opens the driver's side door. "Noah, there is nothing you can say to me anymore. I've heard enough. I've seen enough." She points toward the house. "The minute you let her walk through that door when she showed up on your doorstep was the day we were done."

She slides into her car and slams the door. I watch her drive away until her taillights turn the corner.

"Motherfucker," I shout as I storm back into the house.

Claire is standing in the living room, that snake-like grin on her face.

"What the fuck was that!" I yell at her.

She shrugs. "Poor timing on her part."

"What the hell did you do, Claire?"

She grins at me. "Whatever I needed to make you mine again."

I walk up to her and get in her face. "When are you going to realize I will never be yours?"

Her hands go to my briefs. "That's not what you said last night."

I push her hands off me. "Nothing happened last night. You set this whole thing up."

"Baby, I would never do that."

I clench my fists. "Get out of my house."

She looks up at me and smiles.

"I mean it, Claire. I need you gone. Out. Take all your shit and leave. And get that fucking underwear you planted out of my room."

She pouts. "But where am I supposed to go?"

"I don't fucking care!" I start to walk away.

"You're just like him. You don't care about me."

I stop in my tracks and turn. "Who?"

Her eyes go big and I know she didn't mean to say those words.

"Like who, Claire?"

She shakes her head and runs to the guest bedroom shutting the door behind her.

I can hear my phone ringing upstairs and I take the steps two at a time. Marcus called me again. I text him that I'll be there in twenty and jump into the shower, hoping to wash away the shit show that just became my life.

TWENTY-FIVE MINUTES later I am standing next to Marcus at the crime scene. It looks just like the one from last week. We do our job and my headache slowly dissipates.

We head toward Marcus' car. I had to Uber here since I left mine at Carson's house.

"Where's your car?" Marcus asks me.

"At my brother's," I answer honestly. He knows I was off my game today. And I am sure he knows I am hungover.

He nods at me. "Want a ride?"

"Sure." I know he is going to hound me for my behavior. I just hope he doesn't report it and get me suspended.

I give him the address to my brother's house and he pulls out on the road. "How much did you drink last night?"

I look out the window. "Enough to not do it again."

"I could report you. I know you weren't drunk when you showed up but you weren't one hundred percent."

"I don't usually drink like that. It won't happen again."

"What's going on, man? You were great your first month. But these last few weeks it's like a whole other person is my partner."

I sigh as I hear it. I was hoping I had managed to keep up my appearances.

"And in case you are wondering, no one else has noticed. Just me."

I breathe a sigh of relief at that.

"I know we don't know each other all that well. We've only been partners a handful of weeks but I see this as a long relationship. I don't see either of us quitting anytime soon. So whatever is going on in your head or your life, you can tell me. That's the benefit of a partner."

I know he's right. My first partner I was close as hell

with before he retired. He helped me get through Claire leaving me and the divorce. Niko and I hit it off from the beginning. But for some reason I have kept all this shit under lock and key this time.

"Everything okay with you and Anna?" Marcus asks me.

I clench my jaw as this morning plays on repeat in my head. I can feel Marcus looking at me. I might as well tell him. "No."

"You two looked chummy has hell that day at Jimmy's."

"Things changed," I mumble, my head turning back to look out the window.

"As in?"

"My ex-wife showed up on my doorstep."

"Oh," Marcus says flatly.

"And she claims our divorce is false and is trying to win me back. Of course, she was dismissive and horrible toward Anna. And I didn't defend her."

"Bad move."

I roll my eyes. "Yeah I know that now. We got into a fight and then she left for Nashville." I pause before I say the worst of it all. "And then me being the guy I am let Claire, my ex, stay in my guest room when she came crawling back to me and said she had nowhere to go."

"Another bad move."

"I know. And I didn't tell Anna. Not until the night before she came back. Of course, she came back and we got into another huge fight. Then this morning she came home to pack a bag and Claire staged a whole scene that makes me think I lost Anna for good."

Marcus looks over at me. "Do I even want to know?"

I shrug. "I got shit-faced with my brother last night even though I knew I shouldn't but all this stuff was pissing me the hell off. I've been keeping my bedroom door locked but I passed out last night. Claire threw underwear on the floor of my room. I don't know how she knew Anna was stopping by or maybe it was just luck she did and Claire wanted me to think something happened between us. Anyway, Claire walks into the room in one of my shirts, nothing else, and starts making comments about last night being fun."

"Ouch."

I rub my hand through my hair. "Yeah, so now I feel fucked."

"I don't blame you."

"The worst part is my brother convinced me to let Claire stay with me. It wasn't my idea and now it's biting me in the ass."

"Why would your brother do that?"

"He wants to see if I can dig up dirt on her."

"Why does she say the divorce isn't valid?"

"When she left me, no one could find her. It took a year before my brother's P.I. found her in New Jersey. He tried to get her to sign papers for six months and not once did she respond. The judge filed the divorce. And now she is saying she did sign papers contesting the divorce but we never got them." I am not telling him Carson is a corrupt asshat who hid them.

"Don't those things usually need to be signed for when they are delivered?"

I look at him quizzically.

"I'm divorced too. All those documents required signatures on delivery."

I hadn't thought about that and I'm guessing Carson didn't either, considering he didn't know the mail had been sitting on his desk for a few days. Unless his secretary signed.

"If there is no proof they were delivered, it won't hold in court."

"You're right. I'll have my brother look into it."

"You think she is hiding something else too?"

I nod and tell him all about her expensive car and clothes and the way she is acting.

"She sounds crazy. Did she escape the psych ward?"

Marcus' comment brings a smile to my face. The first I've had all day. "It feels like it."

"But you can't find any information on her?"

"Nothing. His P.I. is going crazy but there is no trace of her on any records."

"I'm guessing you both assume she changed her name."

"That's why Carson wanted me to have her move in. But I haven't been able to get into her purse."

"Does she like to go out for drinks?"

I look over at him confused. "I don't know. I mean she has gone out a few nights."

"I can help, man."

"How?"

He parks in front of my brother's house and turns off the engine. "I could stake your house. See when she leaves, follow her to a bar, and you know."

I laugh at that. "You are going to seduce my ex-wife?"

"If it gets you out of this funk, I'll do what I can."

I shake my head and smirk. "It might be the only thing that works." I look at my brother's house and turn back to my partner. "Carson has a P.I. watching my house. He can follow her and I'll let you know where she goes."

"Nothing like good old fashion police work."

I open the car door and step out. "Thanks for the ride. And listening."

"We're only as good as our partner."

I nod at him and shut the door before heading into Carson's house.

26

ANNA

Seraphina braids my hair as I sit on the floor in front of her sipping a lemon martini.

My fifth lemon martini.

To be honest it's mostly vodka.

And I'm pretty drunk.

I spent five hours crying after I left Noah this morning. Then three hours yelling and being pissed off at the world before Seraphina poured me a glass of straight vodka and told me to shut up.

Now that I'm sufficiently hammered I feel calmer.

Sort of.

I'm not seeing red anymore. But my heart feels like it's been covered in ice and shattered, the pieces melting slowly, no hope of ever being put back together.

I've made Seraphina watch documentaries the last few hours even though she hates them. She tried to get me to watch crime shows but they reminded me of Noah.

Everything reminds me of him.

Hell, I am wearing one of his shirts now because I just can't let him go. He loved me deeply and I felt that love all the way to my bones. I worry that now my heart has shattered, my bones may shatter too. Because his love was everywhere inside of me.

"Girl, you better not be crying again." Seraphina pulls on my hair.

I hiccup and swallow down the tears. "I'm not."

She finishes up the second Dutch braid on my head. "Liar. We need a total subject change. Why don't you tell me about Nashville?"

"I've already told you everything."

She pulls on my shoulders and peers over me. "Not everything. Tell me about that hot singer who you spent the week with."

I roll my eyes at her and push her away. "You make it sound like something else happened besides songwriting when you say it like that."

She raises her brows up and down at me. "Is that what they are calling it these days? Songwriting? I need to get my innuendos straight."

I stand up and grab my empty glass, half stumbling to the kitchen. "You do have a boyfriend. Do you not remember?"

She follows me into the kitchen. "Who, Darnell?"

"Already forgotten after picturing a tall, sexy, blond-haired, brown-eyed cowboy?" I tease.

"Sounds dreamy," she whispers resting her elbows on the counter and placing her chin in her palms.

I throw a lemon at her. "He's twenty years old."

"Age is just a number."

"And what about Darnell?"

She flutters her hand at me as she walks to the fridge and pulls out a bottle of chardonnay. "Darnell who?"

I stare at her in shock. "What do you mean Darnell who?"

She shrugs and pours a heavy amount of wine into her oversized glass. "I didn't want to tell you when you were in Nashville. But I broke up with him."

"What?" I shriek. "But you two were like fire and gasoline."

She gulps down a huge amount of wine and smirks. "It was hot and heavy. Chemistry was never our problem."

"Then what was?"

She bites her lip and looks at me, honesty in her eyes. "I want to be someone's priority. Not their backup plan."

I sip my martini, this one with triple sec in it, figured I should slow down. "I don't think you were his backup plan."

"It was the same shit as last time. He wants me to go on tour with him. I told him I have a business here and I can't leave. He said I wasn't willing to make sacrifices and I told him he wasn't either." She stops and finishes the glass of wine that was half full. "Then he said his music was always first and if I couldn't wrap my head around that then we could never be together."

"He did not say that!"

"Fucking asshole sure did. I slapped him, kicked him in the balls, and stormed out of his house."

"You did not!" I say, mouth agape.

"You bet your perfect peach ass I did."

I wrap my arms around her in a tight embrace. "You are a badass, my friend."

Her arms go around me. "Why are men such assholes?"

"Because they think with their dicks."

"Mmm. You're right."

I pull away from her and reach for the shot glasses she has displayed on a floating shelf next to her kitchen. "We should get drunk."

"You already are."

"We should get drunker. Fuck, men."

Sera smirks at me. "Says the woman head over heels in love with a man who is head over heels for her even with his recent behavior."

"I'm not talking about Noah anymore."

"Fine. But we can't get too drunk, we have to teach tomorrow."

I clench my stomach. "Ugh I think we both have food poisoning from that takeout."

Sera grabs a bottle of tequila out of a cabinet and raises a brow at me. "You're right. I'm not feeling well either. I'll text the other instructors."

We both laugh and take shots to drink away the problems in our love lives.

Sera heads to the living room and turns on the YouTube app on her television. "Now let's watch that sexy singer. Cole who?"

I SHUT my phone off and slam it in a drawer at the bar. Noah has been relentless. Texting me to come home. I want to. More than anything I want to fall asleep wrapped up in his arms and wake up to that sexy smile on his face. But I am not comfortable with the situation. I don't want to be around Claire.

I went to the studio two days ago to work on a song that's been in my head for a while. Mason was able to get me some recording time in so I could send it to Austin. Mason let me know more of what's going on with Claire. I'm pissed that Noah didn't tell me but Mason said he didn't even think he had the whole story. Noah and Carson have been tight lipped on the whole thing.

I wish Noah would tell me everything. But he is too

stubborn. Whatever secret they are keeping, I would keep too. It would help build my trust back with Noah. But I am not giving in. He needs to come to me and let me in.

"Another text from lover boy?" Liam asks me.

"Stop calling him that."

"Fine. Officer McDreamy?" He grins as he dries a glass.

I wipe down the bar and smile. "It's Detective McDreamy now."

"And has he used those handcuffs on you yet?"

I blush as I remember that day with the handcuffs. How special that day was. How happy I was. "I don't want to talk about him."

"He's been texting you ten times a day, Anna. And that's just when you are at home. Who knows how much he texts you when I can't hear that damn chime on your phone go off."

I moved in with Liam four days ago. After spending two nights on Sera's couch and waking up with a stiff neck, I couldn't do it anymore. Luckily, it's the beginning of April and one of Liam's roommates moved out of the house he rents. I have a fully furnished room and a private bathroom. Liam told me I can stay there as long as I want rent-free and that he won't look for someone to move in until I move out.

"Other people text me, you know."

"He texts you more than anyone else."

I prop my hip against the bar. "How do you know?"

Liam gives me a strange look and then heads to the end of the bar to serve a customer before answering me.

Another patron waves me down and I grab another drink order, pondering Liam's lack of response.

We start to pick up and I don't get the chance to talk to Liam much and bug him for an answer as the typical Friday night crowd pours into the bar.

I'm busy making a pitcher of margaritas for a table when I do a double take at a familiar head of strawberry-blond hair. I spill tequila all over the bar when she turns and I see Claire's face.

What the hell is she doing here?

"You okay?" Liam asks me, gesturing toward the spill.

"Yep, okay. I'm just fine," I mumble as I dump the pitcher and start over.

I keep glancing toward Claire. Liam must notice because his eyes follow mine. "Is that the ex-wife?"

I don't know how he figured it out. "Huh?"

"Come on, baby girl, I've never seen so much malice in your eyes as when you looked over there."

I finish the pitcher and set it at the end of the bar at the waitress station. I watch as Liam walks over to Claire, checks her ID, and pours her a glass of wine.

He walks up to me as I pour a few beers for a group of college kids. "Maybe not."

"What?" I ask, not paying attention to him.

"Her ID said Marie and I know the ex's name is Claire."

"Marie?" I ask as I glance back over at the woman I thought was Claire.

"Guess not," Liam says and walks away from me.

I bring the beers over to the guys and stare at Claire. I am so confused. That is definitely her but why would she have an ID that says Marie.

"Am I wrong?" Liam asks me.

I shake my head. "No, that is most definitely Claire. I can tell from the dirty looks she is sending me."

"Weird. Her ID said Marie and it was her picture."

I shrug not knowing why she would have a different ID. "Maybe she goes by her middle name."

"Maybe. There wasn't one on the ID."

"Can you serve her for the rest of the night?"

Liam wraps an arm around my waist. "Whatever you need, baby girl."

An hour passes and Claire is still here. Liam has kept his promise and served her but Liam took a break and a new customer sits down to her right. "Fuck me," I mutter as I walk over to grab their order.

"Are you moving out anytime soon?" she says to me before I can walk away.

"Excuse me?"

She trails a finger around the rim of her wine glass. "Noah and I would appreciate if you moved your stuff out."

I scoff. I know I should walk away but this bitch pisses me off. "As far as I am concerned that is still my home."

"Doesn't seem like it since you look like you moved on."

"What are you talking about?"

"Your coworker. You two seem quite friendly."

I hold back so I don't blow up on her. "Oh you mean my friend."

"The way he wrapped his arm around you looked awfully friendly."

I clench my fist at my side. "That's what friends do when they have your back."

She raises a perfectly sculpted brow at me. "Whatever you say. I just want your stuff out. All those instruments are blocking my way in the sunroom."

"As far as I know, Noah is doing you a favor by letting you stay there."

She sneers at me. "Then why is he finding comfort in me since you moved out."

I take a deep breath as I hold back my anger. "I needed space from you."

"Well Noah seems to be perfectly content cozying up to me while you are gone."

"I don't think Noah is anywhere near you. He is

pushing me to get Anna back home every day," Liam says from behind me.

I look over my shoulder at him, not sure if he is lying or telling the truth.

"My husband is not leaving me for you."

I lean over the bar at that and get as close to her face as possible. "He is not your husband."

"Sure felt like it this morning as he fucked me."

Liam pulls me back just when I am about ready to jump over the bar. "You should leave."

"I am a paying customer. I am not leaving. In fact, I would like another merlot," she says, finishing her glass.

Liam grabs her glass and pulls me away. "She is trying to get to you," he says.

"I hate her."

"Why don't you switch with Cass."

I glare at him.

"Just until she leaves. You can serve, she can bartend."

"Fine," I say as I storm off to find her. I am too old for this petty bullshit.

For the next thirty minutes I wait on tables impatiently waiting for Claire to leave. I have no idea why she is here. Maybe she found out I work here and will do whatever she can to piss me off.

I can't help but watch her whenever I get the chance. She openly flirts with the guy next to her and it drives me wild.

I bring drinks to another table when I see Noah's partner walk in and take a seat next to Claire. I watch them interact for almost an hour before he leaves with her.

Cass finds me and takes over for me and I head back to the bar.

"That was strange," Liam says to me as he grabs some beers.

"What was?"

Liam wipes down the bar. "That she was here, talked a bunch of shit about fucking Noah, and then leaves with someone else."

"That was Noah's partner."

Liam glances at me and stops what he's doing. "Even more weird."

I nod. "I don't think he knows about her or who she is. Noah takes a while to open up to people."

"Well baby girl this just proves my point even more." He uses his thumb to point to the door. "If that woman was dead set on keeping Noah, she wouldn't be going home with random men. I think she knows that Noah only has eyes for you. She is trying to get under your skin."

"Maybe."

Liam grabs both my shoulders and leans over so we are standing eye to eye. "Anna, I am ninety-nine percent sure that man wants to marry you. Don't give up on him."

I gape at Liam. Noah doesn't want to marry me. We've been together for a handful of months. We just moved in together. He can't really think I am the one. Right?

I GET CUT at one in the morning which is fine by me. I am tired. Physically and emotionally. I wish life could go back to how it was on my birthday or our time at the beach. Those moments with Noah are etched in my brain. Both of us with our guards down, opening up to the other. I miss that connection with him.

Hell, I just miss him.

I am in love with the man despite the shit that went down with Claire. I know Liam is right. I know Noah still loves me. I can see it in his battle for me every day. Maybe I should give in. But I cannot deal with Claire. I want it to be just Noah and me. So we can find us again.

I round the corner of the building and walk through the parking lot. I stop dead in my tracks when I find my window smashed in.

Who the hell would do that? My car is a piece of shit and I never keep anything of value in it.

I investigate the broken window and find a note laying on the seat. I've spent enough time around Noah to know I shouldn't touch it. I call the police and then carefully lean over the window to see if I can read the note.

I gasp and step backward when I do.

I loved him and you took him away.

What the fuck? Who the hell would do this?

My mind immediately goes to Claire. She was here tonight and she had a few choice words for me. And it would make sense that she would say those things. I am beginning to think she is crazy.

The cops show up ten minutes later and ask me a handful of questions.

"Where were you? Did you see anyone? How long has your car been here? Do you have any enemies? Did you have sexual relations with a man in a relationship?"

The questions go on for five minutes. And they are all pointless. Considering I am as baffled as them.

"Can you just take the evidence and let me go. I'm tired and I want to go home."

The officer looks at me. "Ma'am, do you know something we don't."

"Give her a break," a familiar voice says.

I look up and see Niko walking toward me. I smile at

him, glad I have a friendly face here instead of this asshole who thinks I had something to do with this. The temperature is dropping and I'm cold standing around in shorts and a light hoodie.

"Hey Anna."

"Hi Niko."

"You cold?" he asks me as a shiver runs through me. "Yo asshat, get the woman a blanket. She's a victim, not a suspect."

"Thanks, Niko."

"You find this when you left work?"

I nod. "Can you guys get it cleaned up?"

The other cop brings me a blanket. Niko shakes his head. "Sorry but we need to call in a detective."

My heart drops to my stomach. "Why? It's just some random attack. Someone who has something against me."

"More than likely," Niko says as he peers into my car. "But, shit, I can't really tell you this. But I am sure Noah will tell you anyway. But that rapist turned serial killer has started leaving notes for his victims before he kills them."

The blood drains from my face. "What?"

He looks over my shoulder and then back at me. "You didn't hear it from me."

"Miss Cooper?"

I turn to see two men in suits walk up to me. They look vaguely familiar. I've probably served them at Jimmy's.

"I'm Detective Wells and this is Detective Stone. I know the cops asked you questions already but we just need to ask you a few more."

I nod and tell them everything I told the officers. Detective Stone walks away to inspect my car as an evidence team gathers the note and whatever the hell else they are doing. The other detective joins his partner and I wrap the blanket tighter around me as my mind goes in a million different directions. *What the hell is going on?*

"Anna."

I stiffen at Noah's voice.

"Are you okay?"

I turn to look at him. He looks miserable. His eyes bloodshot like he hasn't been sleeping, his hair a mess like he's been running his hands through it over and over.

Just seeing him has my heartrate increasing. I want him so bad. I want him to comfort me. I want him to make this all go away.

But I need to stand my ground. I cannot give in so easily.

I shake my head, knowing he wants an answer.

He closes the distance between us immediately wrapping his arms around me. "Baby, you're freezing."

He must feel me shivering. I am not sure if it's because I'm cold or nerves.

"Come sit in my car. It's warm."

I silently agree even though I don't want to.

He opens the door for me and I crawl in. He reaches over me and adjusts the dials on the console to turn up the heat. He opens the liftgate of his SUV and grabs another blanket, wrapping it around my legs.

"Detective Taylor." I hear someone shout.

Noah looks me in the eye, worry etching face. "I'll be right back."

"Okay."

He shuts the door and I watch him walk over and talk to the other detectives.

I close my eyes and lean my head against the headrest. The smell of Noah's cologne infiltrates my nose. I miss that smell. It smells like home.

I must doze off because I am startled when I hear a door

open. I open my eyes and find Noah sitting in the driver's seat looking at me. "They will have your car ready for you tomorrow. I'm taking you home."

"I'm sure Liam will be off work soon. He can take me."

Noah looks over at me, seriousness written in his eyes. "You are coming with me."

That really wakes me up. "I can't, Noah."

"I don't care if you can't. I need to make sure you are safe."

"It was just some random violence."

"Niko told me he told you about the case. I am not taking risks with your life."

I look at him, rage building inside of me. "You should have thought about all those things before you agreed to let Claire move in."

He sighs and rests his forehead on the steering wheel. "Anna, my biggest regret is doing that. It's driven you away. Every day that passes that I wake up without you by my side my heart breaks more."

Godammit. Why does he have to say those things?

I reach over and grab his hand. "Noah, I still love you. I tried not to. I tried to let you go but it's fucking impossible. But I can't be around her."

"I know."

"You know I love you or you know I can't be around her?"

"Both," he acquiesces. "I just want you near me."

"I know." I squeeze his hand and he looks at me with a sad grin. "Claire came to the bar tonight. She's a cunt."

That gets a smile out of him. "She is crazy. She is not the woman I was married to."

"Glad to hear that because I was beginning to think you are psychotic too."

He reaches over the center console and cups my face. "I love you, Anna. And I am trying to make this right."

I press my cheek into the comfort of his palm. "I know."

"I'll take you to Liam's."

"Really?"

He gives me a curt nod. "It's not what I want but it's what you want."

"Thank you."

The drive to Liam's is silent, both of us thinking about everything that's happened. I wish I could go home with Noah. See Brutus' sloppy face. Curl up on the sofa in Noah's arms as we watch some stupid action movie. But the reality is we both need this space and time apart to get our lives in order.

Noah parks on the street in front of Liam's house. We both sit there. I don't want to say goodbye to him. Not after what happened tonight.

"Want to come inside?" I ask him.

He hesitates. And it breaks my heart a little. "I should go home."

"Okay," I say in defeat. "Thank you for the ride."

He nods. "I'll let you know when your car is ready."

"Thanks."

I get out of the car and head up the driveway. My heart breaking. I want nothing more than to feel Noah's arms around me. But he is doing what I asked, giving me space.

I make it to the front step of the house and look for my keys when I feel his presence behind me.

I drop my bag to the ground just as his lips hit mine.

The kiss brings back the chills I had earlier. A mix of need and want tied perfectly with a bow. It doesn't last long but it was enough. Noah grabs my hand and squeezes holding on to it as he walks away. He lets it go and walks back to his car.

I head inside and go straight to bed. I curl up around a pillow wishing it was Noah's body.

My phone chimes with a text and I relax a little as I read it.

Noah: You'll be back in my arms soon. I love you.

27

NOAH

I sit at my desk looking over evidence from the past two murders and comparing notes when Marcus drops a sheet of paper on my desk. It's a picture of three IDs, all with Claire's face on them.

I look up at him. "Do I even want to know what you had to do to get these?"

He shakes his head. "Probably not."

I mock throwing up in a garbage can and Marcus chuckles at me. "I didn't sleep with her, Noah."

"I couldn't care less if you did."

Marcus looks at me strangely. "You seem to be in a better mood."

I smile at him, a genuine smile, not the fake one I have been sporting around the precinct for the last month.

Ever since I took Anna home on Friday night she has been texting me every day. Our conversation gave me hope in us. And I think she felt the same. I didn't want to fight with her. I did just want her to come home with me so I could watch over her but I know she needs her space. I don't blame her. If Kyle were alive I wouldn't want him living with us.

All I needed to hear were those three words from Anna and she gave them to me freely. She still loves me. And the kiss we shared reassured me things will be okay. And that's enough to let me continue to make do in the situation we are in. I know she is safe with Liam. He would never let anything hurt her but the case I'm working on weighs heavily.

As I review evidence that the note in her car is not the MO of our perp, I release a sigh of relief, but I want to know who the hell left that note in her car. She told me Claire was at the bar Friday night. The words on the note make sense with Claire's madness. But we ran some prints and they aren't Claire's.

And now that Marcus got this information for me I am so much closer to having Anna come home. I smile at Marcus. "I am in a better mood. This helps a lot," I say as I hold up the paper.

"Oh, that's not all, Taylor. Not only does she seem to have three identities, but I found something even better." He throws a stack of papers on my desk. "I found multiple credit cards with the name Eduardo Torres on them in her wallet. So I did some digging. Torres is married. Married to a woman named Marie Torres maiden name DeWitt. The same name that shows up on that ID."

"She changed her name. Why couldn't we find this out before? We searched her social."

He points at the papers on my desk. "She changed her name twice. Once right after she left you. I think that must have been the name you found. And then she must have changed it again when she met Torres. But somehow she changed her social because it's a different number. It's why you couldn't find her. Her and Torres have been married for almost four years. He has a huge investment firm. Lives on the upper east side of Manhattan."

Four years? We were still married at that point. Which means this marriage isn't legal.

"I also found court documents. He is filing for divorce."

I scan through all the information Marcus found out. If my divorce doesn't stand with the court, then she would have been legally married to me when she married someone else. We have proof of her having two social security numbers so her new marriage would be null and void. "I'm guessing she was hoping to get money out of her husband."

"It would appear so but she signed a prenup. She can't get anything from him."

"Then why would she come back to me?"

Marcus sits on the corner of my desk. "If your divorce was never legal like you said she is trying to prove then she could be coming to you for the money."

I shake my head. "That makes no sense. She had a good job when I was going through that divorce. She was doing fine for herself. I wouldn't have had such harsh terms if I thought she needed help."

Marcus grabs his chin like he's thinking. "I couldn't find a job history for Marie Dewitt or Marie Torres, at least for the last three years."

"I need to go talk to my brother." I gather up all the papers on the desk and shove them into a manila envelope. "Marcus, you didn't need to do all this."

He shrugs as he stands. "Like I said, you're only as good as your partner. I need to make sure you have my back like I do yours."

I smack him on the shoulder. "I owe you one."

"You owe me more than one!" he shouts as I race out of the precinct.

I BARGE through my brother's office door and find him on the phone. He flips me the bird as I shut the door behind me. I throw the envelope on his desk and he opens it while saying mmhmms and rights on the phone.

He flips through the documents, his eyes bugging out as he reads.

"I need to go," he says into the phone, hanging up immediately. "Where the hell did you get this?"

"Marcus seduced her to get her IDs."

"No shit." He looks up at me for a second with a smirk. "This is fucked up. That woman is crazy."

"No shit."

He mumbles as he looks over the evidence. "If her marriage to you is considered legal still, then this marriage is null and void. What is she after?"

"Marcus found a prenup on that marriage. She wasn't going to get a penny."

"If Torres finds out about this it will make it a lot easier on him. I need to look into his divorce proceedings. I'll contact his lawyer."

"I thought when you finally found her she had a good job. Why would she need money?"

Carson shrugs. "Who knows, but I'll have my P.I. dig deeper into all these IDs." He pauses over the pictures and squints. "Dewitt? Why does that name sound familiar?"

"I've never heard it."

Carson jolts from his chair and runs over to his safe, punching in the code and pulling out a folder. He flips it open and a predatory smile crosses his face. He sits back at his desk and types into his computer. I wait patiently for whatever breakthrough he just had when he throws the papers he pulled out of the safe at me.

"Those are the documents I received right before your divorce was finalized. The papers showing she contested the divorce. But after you said something to me about them needing to be signed for I racked my brain over and over. They came in a regular envelope. Nothing special. But I didn't think too much of it. Look at the name of the law firm."

I glance down and see M. Dewitt Law Offices as the sender. I glance up at Carson just as he spins the monitor around. "They don't exist." He switches over to a new screen and shows me a generic-looking template of a letter contesting a divorce on the internet that looks exactly like the one in my hand.

"She made it up."

"Bingo, brother. That is not a legal document. She didn't have a lawyer."

"My divorce is still legal?"

"As far as I can tell. But I need to find out a few more things. And I need to get in contact with Eduardo Torres' lawyer."

I stand and breathe a sigh of relief.

Carson walks around the desk and gives me a hug. "This is almost over, Noah. You can get your girl."

I PARK in the street outside of Liam's and take huge strides to the door. The text from Liam didn't tell me much just that I needed to come over right away.

Liam opens the door for me, and I am thankful he's been here. I didn't like her living here at first because of his roommates but he's kept an eye on her. And he texts me updates all the time.

I follow him into the living room and find Anna as pale as a ghost sitting on the couch.

"It was in the mailbox," Liam says.

I look at him and then glance at the coffee table to find another letter sitting on it, just like the one we found in Anna's car.

I rush to Anna's side and wrap her in my arms before I look at the note.

You won't get away with this.

"That's it," I say to her. "You're coming home."

She shakes my arm off her. "Noah, I can't. I told you I won't be in that house with her."

I should tell her everything that is going down with Claire, everything we found out, but right now all I see is red for whoever is leaving these notes for her.

"I can't protect you here."

"I don't need protection," she grits.

I gesture to the note. "Clearly you do if you are being threatened."

"And what if it's Claire, what if she is leaving these notes for me?"

I grip the back of my neck. "It's not. We ruled her out. The best place you can be is under my watch."

"No."

"Anna, listen to him," Liam interjects.

"I won't be made a fool of," she says as she paces the living room.

I groan as I stand in front of her. "You won't be."

"I'm not going."

Fuck this. I know she won't listen to me. She never would have told me about this note, it was Liam who texted me. I hate to do this but I have no other choice. I grab her around the waist and hoist her over my shoulder.

"Noah, put me down."

"No," I state as Liam clearly understands my intention

and runs to the door to open it for me. "You are coming home."

"You cannot force me to do this."

"Too bad. I am."

I manage to open the back door of my SUV issued by the police department. It's got a screen and child locks so she won't be able to fight me.

"You are treating me like a child!" she huffs as I throw her into the back seat.

"No, I am treating you like the love of my life and all I want to do is protect you." I slam the door and move around to the driver's seat.

The drive back to our house is silent. I glance at her through the rearview mirror a few times but she sits with her arms crossed, glaring at me.

I breathe a sigh of relief to see Claire's car isn't around. I get out of the car and open the back door for Anna. She jumps out and storms into the house.

I follow her inside, pushing Brutus away as I watch her climb the steps. I follow her into the bedroom. She stops in front of the bed, her fists clenched at her sides.

I shut the door behind me and lock it.

"You going to lock me in this room like some kind of damsel?"

"Anna," I sigh. "I'm not locking you in here. We need to talk."

"I'm tired of talking, Noah. I don't want to hear any more about that bitch living downstairs. I just want her gone."

"She will be sooner than you think."

She rolls her eyes at me and her hand goes to the necklace I gave her. "This is getting old, Noah."

"I know."

"Ugh, why can't we just go back to how it was before?"

she says, flustered. "I keep holding on to this false hope that we can but I am not so sure anymore."

"Anna."

"No, I'm done, Noah. I've had my heart pulled in too many directions. I don't care if you aren't fucking her. I just need peace and I can't have it with her around. We need to just end this. Maybe when it's all over we can find our way back to each other."

"And you think I am at peace in this situation?"

She crosses her arms over her chest. "I don't see you doing anything to change it."

"I'm working so hard to fix this. Fix us, Anna. I need you."

"I don't think you do."

"Fuck," I yell. "We are so close, Anna. The divorce will hold up, I promise you that."

"Can you promise me you don't have feelings for her?"

"Why would you even ask that?"

"Why else would you let her move in?"

I walk right up to her and get in her face. "I don't."

"You kissed her."

"It was an accident." I growl.

She pokes me in the chest hard with her callused finger. "And how do I know there haven't been other *accidents* when I was in Nashville?"

I throw my head back, annoyed. "There weren't."

I can see her grind her teeth and I can tell she doesn't believe me.

"I'm sick of having this conversation with you," I mutter, immediately regretting the words.

"Well I'm sick of you," she snaps.

"Don't say that."

"Or what?"

"Or..." I don't know what to say but the thought of her

leaving pisses me off. I don't think and just smash my mouth to hers.

I think she is going to push me off her but she pulls me in closer devouring me with an all-consuming kiss.

We are animals as we go at each other. She pulls at my shirt, ripping the neck. I push hers over her head, unclasping her bra as my mouth goes to her rose-colored nipples.

Her hands are at my jeans, forcing them down. I kick them aside as I push her on the bed facedown, pulling her yoga pants off in the process. I rip her thong off and throw it to the side, it's damp and I know she is turned on as much as I am. I push her thighs apart and plunge inside of her in one hard stroke. She screams as I enter her, my name a welcome sound on those lips. I don't go slow, I don't take my time, I'm relentless as I pound into her glorious pussy.

Her hands are stretched on the bed in front of her, gripping the sheets with white knuckles as I give her everything I've got.

"Harder, Noah. I need to feel all of you."

I lean over her back and growl in her ear as I thrust into her harder. She pushes back against me, the sound of our bodies smack against each other writing their own song.

"Wildflower," I whisper into her ear. That's all it takes for her to come. I feel her pulse against my dick and I follow her, spilling everything I have inside of her.

I pull out of her and flip her over. She has a goofy grin on her face and I can't help but kiss it off. She pulls me on top of her, her legs wrapping around my thighs. I trail kisses down her neck and across her collarbone as her hands scratch down my nape and back.

"Was that make-up sex?" She giggles.

I chuckle into her throat as my hands make their way down her body. "Ugh, yeah. I told you you'd know."

"Mmm. We should fight more often."

I throw my head back and laugh as I pull back and sit on my knees. "I think we've fought enough the last few weeks."

"Noah," she says softly, her hands trailing down my abs. "I didn't mean it. Any of it. I don't want to wait for you. I'm not sick of you. I know you didn't have sex—"

"Shh." I place a finger over her lips. "I know."

"I love you."

"I love you too, Mayberry. Forever."

She pulls me back down into a needy kiss that turns into a slow and gentle lovemaking session.

Once we are finally sated, I open up to Anna and tell her everything I should have told her from the start. And Anna tells me all about Nashville. We talk long into the night getting distracted by our naked bodies too many times to count.

When we wake up the next morning, Anna is folded into my arms, her hazel eyes boring into me. I trace a finger down her face and there is no doubt in my mind that I will be spending forever with this woman. I want to be with her for the rest of my life. She makes me a better man. She's already helped me let go of the past even when it came back to fight me. I want a family with her. I want to hang pictures of us on the walls in our home. I want our kids running around in the back yard with Brutus as we have all my brothers over for a family barbeque. I want it all because she is the song to my soul.

28

ANNA

I sit in the studio with Mason and Darnell. We want to get one last recording session in before Dee leaves for tour with his band. After everything that happened between Noah and I, a song came pouring out of me. And I think it might be the one. The perfect song. I sent Austin a snippet of it a few days ago and he went bananas over it. He didn't think I could do better than what I wrote in Nashville but I proved him wrong.

It's been a week since I finally gave in to Noah and moved back in. He wasn't wrong when he said Claire would be gone soon. Two days after we had that incredible make-up sex, which like he said I would know when it happened, and I plan on picking fights with him a lot more, Claire moved out. Actually, she was escorted back to New York by a detective. Apparently she bought a second identity to cover up the money laundering and fraud she was doing through a company she worked for and used her status of being married to a huge investment banker as a cover. I knew she was fucking crazy. Not to mention her real husband, who knows if the marriage was even legal, said she was bipolar and had been off her meds.

We still haven't found out who sent me the notes. But I have yet to receive one since Claire left. Noah said it wasn't her but I can't be so sure. The serial killer Noah was searching for was caught. He confessed to the murders but said he didn't even know who I was.

I never thought my life would get this wild but I am glad it's over. I have the two things I need in this world, my music and Noah, the song to my soul as he likes to call me. I told him he should be a poet but I like him more as a detective. Last night he broke out the handcuffs on me again. Best sex ever. Well maybe not as good as the make-up sex.

"Anna, what do you think of this?" Darnell asks me as he plays a lick on the guitar.

I shake my head. "It's too rock 'n' roll. This needs to be softer; it has to build up, and then when it gets to the chorus it blows you away."

I play the melody I came up with on the piano and Mason strums along on an acoustic. Darnell changes the sound on his electric and we come up with the vision I had for this song all along. Within hours we have it recorded and I send it off to Austin.

"You did good, coopcake," Darnell says as he wraps an arm around my shoulders.

"I feel it. This song is magic."

Mason smiles at me. "It's even better than the one you performed in Nashville."

"That song was dope, Anna. Mason showed it to me."

I frown at Mason. "You weren't supposed to show anyone."

He shrugs. "Anna, that song is all over the internet."

"What?" I shriek.

"Yeah someone posted a video to YouTube two weeks ago. I wouldn't be surprised if your phone gets flooded with calls soon. It's got like two million views."

I gape at him as I feel my chest turning red. I grab hold of the necklace around my neck. The one Noah gave me and I calm down. That song was for him. "Did you ever show it to Noah?"

"Nah. I was waiting for the perfect moment. I figured maybe his bachelor party or your wedding."

My cheeks flame. "We would have to be engaged for either of those to happen."

Mason smirks and picks up his guitar.

I reach over to him and pull on his shoulder. "Are you not telling me something?"

Darnell laughs as he watches me and Mason. "Anna May, my brother is head over heels for you. I know he is going to marry you."

I stutter as I try to find words. "But... he doesn't...I can't—"

Mason strums along. "You're already a part of our crazy family. It's only a matter of time."

I am still at a loss when my phone rings and I see it's Noah.

I try to play it cool but Mason's words have me acting like a mumbling idiot. "Hey Detective... Hi... umm how's it going?"

"You okay, babe?"

"Me? Oh yeah, perfectly fine and dandy. Just sitting here—"

Mason pulls the phone from me and talks to his brother. "I told her you were going to marry her and now she is all flustered."

I hear Noah talking sternly to his brother and Mason looks at me grinning from ear to ear.

I rip the phone away from him and hear Noah still scolding him. "...surprise."

"What's a surprise?" I ask him.

"Oh nothing," he responds when he hears me on the phone.

I furrow my brow but let it pass. "Why are you calling?"

"Can't I call my girlfriend whenever I want?"

"Of course. Sorry, yeah I am just—"

"Anna. Forget what Mason said. He's a dick."

"Okay," I mutter into the phone.

I can tell Noah is smiling by his tone. "I wanted to see if you wanted to go to dinner tonight."

I love it when Noah takes me on dates. With our crazy work schedules, they don't happen very often but when they do they always feel special and they usually end in mind-blowing sex. "I would love to but—"

"You got called into work."

I was supposed to be off tonight. "The girl that always covers for me is sick and I owe her one."

He sighs into the phone. "You should just quit Jimmy's."

"I know."

"I'm sick of all those cops eyeing you all day."

I laugh at that. "Gosh, cops are the worst. Good thing I only like detectives."

"Only one detective."

I look up at Mason and he is gagging. I roll my eyes at him. "Mmm I've seen a few that are drool worthy."

"Anna," Noah says sternly.

"There is this one that I would love to rip his clothes off though. Lick down those abs I know are hiding under that suit. Kneel in front of him and take that fat cock into—"

Mason groans. "Stop talking like that about my brother in front of me."

"You just don't like hearing about blow jobs," I tease.

"I am never living that down."

Noah chuckles into the phone. "As much as I want you

to finish that story, I don't. I am sitting at my desk and I don't want to be sporting a tent in my pants the rest of the day."

"I could stop by," I say, biting my lip.

"Don't tempt me."

I watch as Mason follows Darnell out of the room, both of them tired of hearing the teasing between Noah and me.

"I'll stop by Jimmy's after I'm off. I'll sit at the bar and watch you all night."

"Creep."

"Mayberry, I know you like it."

"Only because I know how horny it will make you as I swing my hips all night."

"If I keep talking to you, I'm going to have a big problem on my hands."

"Mmm. How big?"

"Goodbye, Anna."

I smile into the phone and say with a breathy voice. "Goodbye, Detective."

He groans into the phone as I hang up, knowing how much he likes that voice.

I walk out of the room and find Mason and Darnell hanging out in the lounge.

"Please tell me you did not have phone sex with my brother."

"It would have lasted a lot longer than that." I wink at him. "I need to head out. I have to work in twenty."

I wave goodbye to both of them and drive over to Jimmy's.

I CARRY a tray of cheeseburgers to a rowdy bunch of cops. Ever since the serial killer was found, they have all been less on edge and tonight proves it.

It's packed in here. Like every cop who had the day shift decided to come in to celebrate. There are a handful of the detectives Noah works with too. Everyone smiles and cheers.

I hop from table to table, serving drinks and food. Uber is going to make a killing on these officers tonight.

I glance at my watch and see it's half past seven. I'm surprised Noah isn't here. I doubt he changed his mind about coming, especially since all his coworkers are here. But knowing him he probably found a tiny break in another case and fell down the rabbit hole.

I walk past a table by the front door and hear the door slam. "I'll be right with you," I yell over my shoulder. We don't have a hostess and most people seat themselves but it's busier than usual so there aren't many open tables.

I grab an order from a family and turn around to smack right into the face of someone I never thought I would see again.

"Becca, what are you doing here?"

That's when I feel something hard press into my side. I look down and see the end of a gun. *Is she stupid?* This is a bar full of cops.

"Becs, I wouldn't do this here." I look around hoping to catch the eye of someone but they are all involved in their conversations.

"You took everything from me."

I look at her strangely. "What are you talking about?"

"You've ruined my entire life."

I finally take a good look at her and she looks worse than when I saw her in Hartswell. Her hair is ratty, like she hasn't brushed it in days. Huge bags reside under her eyes, her cheeks concave. "Becca, we can talk, I swear, but not here."

"Why not?"

"Look around you. There are cops everywhere." Despite the fact this woman looks crazy and ruined me for a good part of my life, she is still my friend and I don't want her doing anything she will regret. "Follow me."

She looks around the room with understanding. She must not have lost all her sanity.

I make eye contact with the detective who tried to flirt with me last time. I hope he understands my silent plea as I lead Becca outside to the alley behind the bar.

As soon as we get out the door, she holds the gun up to me. I hold my hands up in front of her. "What the hell is going on?" I ask.

"You took everything from me. Why you? Why do you always get everything? It all works out perfectly for you."

"What are you talking about?"

"You took Kyle from me. We were supposed to have a life together. He was going to leave you for me."

I think back to the letter Kyle left me, the one he wrote when he left Becca's house that night before he died. He wrote the opposite. He wanted me to take him back. "I know he told you different. He said he was leaving you that night. That it was a mistake."

"Why do they all love you?" she cries. "Why can't they love me?"

"Who are you talking about, Becca? I didn't take anyone from you." I walk backward slowly hoping she doesn't notice as I try to make my way down the alley.

She flaps the gun in my face, her wild eyes crying as she speaks. "I have nothing left. My husband is divorcing me, trying to get full custody. I have nothing. All because of you."

I look behind her hoping one of the detectives walks out the back door. Or one of my coworkers. I've been gone too long. "I don't even know your husband."

"He is leaving because he found out what I did to you. He doesn't trust me. If you hadn't opened your fat mouth—"

I stop walking backward and instead approach her because she has got me fired up. "Don't blame me for this. For your indiscretions." I look behind her one more time but still no one. "No, Becca, this is all on you. If I had known about you and Kyle, I would have let you have him. Neither of you were worth my time."

"You are such a self-righteous bitch," she screams at me. "And now you think you have it all again. But I won't let you. I won't let you get what you want."

She pushes the safety off the gun and I push forward hoping to grab the gun from her. Her gun goes off and I feel warmth run down my arm at the same time I hear another gunshot and fall back against the brick wall, my head hitting it hard and I collapse to the ground.

29

NOAH

I'm happy we solved the last case. Everyone in the department has been celebrating for two days. But work is work and there is always a case to be worked on. Anna's case is one but I can't touch it. I've been pushing Jon to dig into it but it's not a priority.

I flip through statements on a recent murder and search through databases on my computer to find a ballistic match. I rub my eyes as they grow heavy from staring at the screen.

"You're still here?" Marcus startles me.

I look at the clock and see it's almost seven thirty. Damn. I told Anna I would go to Jimmy's. "I didn't notice the time."

"Stop working so hard," Marcus jokes. "I came back because I forgot my phone but a bunch of us are at Jimmy's."

"Yeah okay. I told Anna I would go. I'll meet you over there."

Marcus walks up to my computer and shuts it off.

"Really?"

"Relax. We all need it after that last case. Let off some steam. You haven't done it yet."

I crack my neck as I push back from my desk. "I'm worried about Anna's case."

"Jon's on it."

I shake my head. "Barely. He sent me over forensic reports on the Duncan case before he left for the day."

"Well I am sure he is still working on it. Besides, she is safe. You are on her like a bodyguard."

I shrug. "Doesn't mean I can't worry."

Marcus nods and I follow him out the door. "I don't blame you. I would do anything to protect the ones I love."

We walk across the street to Jimmy's and the place is packed. Marcus leads me over to a table with some of the other detectives and a few police officers.

I take a seat and look around for Anna but I don't see her. She must be on a break.

"Where is our waitress? I haven't seen her in a bit. She's always on top of it," one of the cops says.

My gut has that funny feeling again where I know something is wrong. My eyes scan the restaurant but still no sign of her. I'm about ready to check the kitchen when Jon chimes in.

"I saw her talking to a blond woman. They walked toward the back. I'm sure she will be back soon," Jon says before taking a sip of his beer.

I can't help but feel on edge. Maybe it was Seraphina but I find it odd she would come here. She never does.

Marcus must notice my agitation. "What's wrong, Noah?"

"Something doesn't feel right."

Marcus scans the room and flags down one of the other servers walking by. "Is Anna on a break?"

"She shouldn't be. She had one half an hour ago."

I stand at that statement at the same time Marcus asks Jon, "What did the blond woman look like?"

"What?" Jon asks confused.

"The woman you saw Anna walk away with," I demand.

Marcus puts a hand on my shoulder. "Did Anna look troubled?"

"Who's Anna?" Jon asks.

Elliot hits him upside the head. "Our server."

"Oh." He shrugs. "I don't know. I made eye contact with her when she left. She had a weird look on her face."

My mind starts filtering through the worst situations. Is she with the person leaving her notes? Did they kidnap her? Kill her? I am sure someone would have heard a gunshot.

"What did the woman she was with look like?" Marcus repeats.

"I don't know." Jon grabs the back of his neck. "Blond, short, thin. Kind of tired looking but if she put makeup on she would be hot as hell."

"Fuck."

Marcus looks at me and must see the terror on my face. "Elliot, you and Jon, go through the front to the parking lot. We'll head out back to the alley."

"What's going on?" Jon asks as Elliot stands up.

"The Cooper case you are supposed to be working on," Elliot says.

"Fuck." The look on Jon's face looks like he put everything together.

"Let's go," Marcus says, his hand going to the gun on his hip but not pulling it out until we are away from customers.

We make our way to the back exit when we both hear a gunshot. We run as we push through the door and find two women in the alley. I see red as I watch blood leak down Anna's arm.

Marcus holds me back as he yells at the blond woman to

freeze. She peers backward for a second and rage takes over. Becca is holding a gun at the love of my life.

She turns around and holds the gun up to Anna as Anna looks confused at the blood dripping down her arm.

Marcus fires hitting Becca in the shoulder. The gun falls as Becca slumps forward into Anna who falls back and hits her head against the back of the building.

Elliot runs around the corner of the alley and gets to them first, kicking away the gun. Marcus and I run. He grabs Becca while I fall to the ground picking Anna up in my arms. The sound of sirens near as a group of bystanders starts to surround the entrance to the alley.

More cops walk out of the restaurant blocking them off as the ambulance pulls up.

I ignore it all. The only thing I care about is the woman in my arms. I assess her wound and breathe a sigh of relief when I see she was only grazed by a bullet.

Her eyes flutter open. "Noah," she whispers.

"I'm here, baby, I'm here." I pull her closer into me and bury my face in her hair, breathing in her lemon and patchouli scent. The scent I don't want to ever not smell again.

"I'm okay," she cries into my chest as her arms wrap around my neck. "I'm okay."

I WATCH the light of the setting sun hit Anna's hair as her fingers dance across the black and white keys of the piano.

My heart has been aching every day for the last week thinking of how I could have lost her.

Becca was arrested for attempted murder. And I know she will be convicted. I worry about the toll it took on Anna but she is strong and resilient, my wildflower, living through it all.

The melody she plays is sad and haunting. A lament of her past.

She doesn't know I watch her. I've been doing it every night for the past week. It's the only way I know she's real, that she is still here with me.

Just as she finishes the melody, she turns around before I can walk away. "Did it sound better tonight?"

I don't know what to say to her. I don't know how long she's known I've been watching her.

She gets up from the piano and walks over to me, her hand going for mine. "I'm here, Noah. I'm still here."

A tear slides down my cheek and I feel her wipe it away. "I know, Mayberry."

"I'm not going anywhere. Whether by my choice or someone else's. This is the only place I want to be."

I wrap her in my arms. "I worry."

She snorts into my chest. "I know you do, old man. I can see the worry lines get deeper by the day on that handsome face of yours."

I press my forehead into her hair. "I love you."

She pulls back as her hands grip my face. "And you have me forever."

She walks to the record player in the corner and turns on a classic. She pulls me to the center of the room and dances with me, her feet tripping over mine, until we just sway back and forth. Her place in my arms forever.

30

NOAH

Three Months Later

I used to hate summer. But the memories that used to drown me have long faded. Anna's carefree spirit has made this one of the best summers of my life.

She quit both of her jobs at the bars and only teaches yoga now so we have more free time for each other. Of course, it's hard to pull her away from her music some days. The days when the melody is flowing through her as she sits in the sunroom writing songs.

I don't hate it though. I like to watch her. Watch how she creates music. I always said it was magic and it remains true. It's incredible to watch her as she puts together words to piano keys to guitar strings.

After everything that happened with Claire and the day that Becca almost took Anna's life, we both feel like we have finally let go of all the ghosts of our past. We are only looking forward now. To the life we are supposed to have.

Together.

Anna still likes to pick fights with me. And I don't mind because the make-up sex seems to get better each time.

Yesterday, she put pickles on my sandwich just so I would yell at her. She knows I hate them. She turned it into a huge fight about nothing. It ended with the jar of pickles crashing to the floor as I fucked her on the kitchen table.

I look over at her now as I drive my International Harvester for the first time in years. Her red hair blowing in the breeze, the sun hitting the freckles on her nose, as she sings along to a song on the radio.

This woman is everything to me. And I plan on letting her know that soon.

I reach across her and grab her hand. She glances over at me and smiles. It still makes my heart speed up. No matter how many times she gives me that look. It will never grow old.

Brutus is in the back seat enjoying the taste of salt water in the air and everything seems perfect.

"This is a new song from superstar Hailey Lane. It's called 'The Fate of Us.' Call in and let us know what you think," the radio DJ says.

"Holy shit!" Anna screams, reaching for the knob on the radio to crank the volume. "Oh my god, oh my god!"

Anna sold the song two months ago. She wrote it the week after Claire left, the day Becca shot her. She told me it was ironic that she would write a song called "The Fate of Us" on a day where both of our fates could have changed. But I think it just proves that we are meant to be.

When her mentor from Nashville called her to let her know someone was interested in her song, she thought it would be some no-name singer and played off the whole thing. But when Austin told her it was country superstar Hailey Lane, Anna about lost it. She went to Nashville a month ago to sing background vocals on the track, per Hailey's request.

I watch her as she freaks out over hearing her song on

the radio for the first time. I am freaking out too. I couldn't be happier for her. All her dreams that she put on hold, that she thought she would never live, are coming true.

I hum along to the lyrics, lyrics that describe us perfectly.

I thought I lost you.
I pulled away.
I couldn't stay.
But now that I am back in your arms
I know I never should have fought
The fate of us

By the time the final chorus comes on I sing along with Anna. She smiles at me as I sing off key and her entrancing voice carries on the wind.

"Oh my god," she shouts again as the song finishes. "I want to hear it again! But please don't sing this time," she jokes. "My ears are bleeding."

I laugh as we drive along the coastline, Anna flipping through stations hoping to hear her song on the radio again.

31

ANNA

I scratch the back of Brutus' ears as the three of us lay on a blanket on the beach watching the sunrise.

Noah's arms are wrapped around me as I sit between his legs. I feel more at peace than I have in my entire life. Not just from being at this cottage that brought me so many memories but that I can finally enjoy my time with the man I love.

After everything we went through a few months ago I didn't think we would ever be here. I thought for sure our fate was sealed with the ghosts of our past. But I was wrong. We fought through hell to get here and I would do it again if it meant that I would get to spend my life with this man.

When we got to the house just before sunset last night, Noah told me to hang out on the porch while he cooked dinner.

I let the waves bring a new melody to my soul as the sun slowly set. When Noah finally let me in the house, he had a candlelit dinner on the table and a fire roaring in the fireplace. Just like that night we spent here when we professed our love for each other.

It was magical. Just like the love between us.

His fingers run up and down my arms as we watch the tide roll in. The beach has yet to get crowded, so it's nice to have the time with just the two of us.

"I love you," Noah whispers in my ear.

I lean back onto his shoulder and press a kiss to his jaw. "I love you too."

He leans in and presses his mouth to mine, my hand reaching up to the back of his neck. His other hand presses between my legs and I groan just as the squeal of a child breaks us apart.

"Maybe we should move this inside," I mumble against his lips.

He bites on my bottom lip. "Nope, I have plans for you today."

I twist in his arms and kneel in front of him. "We finally have all the time in the world together and you don't want to spend it between the sheets?"

He laughs as his arms wrap around my hips, squeezing my ass. "Mayberry, of course I do. But after our plans."

I fold my arms across my chest and pout. He chuckles as his thumb moves across my lips. "We've already fucked twice this morning. I think you can wait."

"Fine," I acquiesce, standing as I do. "Let's get a move on."

He stands up and smacks my ass. "What am I going to do with you?"

"Where do you want me to start? I might have packed some handcuffs," I joke.

"Mmm. Keep talking." He smiles and his lips find mine again.

I wrap my hands around his back, sliding under his shirt. "Maybe a few costumes."

His hands move into my hair as he pulls me against him in a tight embrace. "Now you are just making things up."

I hold him tight before we head back into the cottage. He packs a picnic into a backpack as I grab some treats for Brutus.

He hasn't told me where we are going even though I keep begging him. He puts everything into the back of the Scout and I notice he brought my guitar too.

After an hour drive, we pull up to a forest preserve near Hilton Head. The view of live oak, Spanish moss, and pines picturesque as I take it all in. Noah grabs the backpack out of the Scout and puts Brutus on a leash as I grab my guitar.

"Have you been here before?" Noah asks me.

I shake my head.

"Good."

I look at him as he adjusts the shades on his face wondering why he brought me here. He heads toward the boardwalk that leads through the oak trees, moss hanging across the path. I follow him as I take in the sounds of nature, the beauty of it all.

We make small talk as we head through the swamp. Laughing as Brutus tries to jump into the murky water. I can see a clearing up ahead and Noah stops in front of me, blocking my view.

"I want us to have a space of our own. An escape we can go to when we need to get away. Just us."

I place my hand on his chest and smile. "We have the cottage. That is ours. The only memories I have of it now are happy ones."

Noah leans down and presses a kiss to my lips. As he pulls away, he drags a finger up my arm tracing the wildflower tattoos on it. "I want you to have this too."

He steps away and I walk a few steps more until I am in the clearing. I stop in my tracks as I am greeted by a field of wildflowers. Larkspur, poppies, alyssum, and cornflower flood my vision and infiltrate my senses. It's the most beautiful thing I have ever seen and I know immediately I want to recreate it in our backyard in Asheville.

I lean against the wooden railing on the boardwalk as I take in the vivid purples and bright oranges of the flowers, pinks, whites, and reds, popping up against the other colors. Daisies, baby blue eyes, and Black-Eyed Susans writing a melody in my head.

I turn toward Noah who is smiling at me with a goofy grin. A tear slides down my face as I jump on him and wrap my body around his. His hands cup my thighs as I cry tears of joy into his neck. "This is the most beautiful place in the world. How did you find it?"

He cups the back of my head and pushes my sunglasses off my face so I can meet his eyes. "I would search the entire world to find beauty. Luckily I already have you."

I laugh as I press a chaste kiss to his lips then climb off him. "Suave, Romeo."

He grabs my hand as we walk along the boardwalk. There is a break in the field, a path of grass between both sides of the wildflower sea. He climbs the fence and gets Brutus to slide between the rails.

"What are you doing?" I shriek.

"Breaking the rules."

I look around hoping there is no one around but it's still early in the day and the park is nearly empty.

"You know you took me on private property once. I could have been shot. We will just get scolded here."

I take one last look around before sitting on the rail and swinging my legs around. Noah grabs my hips and helps me down. He jogs down the pathway and I run to catch up. "Why are we running?"

"Don't want to get caught." He laughs.

I roll my eyes even though he can't see them. As the pathway turns, we get closer to the tree line. Once we are out of the vision of passersby on the boardwalk, Noah takes the backpack off and pulls out a blanket. He sets the fruit and cheese containers down and I sit next to him, inhaling the sweet scent of the flowers.

"Are you happy?"

I look over at him and smile. "You make me happier than I've ever been."

He shakes his head and looks down. "Not what I meant. Are you happy here? In a new field of flowers that can be ours?"

"I couldn't ask for more, Noah."

He shifts on the blanket until he is kneeling in front of me. "Are you sure?"

I take my eyes off his face as I look down at his hands. He is cupping a handful of flowers but that's not what stops my breath. It's the sun reflecting off the diamond ring nestled between the blooms.

I look up at him, shocked.

"Anna May, Mayberry, my wildflower. You've given me my life back. You've let my heart bloom in ways I never thought were possible. I thought it was forever wilted. That I could never love again. But every second I spent with you, you brought it back to life. You gave me hope and the promise of happiness. I keep telling you that you are the song to my soul. Will you let me be yours?"

Tears are streaming down my face as he pours his heart out. He didn't need to give me a speech. He could have just asked me the four simple words. Because I could never say no to this man.

He picks the ring up out of the flower display and holds it in front of me. "Will you marry me?"

I nod my head as he slides the ring onto my finger. The diamond set on a silver band glistening in the sunlight surrounded by two aquamarine stones. I grip his hand before he can let go. "Noah, you are the song of my heart and the soundtrack to my soul. I don't need to marry you to know you are my forever, but I'll do it anyway because I love you."

He grabs the back of my neck and kisses me fiercely. We mumble I love you as we strip our clothes, not caring we are making love in the middle of a field of wildflowers, not caring if we get caught.

Because our love is wild and fierce and will continue to bloom like the flowers surrounding us.

And I know without a doubt this love is forever.

EPILOGUE
EIGHT YEARS LATER

Noah

I toss a football to our five-year-old, Cypress. He catches it and runs deep, bypassing Hunter's son before crossing the end zone.

"Touchdown," he screeches, doing a crazy dance of punches and kicks at the end zone. The kid is fast as hell for a five-year-old. I have no idea how he outran Hunter's twelve-year-old. Cypress is obsessed with football, no thanks to Asher who has had him watching it since he was old enough to watch TV.

"Cypress, you better be careful. You don't want Uncle Hunter to fix a broken bone," Anna yells from the deck where she is sitting with the wives of Carson and Hunter. She is just as beautiful as the day she came running across the driveway asking me to fix her shower. Even after two kids and a third on the way.

I smile as I see that raw aquamarine stone still hanging around her neck.

I give my kid a high five before he runs to the porch and grabs a juice box.

"Dada!" I see my two-year-old in my mom's arms reaching for me.

"Hi baby girl," I say as I grab hold of her, smothering kisses all over her face while she laughs. "How's my favorite Azalea?"

"Snacks. I'm so hungryyy," she cries and I chuckle as I set her in her booster seat next to my wife.

"I swear that kid eats more than all you boys did at that age," my mom says as she carries a plate over to Azalea.

"She's a growing kid, Ma, what do you expect?"

I sit next to my wife as I take in the scene around me. All my brothers are here, even Everett. I never thought the day would come, but he met someone who encouraged him to stop letting his past hold him back.

I smile as I watch the family banter back and forth with each other. Asher fakes a smile at me and I know he is dealing with a lot, being put in a place he never thought he would have to deal with. But I give him a reassuring nod. I know he will succeed.

Carson wraps his arm around his wife. His hand going to her belly. She is due the same week as Anna. Hunter and I have a bet who is going to be born first. Anna would kill me if she knew we were betting on the babies but I only did it because I know Anna is going to give birth to our second baby girl first. This pregnancy has been rough on her, the doctors think it's because of her age. We know this will be our last child but we are both happy. We've already named her, Dahlia, another flower to add to our wild bunch. And she is living up to her name, no doubt she will be a feisty one I am going to have to keep a close eye on.

Hunter laughs with Mason as the two of them give each other a hard time over who knows what. Hunter's wife and Mason's fiancée snicker at them as they sip on wine.

Anna pulls on my arm and I hold her hand as she

waddles down the steps. "Ugh, is this baby going to come anytime soon? I feel like a balloon."

I chuckle as I wrap an arm around her. "Mayberry, you still have two more months."

"Remind me why we wanted to have another kid?"

I press a kiss to her cheek as I whisper in her ear. "It was an accident."

"Because you and your penis can never leave me alone."

I pull her into the field of wildflowers she planted at our new house. Once she was pregnant with Azalea, we knew we needed a bigger home. I miss our first home together, all the memories it had, the good and the bad, but this one is completely ours.

We picked it out together and made it our own. It's nestled into the mountains at the edge of a valley. The back of the house overlooks the ridges, but the best part was the open field that came with our property. Anna spent months prepping the field so we could have our own wildflower field like the one where I proposed in South Carolina.

I think this one is even better. On the outskirts of the field you can see a small building that we built as Anna's recording studio. Ever since she sold her first song, she has been sought out by labels, producers, and bands. She doesn't choose genres but let's the music write itself. She's helped with writing for rock bands and pop singers. She even helped launch the career of a young country singer a few years ago that led her to win a few Grammys. I've always said her music was magical.

As for me, I recently accepted a promotion as lieutenant. It gives me the stability to provide for my family and not risk my life every day by being in the field.

I pull Anna into the wildflowers, far from view of our family. "I don't think it's my penis that's the problem. Not to mention the date of conception for Dahlia was

Halloween and I recall quite clearly you putting on that police officer costume for me."

"Is that what happened, Detective?"

"It's lieutenant now."

She twirls in my arms, her dress spinning up to her waist, revealing green lace panties, my favorite. "Mmm I like detective better," she says, her voice raspy.

I pull her into me, her round stomach pressing into mine. "Whatever you say, my crazy wildflower."

THE END

ALSO BY TORI FOX

Saints & Sinners

Black Hearts

Cruel Promises

Dirty Secrets

Wicked Lies (coming 4/27/23)

Broken Vows (coming 6/29/23)

The Partners

Atonement

Repentance

Redemption

The Taylor Brothers

(Every brother's story can be read as a standalone)

The Ghost of You (Noah's story part 1)

The Fate of Us (Noah's story part 2)

Burnout: An Everyday Heroes Novel (Everett's story)

Fall From Grace (Carson's story)

The White Creek Series

Missing Pieces

Broken Pieces

Forgotten Pieces

Standalones

ACKNOWLEDGMENTS

I can't believe this is book five! How the hell have I written five books?!

I am so grateful for each and everyone one of you who have read one or all of my books, you are what keeps me writing. And I have so many more stories to tell!

Bill, another book down. One step closer.

Ellie at My Brother's Editor, thank you for dealing with my constant emails and making this book what it is.

Juliana at Jersey Girl Design, you killed it again!

Amanda Walker, thank you for all you do.

Kiki , Kristina, and everyone at The Next Step PR, thank you for your hard work on this series. I promise one day I will answer all my emails and messages faster! You all are amazing!

ABOUT THE AUTHOR

Tori Fox is the author of romantic suspense and contemporary romance with a little bit of angst and a whole lot of sexy. When she isn't writing, you can find her listening to true crime podcasts as she tends to her plants or singing along to Taylor Swift as she drinks champagne. Tori is living her best life in the magic of New Orleans with her dog.

You can find Tori on Facebook, Instagram, and TikTok
@ToriFoxBooks

For the latest news and releases visit
torifoxbooks.com